Had Livio been the dagger man of last night? But if so, why had he not killed me during those moments when I knelt over the captain's body? He had ample time, and no witnesses.

What was it he had told me? *"But for your sudden movement, you would have received that dagger. And you wore no bandolier to deflect the blow. You would have died."*

Was that the warning of an assassin?

Fawcett Crest Books
by Virginia Coffman:

MISTRESS DEVON
THE DARK PALAZZO

The
DARK PALAZZO

Virginia Coffman

A FAWCETT CREST BOOK

Fawcett Publications, Inc., Greenwich, Connecticut

For those dear partners in all my work,
my sister Donnie and her husband,
Johnny Micciche.

THE DARK PALAZZO

THIS BOOK CONTAINS THE COMPLETE TEXT OF THE
ORIGINAL HARDCOVER EDITION.

A Fawcett Crest Book reprinted by arrangement with Arbor
House Publishing Co., Inc.

Library of Congress Catalog Card Number: 72–94015

Printed in the United States of America
May 1974

CHAPTER ONE

ALTHOUGH A LONG, hazy blue twilight already shrouded the Grand Canal in the distance, I could see that the red and gold banner of the Serenissima still floated over the Venetian Customs Barrier. As my companion and I were assisted out of the felucca and onto the quai, a uniformed guard signaled us across it for inspection of our papers.

"Eager for a bribe of a few ducats," grumbled Miss Dace.

But I could not complain, I who had so recently felt the chill of Sanson's shears upon my neck and known the ghastly hospitality of the Conciergerie in Revolutionary Paris. Now, with all too vivid memories, I trembled inwardly for fear the supremely aristocratic Republic of Venice would find my passport from democratic France inadequate. France, having been attacked by the Austrian Armies, was now pursuing its reckless enemy across the Austrian-controlled lands of Northern Italy. In this carnage only the independent Republic of Venice remained outside the fighting, though sought after as a bulwark and ally by both sides. With France's Revolutionary Armies on her west borders approaching the Austrians, and the Austrian Empire in the north hoping to snatch her as a battering ram against the French, Venice was not desirous of admitting further troublemakers. My only consolation was that France's enemy was Austria, not Venice.

"Don't you be fretting, my dear," Miss Dace comforted me staunchly. "Your mama may have been one of them nasty Frenchies, but this watery little patch of islands isn't going to refuse the daughter of their British Ambassador."

I had seen enough in Paris during the last few years to dismiss her confidence as naive, but I did not say so. Poor Dacey! Lucky Dacey! I do believe her British self-confidence had not even been dented by the world-shaking events of the last six years. No need to upset her with the reminder that many Italians were joining the French, hoping for freedom from the ancient Austrian yoke. Venice had diplomatic relations with all sides in the war, including the British who were at war with France; but I had heard that aristocratic Venetians, while accepting all embassies, rather volubly despised the new democratic French government.

"Bless you, Dacey. I may need your confidence. And your prayers." I squeezed her gloved hand, thankful for the very innocence that kept her imagination from dwelling on horrors and her mind free from conceiving doubts of its own sanity.

Another handsome Venetian officer met us on the steps of an ancient building whose elegant interior, with its marble and parquet floors, I glimpsed in the flare of candlelight behind him.

His polite smile did not deceive me, and I was made more uneasy than flattered by the interest he took in my person, from my plainly frilled black bonnet to my morocco slippers.

"The Signorina must be aware that she will not be permitted to cross the Canal into the San Marco district until first light. Your papers, Signorina, and those of the Signora, if you please."

He held out one hand, and I knew everything depended upon our passports. Dacey's papers, being British and countersigned by the Prime Minister, Mr. Pitt himself, presented no problems. But the minute he saw mine, with the seal of THE REPUBLIC OF FRANCE, ONE AND INDIVISIBLE and the tricolor ribbon attached, his expression chilled.

"How like the French butchers! Now they send a beautiful female to spy out our defenses. But I must tell you, Signorina, your beauty will avail you nothing with the Serenissima."

The compliment annoyed me in such a threatening context. I had enough of threats, after months in the Abbaye Prison, climaxed by the weeks in that antechamber to the

guillotine, the Conciergerie, until I was released under constant surveillance to care for my dying mother in a single,
unheated room hard by the Left Bank of the Seine. It was the
Cordeliers Quarter, teeming with Republican nonsense, and
was the last sight my mother beheld of her beloved Paris.

"My name, if you will trouble to note, Messire, is Rachel
Carewe. I have been a prisoner of the French Republic." I
heard in my voice a cool hauteur for which I was ashamed
almost immediately after. "I am the daughter of Sir Maitland
Carewe, British Ambassador Plenipotentiary to the Serenissima." As a sop to the officer's pride I gave Venice its ancient
and glorious title, now sadly tarnished; for we had all fallen
on less glorious times in these winter days early in 1797.

Startled by my claim, the Commendatore studied my passport papers by the flickering lights behind him. His attitude
changed rapidly. There was deference now, and enthusiasm,
due, no doubt, to the Venetian hope that Britain would defend
them from the encroachments of powerful, autocratic Austria
as well as the new taint of democracy from Revolutionary
France.

"But Madonna Carewe—" I was the noble "Madonna"
now, "—you should have revealed your identity at once. The
Serenissima welcomes its friends—of whom none is more
valued than your noble father."

Immensely relieved, I managed a smile and gave him the
hand he sought, which he brought gallantly to his lips.

"And now, Madonna, if you and your companion—" He
glanced at Dacey's papers, "—the Signora Dace, can occupy
yourselves for a so-brief hour, we will have the return of one
of our gondolas from the Piazzetta. It was found necessary
to send officers to the Caffè Florian for examination of some
papers. A French spy."

Feeling that I had barely escaped this fate, I asked uneasily, "What will be done with him?"

His shrug was eloquent. I could guess the answer even before it was spoken, yet I shuddered.

"Ah, that now! But he will be delivered to the Stranglers,
Madonna, upon order of the Council of Ten. The strength
of the Serene Republic has been built for a thousand years
upon swift justice."

I winced, and my companion caught her breath in British
horror. Dacey asked indignantly, "Why does the Doge
permit such awful things?"

"His Serenity's power, Signora, is—how can one put it?

—a matter of externals only. Appearing at Feast Days, signing treaties, representing the glory of Venice in his presence. . . . His Serenity, Doge Ludovico Manin, is a very gentle man. He wept when he was elected to his great dignity. It is said he would go to any length to keep us from becoming embroiled in this terrible war that goes on around the borders of Venice. But he would never be permitted to interfere with the Council of Ten. Indeed—" he looked over his shoulder nervously, "one hesitates to mention their names aloud. Their spies are everywhere." Then he added with haste, "But that need not concern your gentle hearts. While you wait, let Capitano Dandolo take you over to visit the little casino, within walking distance along the Canal. It will amuse you and perhaps—" though his smile belied his words "—you will be lucky with the cards."

I could not have felt less like appearing at a fashionable gaming den. I was wearing the only modern and respectably unsoiled muslin chemise gown left to me after my imprisonment and the long period of poverty after my mother and I were freed. It was far from the heavy, panniered, and elaborate ball-gowns still in fashion at Venetian ridottos.

But I had not reckoned with Dacey. She clapped her hands, her dear, faded eyes alight. "I should love it above all things, Rachel. Do let us pass the hour at a casino. I promise not to overspend, but I have my reticule full of *scudi* to be rid of. Coming down the Brenta I asked that silly boatman to give me good British coins, but what can one expect of these decadent heathens?"

Embarrassed, I glanced quickly at the officer but was met by a flirtatious grin. I suspected he did not understand Miss Dace's English. In any case, I hoped so. He had been most courteous.

"Capitano!" he called, snapping his fingers, and making one of those dramatic gestures that I found so amusingly graceful. "Escort the ladies to the Casino Giudecca." As the officer in question proved flatteringly prompt to oblige, the Commendatore added, "The Republic will, of course, play host to the ladies for a supper, if they are so inclined. The food is delicious, Madonna."

"You are too kind, Messire." I gave him what I hoped was my best smile before joining Dacey and the waiting Captain at the foot of the steps.

"My respects to His Excellency, Madonna," the Commendatore called after us as the young captain escorted us into the starlit darkness behind the little Port Customs Building.

The Captain asked politely, "You and the Signora were the only passengers on the little boat down the Brenta, Madonna Carewe?"

Dacey said at once, with her usual decisiveness, "Only we ladies. Such nonsensical fears as these Italians have! None across Italy would come into Venice. They fear the French will conquer you. What an absurdity while—"

"Absurd, indeed, Signora!" put in the Captain.

But Dacey went on, undeterred, "While the British Lion protects you."

I betrayed a ghastly cynicism by laughing and immediately I had to cover it with a sharp coughing spell.

Captain Dandolo had better manners and managed to murmur without offense, "Your pardon, Signora, but we hope to save the Republic with our own Lion of St. Mark, rather than with some—some foreign beast."

Dacey nodded with perfect understanding. "One lion is very much like another, I daresay."

This time I did laugh without camouflage, and was rewarded by the delighted sympathy of Capitano Dandolo who glanced at me, his brown eyes alight.

"Madonna Carewe has the Venetian heart, I think; isn't it so?"

Since I was newly come to the ancient Republic, I could not honestly express an opinion; but in any event, Venice had given me refuge in a dreadful, mind-shattering time, and I was truly grateful to this ancient Serenissima, this *Most Serene*, as Venice was called by all who had loved and respected and feared her through a thousand dangerous years of her life.

I looked around while we crossed a tiny square of garden behind the Customs House. The blue-dark did not conceal the perfume of its mysterious and subtly scented early flowers, nor the aura of light on the north horizon that could only be that heart of decadent, laughing, eternally masquerading Venice, the Piazza San Marco. I was thrilled in despite of my previous fears—fears that, somehow, I would be pursued wherever I went; and that in the end, I would meet the fate I had so closely cheated on the guillotine. It had been terrible; but I had been told by a friendly physician in Padua that such fears would fade, once I reached the haven of light-hearted Venice.

Already, however, I sensed that the aristocratic Venetian laughter had been somewhat stifled by the unbelievable success of the ragged, barefoot, untrained Armies of Republican France under General Bonaparte. The idea called "liberty" spread by the French had an all too electrifying power, I found. My own tastes, perhaps built upon experience, were not so radical. I would be quite content, I felt, to return to countries where the idea of liberty was not so persuasive.

"Dear me," Miss Dace remarked, staring ahead along a narrow lane between buildings with barred, secretive windows that looked for all the world like a Sultan's seraglio, "One might as well be in Constantinople. It looks most mysterious."

Captain Dandolo, fumbling carefully for words, tried to excuse the ancient oriental architecture which made Venice so splendid, and I tried, as best I could, to help him out. "We are not in the center of London now, Dacey. Venice is the gateway to the East. Think of all the Crusaders, the pilgrims and merchants, who have taken ship from Venice."

"And bleached their bones on those heathen shores across the Mediterranean," Miss Dace muttered, but then cheered almost at once. She had noticed the sounds of laughter, the tinkle of glass and silver from the lower story of an otherwise dark and shuttered house on our left.

"The Casino," explained Captain Dandolo. "This way, Ladies. Certain formalities are necessary—to prevent undesirables from entering."

Dacey said wisely, "Those Frenchies."

But the Captain smiled. "Not at all. The safeguards are against those Venetian citizens who lack the ducats needed at our better casinos. We do not countenance such nuisances in the Republic. In plain truth, there are too many of the poor for our liking."

How different from France, I thought, faintly troubled and surprised that I was troubled. In Paris, until the last few months, it had been a crime to be rich, not poor, And yet, the Venetians called themselves a Republic. The old, proud name of Serenissima more truly described this little heap of islands floating between Eastern and Western worlds. I kept thinking of these things as Captain Dandolo mounted the three wide steps of the stone building with its curious pink stone that gleamed faintly in the flickering lantern light. Whatever his signal at the door with the judas window, it succeeded of its purpose.

Miss Dace squeezed my hand. "Isn't it exciting, Dear? A genuine Gaming Hell!"

For her sake I managed a pretense of enthusiasm, but this last long wait before I reached my father in Venice was remarkably irritating to the nerves. And before my departure from Paris there had been many sleepless weeks while I waited to discover if I would be permitted to leave France with legitimate passport papers. I had been reasonably sure, and yet, there was always the possibility that in bringing myself to the attention of the government, I would remind them that they had once thought of beheading my mother and me. So now I stifled a yawn, tucked my nervous hands behind the folds of my cloak, and allowed myself to be ushered into the foyer.

It was a dazzling marble display with veined pillars, a beautifully designed parquet floor and much lighting. There must have been dozens of candelabra, hundreds of candles, all reflected in gold-framed mirrors and in the pillars themselves. I hesitated, aware that I was far from resembling the daughter of a British Ambassador, but I reckoned without Captain Dandolo, and without the gambling fever that gripped these aristocrats.

Like their surroundings, these gamblers radiated light, their jewels blinding me. Male and female, they were an astonishing sight after the modernity and simplicity of French Directoire Fashion. There were great powdered pumpkin wigs, enormous skirts, breeches and elegantly clocked silken hose. . . . It was as if they had never heard of the upheavals throughout the rest of Europe. They lived in their fairy tale, diamond-bright world with no sense at all that it could be shattered by one cannonade from Bonaparte's Revolutionary Army. An army inexorably approaching, day by day, seeking a pitched battle with the Austrians, whom the sly Venetians were aiding with an eternal eye for good business.

The Captain said gallantly, "Will you play, Madonna Carewe? And the Signora?"

I refused, trying to sound gracious, but in any case, I hadn't the money for this sort of pleasure. Dacey, however, was thrilled and highly impressed when he introduced her to the elegant gamblers huddled around an ancient, bejeweled crone pushing cards out of the "slipper." I noted several glances in my direction—contempt from the women, curiosity from the men. Feeling conspicuous, I moved into a poorly lighted antechamber beyond. Others had shared the room before me and had returned to gambling, their plates and glasses being collected by footmen so richly uniformed they put me to shame. The dining salons opened out of the back of the antechamber, and when Captain Dandolo obligingly fetched me a plate of almost unidentifiable delicacies popular in a sea-faring state I began to take a genuine interest in my surroundings.

Almost at once the good Captain was back. "May I tempt you with a glass of champagne?"

I thanked him. The champagne was welcome, indeed, after the last long, tiresome link in my coach ride across Italy only a few leagues below the fighting zone. I caught a glimpse of Dacey, greatly excited, tapping her cards and looking triumphant. Beside her, a beautiful woman of a certain age was equally excited, though her luck was out, I suspected, judging by her tight mouth and the way her eyes sparkled angrily behind a small, jewel-studded eye mask. Her hair was powdered and elaborately fashioned, which was a pity because I suspected her hair was red, a far less aging color than the old-fashioned powdered look. She shot a quick glance around her, then through the doorway at me. I do not think she saw me. I did not want her to feel, however, that my gaze affected her luck, and I glanced quickly away, toward the white and gold paneled doors standing open to the dining salon.

Only one other person shared this antechamber with me, a male stretched out asleep in a milord chair, probably shunted off to this room because he was wearing buckskins and topboots and clearly would not be permitted to mingle with the grandiose wigs and breeches in the gaming rooms. He had a gold-fringed towel over his face and was apparently asleep. But for his slim figure and his hands, one of which precariously balanced an empty champagne glass, I would have supposed him an elderly man. But the hands, while thin, were vigorous. Very like the man himself, I suspected, wondering at the same time what I found so interesting about a person whose face I couldn't see. His hair was dark, the ends swept back carelessly, almost long enough to queue. I could see it also above his forehead, where it was tangled and seemed inclined to curl. I wagered with myself that the face behind that towel was more than ordinarily attractive.

I was soon to discover; for the striking woman at the gaming table beside Dacey had left it and was approaching my antechamber, followed by an attentive lackey.

"Champagne for Madama?"

"As you like. You would do better to bring me luck at faro."

Although he had doubtless heard this a thousand times, he managed to bend sufficiently to wish her "Better luck, Madama, indeed. I often note that the luck changes very near upon the hour."

The red-haired lady received this with an understandably cynical smile but sent the lackey on his way and strolled slowly toward the dining salon. I was more or less in the shadow of a marble pillar and I supposed she did not realize that she had passed me. A curious thing happened then, as she reached the sleeping man near the open doors. The man gently removed the towel from his face, and spoke to her.

I was surprised to note that he wore spectacles, an uncommon sight in my experience. Perhaps they were necessary, but they also effectively disguised his eyes. But for the spectacles, he might very well be the attractive man I had thought him. So he was ordinary, after all. I wondered why he had intrigued me in the first place. And yet. . . . I had seen many remarkable men in Revolutionary Paris. I was used to them. I thought I could recognize a man of unusual qualities, even when I judged in ultrafeminine fashion, by externals. This man, somehow, had deliberately contrived to look like something he was not—an ordinary young idler, a wastrel of sybaritic Venice.

The lady gambler exchanged brief, low words with the man I found so interesting. I could not decide whether they were previously acquainted. The lady shook her head and went into the dining salon. I had an odd feeling—self-protective—that it would not be sensible for me to be seen watching them. I remained behind the pillar. The man settled back in his chair with his legs stretched out before him and crossed at the ankles as if he were about to indulge in another nap, but I knew now that his negligence was merely a pose. I discovered, belatedly, that I was afraid of him, although there was nothing obviously frightening about his look, or indeed his expression, what I could judge of it. It was simply that I had become convinced he was not what he pretended to be. In all probability, I should not have thought twice about his situation had I not come fresh from Paris, where anyone who was not what he pretended to be must be either a spy or an aristo, or both, and until very recently would have found himself headless in short order.

The faro tables and the dicers and the other gamesters broke up occasionally, while the pairs strolled out of the gaming salon, into the dining salons or onto a terrace at the opposite side. But Dacey seemed still wrapped in the wonders of beginner's luck and so long as Captain Dandalo did not signal to us, there was nothing for it but to sit there and finish my champagne. Shortly after the dining salons became crowded with those going to the suppers, the glamorous woman I thought of as the Gaming Lady returned to my antechamber with a plate and sat nibbling at the tidbits while her thoughts seemed to be elsewhere.

I was sure the gentleman pretending to be asleep now watched her from under his dark lashes; for he had unobtrusively removed his spectacles and rested his head against the high back of the chair while the spectacles dangled carelessly from his fingers. Then, as if awakening, he put them on, thus effectively dimming what I had briefly glimpsed as dark eyes.

The Gaming Lady sighed, and considered a ring she wore. I wondered if she considered also the prospect of risking it upon her luck at faro. Then the "sleeping" gentleman spoke to her, his voice apparently persuasive. I heard her laugh and, as some large paper money changed hands, she agreed: "Very well then. For luck. But yours is the risk, Messire."

She set her plate upon the stone mantel, the contents of the little supper scarcely touched, and she swept past me, stopped for an instant, stared at me, and then went on hurriedly, toward the faro tables, as I supposed. I glanced at the young man. He was smiling. He took off his spectacles and polished them absently while gazing after her.

At the same time Captain Dandolo and Miss Dace came to fetch me. Dacey was wildly excited. "My dear, you'll never guess."

"You have won."

"I banked. I took the bank. I—Adelaide Dace. Did you ever! And won a snug little sum. Look. My reticule is so heavy, I can scarcely lift it. The kind Captain says it is time to go. The gondola has arrived."

I was genuinely pleased at that. I started to set my glass down when it was politely removed from my fingers. Startled, I looked around, and found myself staring into that perfectly odious set of spectacles which reflected my own image back to me.

My bête noire, the young man whose antics had aroused my curiosity, smiled, relieving me of the glass. "Allow me, Madonna."

Miss Dace waited until he had stepped back—out of hearing, I hoped—and she murmured, "Heavens! What was that?"

Captain Dandolo shrugged, ushering us out of the antechamber. "One of the idlers who hang about the gaming halls. Doubtless hoping to catch a few *scudi* from some lucky winner."

I opened my mouth to correct him, then, for some obscure reason, looked back at the antechamber and changed my mind. The man with spectacles stood watching us from within the shadow just beyond the doorway. Dacey did not miss my gesture.

"Really, Rachel! Your dear Papa is not like to approve your taking such notice of a—a wastrel."

I felt mischievous and infinitely better than I had felt half an hour ago when we had entered this place. It may have been the champagne; I cannot be certain.

"All the same, Dacey, I discovered something very odd a moment since. He has remarkable eyes, and he keeps them hidden. Don't you find that interesting?"

"Interesting? That wretched snirp of a man?"

"Snirp?"

"A creature most unprepossessing in every way. Why, he puts me in mind of one of those Venetian alley cats!"

I teased her, "But I am fond of alley cats."

The Captain glanced at us and Miss Dace preened herself. "I must say, I prefer a man with good British beef on his— ah, that is—"

I laughed and so did the Captain. Flustered, Dacey added sternly, "You are besotted by that snirp's eyes, my child, but mark me . . ."

We were being bowed out and she broke off, but I had a horrid little notion that my mysterious Idler guessed the subject of our discussion and was amused by it. We were on our way across the silent, dark little square when suddenly I remembered and wondered aloud, "Did she win, after all? And with his money?"

My companions were far from understanding me, and I did not explain. It was all part of a little mystery that intrigued me and roused me for the first time from the depression I had felt since my mother's death.

CHAPTER TWO

ALTHOUGH THE EVENING was now well advanced, the entire area around the lacy, pinkish Doges' Palace, the Piazzetta, and the Square of St. Mark's cast a glow nearly as bright as sunrise over the lagoon. The glow reached out long solid lights and shadows across the waters and Miss Dace remarked upon the reflections she saw over the side of the gondola.

She removed a glove, reached over and trailed her fingers. "How deep it looks! And murky, even through the lights of the square we are approaching."

"The Piazzetta," said Captain Dandolo. "It is the open end of the Piazza San Marco. There is another open end, beyond the Campanile, the tall tower you see."

"Is it very deep?" As the Captain looked his surprise she went on, sighing romantically, "The canal hereabouts, I mean. Or is it the lagoon? I daresay, star-crossed lovers throw their rivals into water like this. And yet it sparkles so beautifully."

"Don't!"

They both looked at me and I felt absurdly ill at ease. "That is to say . . . it does seem deep. And—" I tried to turn off the awkwardness with a laugh, "I am not the best of swimmers, at any time."

"But I am," the Captain assured me, playing at romance, for he was a man who knew his own talent for dalliance and used it. "And it would be an extreme pleasure to rescue the beautiful young Madonna Carewe."

My mood lightened and I felt infinitely better. The Captain was still flirting when he gave the order to the gondolier, "No, Giacomo. Not the Piazzetta. We shall escort the lady, the ladies, directly to the palazzo of His Excellency, the British Ambassador. You know how to reach it? On the little canal of the Contarini-Zambetta."

"Yes, Capitano. By way of the Rio del Palazzo, between the Doges' Palace and the Prison of the Deep Wells."

"The———the deep——" Miss Dace sat up straight, shifting us all in the carefully balanced gondola. "Heavens!"

The Captain smiled. "We will not pause there. We simply glide underneath the bridges between the Prison of the Wells and the offices of the Ten in the palace. The Wells are the dungeons where prisoners are garroted. Such places can hardly concern two ladies like yourselves."

Oddly enough, though Dacey was shocked and gave me another quick, worried glance, I was less disturbed than I had expected to be by the mention of prisons. Nothing seemed more alien to my new life in Venice than a prison where malefactors were strangled. After all, malefactors were far from my life at that moment, and I hoped they would always be so.

"A pity you must wait another day to see the glories of Piazza San Marco and the cathedral," Captain Dandolo remarked to me. "The sight will remain with you all of your life."

But there was no denying that I was tired, and I felt, though I did not say so aloud, that the glories of the piazza would surely seem even more impressive when my spirits were fresher, in the morning.

We passed the Piazzetta, rocking uncertainly in the wind-swept current around the mooring poles, and in a minute or two turned sharply into a tiny, shadowed canal behind the Palace, under humped bridges. One dim lantern above a heavily scummed set of steps revealed a black cat, staring at us as the prow light of our gondola passed.

His eyes gleamed as they caught the light, and Dacey shuddered. "How very weird the creature looks! And black, beside all else. A bad omen."

"Rubbish!" I said quickly, sympathizing with the lonely,

defiant little feline. "He is merely hungry." But suddenly I remembered the dark alley cat of the gaming hell, Miss Dacey's "snirp," and I laughed. Everyone looked at me and I sank down a little in the confines of the gondola, remarkably self-conscious.

Thanks to the extraordinary maneuverability of the gondola and the skill of our gondolier, we moved rapidly through a darkness all the more dense and mysterious after the bright illumination of Piazza San Marco. Several times I found myself blinking to see better into the cross streets we passed, those intricate, narrow alleyways between the walls of four-hundred-year-old palaces so forbidding, so lacking in windows or welcome lantern lights that they seemed an omnipresent haven for cutthroats.

We turned out of the desolate, alarming little canal into one slightly wider. This canal was immediately lighted by twin lamps above a doorway that opened onto the usual green-scummed steps. The gondola bow scraped the nearest wall, throwing Dacey against me. While we were recovering our equilibrium, the Captain apologized and tried to assist us.

As he did so, I reminded him that we were already behindhand in our thanks for his great assistance tonight. "I had written to my father of our arrival, but with the French Army and the half of Europe moving across Italy, we were uncertain even of the day we should arrive. Nor have we heard from him. Poor Papa! I only hope he has not totally lost hope of our arrival."

"You have been long apart?"

"Heavens!" Dacey put in quickly. "He lost Rachel as little more than a child. They have been apart for eight years, thanks to those horrid Frenchies and their Revolution."

"Hush, Dacey! It was no fault of the French, but of Papa and my mother. The English and the French of it. They were never meant for marriage. And when Mama returned to Paris to be with her kind, she took me. It was the last time I was permitted to see my father. Although, of course, we corresponded when the long wars between Britain and France made it possible."

"A sad life you have had, Madonna." The good Captain smiled at me in his likable way. "But we shall make all that different in Venice. No tears under the Serenissima."

I gave him smile for smile, but I knew what he seemed unaware of, that the laughter of the Serenissima was hollow, that its ancient freedom and independence were threatened with extinction any hour, though still they laughed. But maybe it was brave laughter, not blind, nor ignorant or indifferent. As we sailed along through darkness and light that evening, I determined to be like them, the Venetians—to relearn that remarkable gift of laughter these people knew so well, and which I'd almost lost in the last few years.

"His Excellency must be in daily expectation of seeing Miss Carewe, however," Dacey broke in crisply. "I was once governess-companion, when the Carewes all resided in London. What a pity that dear Mrs. Carewe chose to return to that barbaric birthplace of hers! But then, she was always . . ."

"Dacey," I said, and she sniffed and recalled herself.

"Well, I'll say no more on that head. But how anyone could prefer Paris above all the amenities of British life is more than—" She caught a glance from me, tightened her lips, and ended, "Hm . . . no matter. How forbidding these palace walls appear from the water line. And at night! Nothing but these dreary little mooring lights."

Captain Dandolo was quick to defend his native watery heath: "Ah, but I assure you, Signora, the interiors are another matter entirely. Nothing in Europe can equal them. One must go to the East, to Constantinople, to see their equal. The Ambassador entertains only infrequently, due, I believe, to the loss of his family, but now that Madonna Carewe is joining him, we shall expect prodigious gaiety."

I promised him as much as I could. "I hope I may assist my father in any way possible. He has been a lonely man these past years." For some unaccountable reason, I felt the Captain's quick look in my direction, but when I gazed at him he was peering over my shoulder at the endless series of dark buildings of three storeys or so, looming up to line the curving canal, each building separated from its neighbor by an alley or canal so narrow it fairly shrieked to be a cutthroat's lair.

The gondolier grunted, and with both hands tight-locked around his huge sweep, nodded toward the small, humped bridge so low we all had to duck our heads.

"This will be the Palazzo Androtti, beyond the bridge and on the left side," the Captain pointed out, "currently in use by the British Ambassador. An elegant situation for balls, ridottos, and formal events. Perhaps now that his beautiful daughter arrives to play the hostess, we will have a return of those elegant days and nights."

Past the bridge I sat up, rose to my knees on the cushioned pad, as Dacey did also, and we studied the palazzo, of rose-red stone or perhaps overlaid with red plaster, the entire facade straight, severe and secretive, with cellar gratings on the ground floor, where the occasional high tides of the lagoon had easy access. There were no windows below the first storey which we could see above us. These long windows from Renaissance ceiling to floor opened upon narrow metal balconies in two pairs, the only interruption of the facade that faced on our canal. The facade facing the narrow, side canal beyond the building was even more severe—a huge, black-shadowed wall with its lowest long windows again high above the water.

A grim place for my father to have spent so many years alone. I remembered him as a vigorous, popular man, skilled at the political handling of associates and his foreign counterparts. It revealed how much he had needed my brilliant, witty mother, that her departure from his bed and his drawing rooms had so changed his life.

We tied up between two mooring poles bearing the red stripes which I assumed were in some way representative of my father's British post. The striped poles, as it turned out, were actually the heraldic colors of the original palazzo owners, the Androtti family. Two faintly flickering lamps cast the heavy canal door in a sickly array of gloomy shadows.

"Not very promising," murmured Dacey in some concern. "Dear me! I trust His Excellency is not gone off to bed. I have no notion what his habits might be in the last half-dozen years and more, but he was never used to retire so early."

I speculated that perhaps, in his single state, he had grown to be a bit of a valetudinarian.

"Just so, Madonna Carewe," the Captain put in. "Nor does he venture out to his affairs of business as do some of the younger plenipotentiaries. The French Ambassador, for example, is wherever the lights are brightest and the dice the liveliest. Curiously enough, he nearly always loses." He added sharply, "That popularity of his will be at an end if war should come."

Dacey said, "Heavens, I should hope so!" but I made no reply. I was too anxious, too nervous over possible changes between my father and me after nearly eight years. It was very well for me to hope to resume my old relations with Papa after so long; but the truth was, I had been a mere child of twelve at that time and now felt a very old and experienced twenty. Father had been a youngish man in his late forties, and would now be shortly facing sixty. He was at an age when he might be anything from a vigorous diplomat to a tired and embittered hermit. But I was certain the latter could not be true. Diplomacy and the ability to get on sociably with others had been two of his predominant characteristics. He could not have changed that much.

The Captain assisted us out of the gondola to the top step where, after an inexplicable little shiver—of anticipation? or premonition?—I raised my hand to the brass door knocker. My fingers shook and the knocker's echo seemed to reverberate through the ancient palace. Behind me, Miss Dace cried out, making me jump. I looked around, saw that the gondolier was setting our bandboxes and our portmanteaux on the lower step where the green slime trembled as the black waters of the canal washed over it and back. The gondolier ignored Dacey, but the Captain apologized and removed our things to the top step just as the huge, brass-studded door opened inward a few inches. From the scene around us, the atmosphere and the lateness of the hour, I half expected to see in the doorway some preposterous and sinister retainer escaped from Mr. Walpole's ghastly romance, *The Castle of Otranto*. What I did see was, in a few minutes, to prove a good deal more startling and even less believable to me.

A woman's voice, abrupt and crabbed, greeted me in Italian from behind that stingily opened door. "Yes. What is this disturbance at such an hour?"

Holding tight to my patience, I said in conciliatory tones, "I am Rachel Carewe. I am the daughter of His Excellency, Sir Maitland Carewe. I have reason to believe he is expecting me. Is he at home?"

Behind me, the Captain came to my rescue with some sternness and more arrogance that clearly shook the woman, who was undoubtedly my father's housekeeper.

"Signora! You will stand aside and admit the Plenipotentiary's daughter. At once!"

The woman obeyed, and at once. As I stepped into a foyer with an immensely high roof, and a hall singularly bare of furnishings, I looked at her for the first time. To my astonishment, the woman in her little, old-maidish linen cap and her neat black clothing was extraordinarily like the red-haired Gaming Lady I had seen at the Casino while we had awaited the gondola. She had evidently removed the ring I noticed earlier, and this woman's red hair was not powdered. Her figure, excellent for her age which I took to be the late forties, was muffled by the uniform quality of her full-skirted black gown. Her eyes were green, I noted, and oblique, almost oriental in shape. But most puzzling, even shocking to me, was my firm conviction that the same woman could be in two places at opposite ends of Venice at one and the same time. And, of course, garbed so very differently. I've no notion, even now, why I feigned ignorance over my previous sight of her.

She said reluctantly, "Very well then. Come in. But His Excellency has retired and you must wait until first light to see him."

Captain Dandolo kicked open the door with his boot, motioned for Dacey and for the gondolier with our boxes to follow the red-haired, surly housekeeper.

"Wake your master! Tell him to open his eyes to his daughter's arrival."

"No, no!" I protested quickly, waving away the idea. "He may be ill, or—"

The housekeeper seized the excuse I presented. "He is ill, Signorina. That is the truth on it. But I can arrange for your keeping overnight. And in the daylight—" She shrugged eloquently. "But that may be settled later. Capitano, you may leave the Signorina's things to me. I will see to everything."

I tried to make peace between them, having no wish to provoke more difficulties over what was clearly my unexpected and unannounced arrival.

"Please, Captain, I thank you, but I am persuaded it would agitate my father if he has retired. Undoubtedly, he has not been told of my arrival. Miss—Madame . . . did my father not receive a letter from me, sent under cover of another from a former employee, Miss Adelaide Dace?"

The woman's green eyes flashed in the light from the gondola lamp held high in the gondolier's hand. I could not but feel that the news was a shock to her. She recovered rapidly. "I am Mira Teotochi. His Excellency received no such plesasant news. He has been of the impression that his unfortunate daughter was guillotined more than a year ago. His last information was that Signorina Carewe remained in the Conciergerie, awaiting her trial. All his efforts to contact her afterward failed. We have heard nothing since. This will be a great shock to him."

It was crushing to me as well. I could appreciate the difficulty of breaking this news to my poor father. The woman was right. We would do well to wait until he had been gently prepared. I explained this to Captain Dandolo, trying at the same time to hush Dacey who had taken instant umbrage to the woman with the aristocratic name of Teotochi.

"I've a mind to announce our arrival to His Excellency myself. He ought to know."

"Do be still, Dacey," I said and turned to the Captain. "This would explain why no preparations were made to meet us. At all events, you have helped us far more than we could ever hope for, or expect. I trust we shall meet again, Messire."

He grinned and saluted my hand with an elaborate old-fashioned kiss upon my knuckles.

"Madonna, I shall make it my particular pleasure to meet again the lady with the so-lovely eyes of the violet."

I blinked, embarrassed at his absurdity, and stood in the doorway until the Captain stepped down into the tilting gondola, waved to me, then gave the signal for his gondolier to push off.

The Signora Teotochi studied me a moment or two, puzzled, I think; and for some odd reason I suspected she was alarmed. Or maybe it was only that in her capacity as housekeeper, she was considering all the endless problems of housing two females who arrived unannounced.

"Come, Signorina," she said to me when Dacey had coughed, cleared her throat and showed every sign of marching ahead to find our own chambers. "And the Signora. Your boxes will be brought to your rooms immediately. Since we were not expecting guests, I trust the Signorina Carewe will forgive the dust and rats. Most of the palace has been in disuse these many years."

"Rats?" Dacey echoed, standing stock still.

For the first time Signora Teotochi smiled. I thought it a sinister smile in despite of her carefully disguised beauty.

"But yes. In a city floating on the water, as the Serenissima is said to do, one must expect a few slight inconveniences Come. If you permit, I will lead the way."

"*Slight* inconveniences!" Dacey whispered to me in an audible aside which amused me a little. At one time in my life, I had seen a rat trained to entertain several of us in the Conciergerie. Rats had their uses, I supposed. And besides,

I had a great deal rather think about the possible rat population of Venice than the dreadful truth: In all these many months my father had never heard that I had been spared the guillotine. I was in the position of restoring myself to the life of a man who had learned to live very comfortably without me.

The Signora Teotochi led us from the dank hall smelling faintly of sewage into an entrance vestibule large enough to serve as a reception salon, or even a ballroom. Light from highstanding torchieres, one on either side of the doorway, gleamed upon the marble floor whose harlequin pattern of dark and light was carried out in the stucco stripes running vertically on the lower half of the halls. There was a certain grandeur to all of this but nothing more. There were no furnishings whatever, and the very pattern of the floor itself, austerely black and white, added to the excessive cold and dampness that I felt as we crossed this curiously large vestibule. There were elaborately grilled windows set very high in the west walls, facing on the tiny canal at the far side of the building. These windows were hardly utilitarian, except at sunset, and certainly no one could look out of them at that height; but at this hour of the night they served only as two dark eyes, staring at us, following our movements.

I must have remarked this aloud, because both Dacey and the housekeeper turned to stare at me. I colored a little, I think. It was such a stupid thing to have said. One would think I had run mad!

The housekeeper said abruptly, "The staircase. This way."

Three-quarters of the way down the room she opened a door and we found ourselves climbing a winding stone flight of steps so dark and cold I decided the entire affair was lighted by the heavens high above the stairwell.

Indeed, Dacey pointed up at the starlit sky seen through a circular opening above. She smiled wryly, "Even the roof is missing."

Signora Teotochi looked down at us, the slant of her glittering eyes accentuated. I suspect she believed Dacey was serious, but in any case, she remarked, "I fear I cannot place the Signora beside your chamber, Signorina. But you will both find yourselves upon the second storey. That is to say, you are three floors above the odors of the canal. This is not a large palazzo, but very distinguished and with an exciting history. One more storey; it is the top."

On the narrow stone landing we were about to pass

through the heavy door onto the first storey, but the Teotochi had already begun to mount the final flight. Dacey was breathing heavily, and I confess I myself was not in much better case. Meanwhile, we had seen no servants since we entered the building, and there was our luggage left on the canal floor. I wondered if Teotochi would bring up our boxes herself—and if so, where were the other servants in this house? There had been a strangeness about this business from the moment I realized she was the woman I had seen at the gaming casino. Or was I mistaken? Could they be two entirely different women? Then too, it was extraordinary that a palazzo of this size should produce no inhabitants, even though the hour was late. It was as if it was never used, had no visitors, transacted no business. It was most unlike my busy father.

Now and then, though, I heard a sound, a creaking door, even a possible footstep on the steps we had left below us, and I assumed that like all curious servants, those in this house were peeking out to see what we three females were about at this hour.

"The door," said Teotochi, ushering us through into a large dim corridor furnished with two imposing fifteenth-century armchairs, some noble pillars of beautifully veined marble, and a branch of candles which someone—the housekeeper herself?—had left on the red-cushioned chair before hurrying down to the canal door. In the circumstances, I did not quite have the courage to make any remarks about the condition of a household in which the only staircase appeared to be open to the uncertain elements of a maritime city like Venice.

No matter. My chief concern at the moment was to find a bed with even the poorest pretense of a mattress. Tomorrow must be left to fate, the fate which had saved my mother and me from execution and given me, if not my dear mother, a new life. Rather a dubious one at the moment. But I could not ask for everything, merely a chance to begin that new life. I counted upon my own fortitude to give me conduct from here.

And Dacey. I glanced at her. She was trotting along beside the housekeeper, paying very little heed to her surroundings. She even yawned as Teotochi turned at the end of the hall and stopped before a heavy, reinforced door opening off the wide corridor. I do not think poor Dacey was quite prepared to be shunted off into this dark place, cut off from anyone or anything familiar.

The Teotochi, having whipped out an enormous ring of keys, unlocked the door and with difficulty pushed it open. She gestured toward the interior. "But for a trifling of dust, this chamber should serve adequately, Signora, ah—"

"Adelaide Dace!"

"Just so. Just so. Here is your light." She went over and picked up the branch of candles from the chair. To my startled amusement she wrested one lighted candle out of its socket and offered it to Dacey. "You will find a holder in the armoire. Should you wish anything in the night—ah, but I had forgotten. The bell pull is broken. Well then, perhaps you will not find difficulties until the morning."

"Really, Madam! I'll have you know—" Dacey exclaimed in haughty surprise, but I caught her waving, indignant hand.

"Please, Dacey dear . . . not tonight. We will settle matters tomorrow."

"But you need me. I should be perfectly content with a truckle bed in your chamber. I don't like the way they are separating us. It smacks of chicanery."

"We have no truckle beds," said the Teotochi, who definitely had the last word.

I asked, as pleasantly as possible, "And where am I to be?"

She took me the full length of the corridor to the elaborate apartment upon the front of the building, overlooking the canal by which we had approached my father's palazzo. This room was not locked and was clearly intended for very special guests. I was suitably impressed. The woman brought in and set down the candelabrum, smoking now from the joggling she had given it when she wrested out Dacey's candle.

"You will be comfortable, I think, Signorina."

Smiling, I asked, "Is this too a broken bell cord?" She was not amused, shrugged and left me there in a large room darkly and heavily hung with green velvet. The bed was huge and made even more impressive by its curtains which I ached to draw apart. It looked frightfully confining in there, and while I had no particular prejudice against rodents, I had an absurdly violent distaste for spiders, of which I suspected there were an unconscionable number around that bed.

And so, having bid the woman good night in my turn, I was alone.

While I drew the heavy hangings back from the bed only to note the coverlet, likewise a dark green velvet, heavy enough to choke the unwary tenant, I heard Dacey's blessedly sane voice calling to me from the corridor outside. I called to her to come in. She had removed her fashionable dark pelisse and bonnet and was fluffing out the stiff little curls that had been light to begin with and now remained naturally yellow with the great good luck of many blondes in my acquaintance. She would have looked welcome to me if her curls were green as my bed coverlet. Though older than my mother, she had been my companion and guide in many a childhood adventure, and now dear Dacey was making every effort to assure herself of my present comfort. Having come from England to meet me in Genoa, she appointed herself my guardian from that moment.

"Would you like something to make you sleep? I have some laudanum drops," she suggested as she looked around my room, investigating nooks and crannies. She began to force open the warped doors leading out onto the tiny metal balcony which I had glimpsed from the gondola. She sneezed. "What a housekeeper that woman is!"

I went out and closed the hall door. While I assured Dacey that I preferred not to take laudanum and was tired enough to rest after the long day's ride, Dacey got the two glass doors open and crowded her way out onto the balcony.

"Foul air. Do you smell the odor of garbage?"

"Not in here," I reminded her. "Are the stars still out?"

"In splendor. It is truly beautiful. If one allows for that faint odor of—oh! It was a barge full of refuse going down that wretched side canal. It's gone now. That's better. . . . Hello! What's this?"

At her sudden change of tone I stopped rolling back the coverlet and looked over at the tiny balcony.

"What is it?"

She ducked quickly into the room, bringing the doors together with the utmost care not to make a sound. I stared at her, astonished.

"My old valise. That gondolier left it on the step."

I was a little puzzled at her excitement. "It must have been in the shadows. But it will be quite safe. Shall we have someone bring it in?" She stopped me as I reached for the faded petit-point bell pull beside the bed.

"That won't be necessary. Rachel?" Her large, friendly blue eyes narrowed in so sinister a fashion I had to smile at the absurd effect. "Rachel, my dear, my valise was just taken inside."

Bewildered, I said. "Then it is of no concern. It will doubtless be in your room shortly."

"Exactly. And brought up by something out of a Barbary pirate ship. Wait 'til you see the fellow."

"Well, perhaps he is a night guard. Mrs. Teotochi probably doesn't want to rouse any of the regular servants. Do you realize it is nearly midnight?"

"Hush!" Dacey was now hanging about my hall door, being most mysterious. She motioned to me and I joined her, somewhat reluctant. I confess I thought her conduct a bit absurd. Dacey's door was open and the light from the candle in her room, though leaving most of the hall in deep shadow, was still enough illumination to permit us to see what went on. Halfway down the wide hall the staircase door was kicked open and an enormous, bald male in well-worn, grease stained livery appeared in the corridor, setting several of our bandboxes on the ancient parquetry of the floor. The oblique slant of his eyes and the greenish-bronze glow of his flesh suggested Tartar blood. Below his livery tunic he wore baggy Turkish pantaloons. He reached behind him, and set two portmanteaux beside the bandboxes. Dacey was right. He was a true exotic, though perhaps not so unusual a sight here in Venice, the gateway to fabulous Constantinople.

Except for my as yet unseen father, we appeared to be alone in the enormous palazzo with this intimidating fellow and the equally intimidating Mira Teotochi.

Dacey whispered to me, "What sort of place is this? We seem to be the only normal human beings in the entire place."

"Except for Mira Teotochi," I corrected her.

"I make no exceptions," she said, sealing her lips firmly. I smiled, but I was much more inclined to shiver.

CHAPTER THREE

PARTLY OUT OF CURIOSITY, and partly too, from a feeling I shared with Dacey that there was something eerie about this exotic household, I remained in silence beside her, watching the Turk's behavior with our luggage. Just as Dacey predicted, he took her boxes to the room at the far end of the corridor, and seeing the open door, looked in, then toward the front of the house, toward my door.

"He guesses where I am," Dacey whispered.

I nodded and then, having shut the door in silence, we waited. The creature moved along the corridor with the utmost care not to make a noise and left my own cases in front of my door. We gave him a few minutes to disappear from sight, then looked out. I brought in my cases and we stood there staring at each other.

Dacey broke the silence, expressing our mutual wonder. "I shall bolt my door tonight," she said in a shaky voice unlike positive, confident Dacey. "And I strongly advise you to do so as well."

"Thank you. I intend to. . . . Good night, Dacey dear."

In the doorway she looked back. "Rachel, I should sleep a deal more comfortably if I knew there really was a Sir Maitland Carewe in this great palace of horrors."

"Dacey! Good God! What are you suggesting?" But of course, I knew. And I was beginning to share her strong uneasiness. "At all events, we shall know in the morning."

We whispered our good nights again and I waited until I saw her door close and heard the rusty screech of the bolt being thrown. Then I stepped back and bolted my own door. After that, for the first time I went about studying the big chamber in which I had been placed. Against the west wall, between two high grilled windows, there was an armoire, large enough to hide at least three assassins, and of dark enough wood to depress the room and its occupants. There was a piece of furniture of quite different period and type beside the double doors opening onto the little balcony. This was a comparatively modern marble-topped commode of the present eighteenth century. On the other side of the doors was a kidney-shaped writing desk so exquisite and so familiar, I felt a sharp pain about the heart; for it had been my mother's desk, left behind in England when she deserted my father. It was the first actual sign that my father had ever been in this curious and desolate house.

"At least that is something," I told myself, and upon further examination found in its small, unobtrusive drawer a charming white-enameled snuffbox of an oriental motif done in gold, which I recalled having seen in my father's hand as he took snuff with a gesture surprisingly graceful for a man who was not a dandy or a fop. I assumed from these little reminders that father had slept in this room at one time, or that the articles had been removed from his own bedchamber. This latter thought was disconcerting, in view of everything else that had occurred.

No matter. The painful events of past years had taught me one thing: to take my repose where I could find it. A sleepless, nervous, silly female was in no case prepared to face problems much less the danger that might appear to threaten us on all sides in this place. I unpacked my immediate necessities from the top of my portmanteau, reflecting on the impropriety of my appearing at my father's palazzo without a maid to lend me countenance. My father, though genial, had always been a high-stickler, and would think me lost to all decent society. He would never understand the new French democratic way of doing things. But so be it. I must go to bed without having washed so much as a finger, since, clearly, there would be no water in a chamber like this, set aside for infrequent visitors.

Oddly enough, I was mistaken. Upon the spur of the moment, I glanced inside the armoire's high shelf and found a pewter carafe. I smelled the pewter cup beside the carafe, I drank a little water. I had considerable experience with brackish water in prison, but this was fresh. I wondered. Then I ran my hand over the furniture. It had been dusted recently. So this chamber must be in general use. By whom?

Just to be certain, I went over and checked the door's bolt before washing away the dust of the day's journey and dressing for bed. Before what appeared to be a shaving mirror I brushed my hair, happy indeed to see that regular treatment and a good sound brush were finally restoring some of the dark luster of which I had been vain as a girl.

A gondola full of singing, laughing revelers disturbed the night's eerie silence and I looked out through the long glass doors, envious of them. Both males and females were masked and enjoying this journey over the dark, sparkling waters that had seemed so sinister to me only an hour before. I finished brushing my hair and I got up to close the heavy velvet portieres over the balcony doors. As I did so, I became aware of a slight movement just on the edge of my vision. I blinked rapidly and paused, straining to see through the darkness.

Eastward on the canal, just beyond the palazzo, was the curving little footbridge under which our gondola had glided before tying up at the palazzo's mooring poles. On the far side of the bridge, leaning on the stone railing, was a dark figure, a man, I thought, studying the facade of my father's house. Watching my room as well, no doubt, perhaps noting when my light went out. A thief? Venice was full of them, I knew. Or something more terrifying than a thief? Upon learning of my imminent departure for the Venetian Republic, the officials in Paris and at the border had told me chilling tales of the way in which the mysterious and secretive Council of Ten governed Venice. Answerable only to the Great Assembly which had never in its history impeached any one of them, these aristocrats held sway by secrecy, terror, and, it was whispered, by summary justice, or as near to it as made no matter.

"Spies everywhere," said my French friends. "One false step—even a faint suspicion against you, and if you are a nobody, you are stabbed some night and rolled into a handy canal. If you are a member of the Quality, you will be brought before one of the Ten's Inquisitors, Old Red Robe, or one of the two Black Robes, and say what you will in your own defense, all it needs for your undoing is a hint from an enemy. You are taken to a dungeon and strangled—a nasty way to go."

I made no doubt of it. For all its decadent splendor, the Serenissima was an anachronism, left over from the barbarous days when the fires of the Inquisition had ruled Europe.

And this creature now, slinking there in the shadows, with his form only faintly etched by the stars, was he a spy from the Council of Ten? I shivered. I did not like to move lest I call his attention to me, for he might have had his eyes upon the lower floors; but I could not stand there all night in my thin night-rail, with my hair tumbling around my shoulders like a hoyden. I snapped the portieres closed and went to bed.

Save for one curious and inexplicable incident—dream or mental aberration, if you will—I found this heavy bed surprisingly comfortable, once the depressing velvet hangings were pushed apart. I was aroused late in the night, an hour or so before dawn, by a voice out of my dream, calling to me. In those first seconds of half-sleep, it seemed reasonable that I should hear the childhood name by which father had addressed me long ago:

"Shelly . . . Shelly, my girl . . ."

I turned my head upon the pillows, wondering where I was, and opened my eyes. The size of the bed confused me and I supposed I must still be dreaming. I tried to recall what it had been, that pleasant snatch of life borrowed from the days of my childhood when Mother and Father were together and we lived outside London, on a Surrey estate that overlooked the winding Thames far below our green hillside.

"Shelly . . . Shelly?"

The sound was only in my head. I was awake now. I sat straight up in bed, badly shaken. Silence ensued.

Gradually, I made out the faint creaking noises of age, timbers and the wind rushing through the narrow side canal and across the canal that acted as the palazzo's main street. There were no more voices absurdly materializing out of my dream. By the time I made up my mind to this I was so relieved that my thoughts reverted to the last curious sight I had witnessed before retiring. The bed was so high I was forced to use the steps beside it to reach the floor, but from there across the room it was easy enough to make my way.

The portieres I had closed so hastily and carelessly, out of temper with the spying creature in the bridge, had fallen a little apart so that the faint glow from the lamps above the mooring poles crept into the room. Every object of furniture lay in heavy shadow but there was a path of light across the floor. I went to the long glass doors and peered out between the portieres.

Our spy must have tired and gone elsewhere. At all events, he had vanished from the bridge and the abutments on either side. I pressed closer against the glass, trying to see below the water line. No sign of him. He had certainly retired to his own lodgings like a sensible man. Or he may have gone to report whatever developments were of interest to the Inquisitor for the sinister Council of Ten. Ugly thought.

As I climbed back in between the rapidly chilling bedclothes, I had another thought: Was it possible he had disappeared into the palazzo itself? But why? It was too absurd.

A surprisingly short time later I fell asleep again and was aroused after sunup by a sharp-knuckled rap on the door.

"Now, we'll see what we shall see," I promised myself, putting my feet over the side of the bed and dropping to the floor without regard to the bed stool. I snatched on my robe and hurried to the door, trying at the same time to restore an inner calm I was far from feeling.

It was the swarthy man with the large, shaven head and livery and trousers vaguely Turkish, and he was offering me a covered tray. I thanked him, but he merely grunted. With the pupils of his eyes like chips of onyx, he observed me and the room behind me. It was an interest that made me more than a little uncomfortable. I turned away with the tea tray, hoping he would accept this as a hint to depart, but to my annoyance, he shuffled a step or two toward me in his peculiarly curved slippers, and made an odd, mumbling sound in his throat. I set the tray on a tilt table near the door and looked at the man sternly.

"That will be all, thank you."

Whatever interest the Turkish fellow had in me, it was not either pleasant or flattering. I wondered what I had done to earn his dislike and decided that he must have resented bringing me the tea tray. Since the household had not expected me or Dacey, it was small wonder that my Turkish friend disliked this unexpected trip up three storeys to wait upon a stranger like me.

I relaxed a little and asked him as he shuffled reluctantly

backward into the hall. "Is my father . . . Is the Ambassador awake yet?"

He replied in the same manner as before, with the rattling noise and pointing to his throat. Belatedly understanding that he was mute, I begged his pardon and watched him move away. When he had disappeared through the door opening onto the stone staircase, I saw Dacey's door open at the far end of the hall. With her faded golden locks still in curl papers, she waved to me. I asked her if she had her tea tray and if she would join me. She did so, kicking my door closed to give us some privacy, and informing me, "It is not tea, but chocolate. These Venetians!"

I smiled at her expression. "But it is hardly a death potion. We shall contrive."

"I shouldn't be at all surprised to discover that death potions are all the crack with these creatures in this household!"

As she was out-of-reason cross and threatening to spill everything by pulling out the table over the lumpy carpet, I hurried to the rescue, got the table away and asked her to fetch two chairs. By the time we had arranged ourselves in front of the balcony doors with the portieres drawn back and the sunlit tile roofs of Venice before us, Dacey was in better humor.

"You see," I pointed out presently when she had emptied her little chocolate pot and was finishing her third cup, "it is not poison, after all."

She looked around furtively, as though she suspected the very walls of eavesdropping. "That's as may be, but I have my suspicions. Nothing concrete, mind. Yet it would not surprise me to find poor Sir Maitland bound and gagged in the moldy cellars under this place."

"What? Bound and gagged for five years?" I laughed in despite of a little nagging fear that underlay all my thoughts.

"You may scoff, but it would not be the first time such things have happened. My window overlooks the area toward St. Mark's Square, and I saw a most suspicious ship at anchor out in the lagoon. The sort with triangular sails of that creature's heathen shores."

"The Teotochi woman?"

"No, no, dear. Do pay attention. The Turk. Every day people are captured and taken to Barbary to be sold into slavery among those heathen countries." She lowered her voice discreetly. "Especially pretty females."

It was perfectly true, of course, but as it had never hap-

pened to anyone of my acquaintaince, it was difficult to
believe it could occur here in civilized Venice, even though
rumor said otherwise. Adelaide must have seen my skepticism
because she reminded me, "Incidentally, where did he come
from, that Turk? Why does that redheaded female make hire
of such a creature? There are enough Venetians out of work.
Is she up to something, that she wishes her servants to be
silent?"

"It may be that Mrs. Teotochi prefers silent servants to
chatterboxes."

Dacey thought little of my reasoning and said so as she
reached absently for my pot of chocolate, and poured the
dregs into her cup. "No. You must know, if you will think
a trifle about it, that the Plenipotentiary of a great nation
does not reside in a great, dusty palace with nothing but
that detestable redhead to care for him."

But I found myself still resisting this expression of my own
secret fears. It wasn't until Dacey had returned to her room
to dress than I remembered my disturbing dream of my
father calling to me. I stood in the middle of the room just
below the foot post of my bed and studied the walls, the two
small barred west windows above the armoire, the walls
darkened by age but severely beautiful with their panels of
damask covering. I gained nothing from the study except to
realize that however ancient this building might be, it was
basically rich in artistry and decor and even in furnishing.
Exactly the sort of home my father would have chosen.
Father was always greatly attracted to the beauties of the
antique, and especially articles used during the period of the
early Renaissance.

And where was Father amid all this Renaissance splendor?
If I did not see him this morning, I was determined upon
reporting the entire affair and our suspicions to the local
policing force of the Ten, an organization familiarly called
the *sbirri*. As nearly as I could see, none of the affairs of the
British Embassy were being conducted here. No ceaseless
comings and goings, none of the crucial matters that must
concern a Britain currently at war with France and operating
her essential intrigues and spying in neutral Venice. The work
of the embassy must be handled elsewhere at present. That
too I would find out.

I dressed in one of my better gowns made in the new
French style, with long, tight sleeves, buttoned four times
at the wrist and lower arm, a high waist, and the straight

folds of lilac crepe skirt, the whole silhouette uncluttered by hoops, panniers, sacques or towering headdresses. I was shaking out my new shawl which had been sadly crushed, when I I became aware that I was being watched by two females in the doorway. One was a harmless, pitifully thin, big-eyed young chambermaid. But the other female—I was so angry at this silent spying that I swung the shawl rapidly over my head and around my shoulders, flicking the fringe across the face of Mira Teotochi.

For just an instant the woman's glittering eyes narrowed. She brushed her shaking fingers across her nose and cheeks. She said, "You—startled me."

I smiled. Thank heaven I had not been forced to say that myself, as I felt sure she had intended, in sneaking about like that. Her shaking fingers might have been mine, had I not by the merest luck seen her standing there with the chambermaid, watching me so silently. She understood my dry smile and reddened a little.

Bearding the lioness, I asked directly, "Have you come to take me to my father, Signora?"

"Yes, Signorina."

That took me aback, it was so unexpected. I had stiffened and clenched my fists ready to do battle, metaphorically speaking. Now, I should relax, be glad, be enormously relieved. I told myself I was all of these things, but truth to tell, I was almost as unnerved as before. "Then I must thank you. This is welcome news."

Odd, though, that my father had thus far made no effort to approach the daughter he once believed lost to the horrors of the guillotine. Unless, of course . . . unless he was seriously ill. Poor Father! That would explain everything, even the reason why the affairs of the embassy were not conducted here in the palazzo.

"I shall come at once."

As the chambermaid went in to clear away my breakfast, Mira stepped back into the wide corridor, and as I joined her, closing the door behind me, she said in a perfectly reasonable, almost friendly voice, "It is as well if the Signora does not join us for your first visit. You will understand?"

"I am afraid I do not. I agree that I should be alone with my father for a first meeting, but is it because he is more ill than I supposed?"

"That—possibly. His Excellency was first stricken more than a year ago. The water here, and the diseases spreading from the Barbary shores. We are not precisely a healthy city for gentleman foreigners like your father. And hard upon the typhus came a blow of the brain."

"A blow of the brain! You mean he was attacked?"

"No, no. A pressure upon the brain caused by the breaking of a vessel of the blood." As I gasped and felt ready to sink with aching pity for him, the woman reassured me in part. Having learned suspicion in my later years, I wondered now if she had deliberately contrived to discourage me before giving me a single bit of cheerful news.

"But he is much improved, Signorina. He is able to move and to speak now, with occasional difficulty, but unquestionably to speak, and to walk, if he is cautious. Of course, he oversees the more important matters of the embassy. Routine problems are conducted at the Palazzo Correra on the Grand Canal. Naturally, His Excellency's secret is known to very few."

I wondered how much the English Prime Minister, Mr. Pitt, suspected of Father's illness. In these crucial times, his condition would be disastrous to British interests with the Serenissima, and with the archenemy, Republican France. I was torn between love for my father and the knowledge that by being party to this deception I would betray his country's interests abroad. Curious—and unsettling—that I could refer to the land of my birth as "his country!"

"Does he know I am in this house?"

"He knows, Signorina."

And suddenly, as she opened the door onto the stone steps, I recalled my dream in the night. Although the sky far overhead was a piercing blue, and the day obviously sunny, there was a brisk breeze blowing off the Adriatic.

I wrapped myself more closely in my shawl as I asked Mira Teotochi, "Does my father often wander through the house at night?"

She stopped, staring at me. "Certainly not, Signorina!"

I watched her. I think my close gaze alarmed her a little. I did not know why. "When did you tell my father of my arrival—my . . . resurrection from the guillotine?"

"But this morning! Only an hour since. Had he known earlier, I am persuaded he would have come to you himself, difficult as it might be. It was a great shock, however, and when I had told him, he tried to leave his bed to see you. But I fear he was a trifle confused and he stumbled as he stepped onto the footstool. We put him back to bed."

So it had not been Father I heard last night, somehow penetrating or giving life to my dream. "Who is *we,* Signora?"

"But—Achmed and I. His mother is our cook here at the palazzo. A gypsy from the Taurus Mountains in the Ottoman Empire. Achmed is a mute. The Emir of Bokhara caught him too close to the Seraglio and deprived him of his tongue."

I exclaimed something, more horror than sympathy, I believe, when the door behind us was thrown open abruptly and Dacey's voice, shaken but angry, hurled after us down the steps, "What are you about? Where are you taking the child?"

I wanted to smile at Mira Teotochi's startled expression. "The—the child? Ah, but you mean the Signorina, of course!"

"Hush, Dacey dear," I called up to her. "I am going to see my father."

"If you are not returned in half an hour," Dacey warned us, "I'll be coming for you myself, and will not take no for an answer! Half an hour!"

Alarmed at her vehemence, I begged her to give us forty-five minutes at the least, but she hung over the top of the stone balustrade, determined not to budge from the spot.

My father's apartments were upon the first floor, in the back, a bedchamber and sitting room. The wide hall similar to that on the second storey was here used as a gallery. There were numerous dark, gloomy portraits, several of them of men in a doge's bright robes. I supposed my father must have taken the palazzo simply in its patriotic Venetian state. There was nothing English added. Nothing that I could find, in any case.

Shaking with nervous excitement at the prospect of our meeting after eight eternal years, I followed Mira Teotochi into my father's sitting room. Like the gallery, the room appeared to be a museum piece for the fifteenth century. In a general way, and within limits, I found museums interesting, but the thought of my vigorous, life-loving father confined to ancient, dark, velvet-hung quarters that were damp and smelling of age, sickened me. My heart was wrung with compassion for him and I longed to open those side windows, tear down the heavy draperies and bring fresh life to him.

But first, I longed to see him. I ran past the housekeeper, drew down the latches on the double doors and swung them open into the bedchamber. The curtains around the bed were pushed open and I saw my father propped up against a half-dozen pillows and leaning toward me, stretching out his arms, even his fingers, spread and reaching for me. As I ran across the thick carpet to him, I heard the housekeeper pass me, breathless, as she reached for the portieres that kept the daylight out of the high, side windows. She reached for the long cords, pulled them open and I was shocked at the age that had settled upon my father during the time since I had left him as a girl. And I did not doubt that poor Father found me also considerably aged from the child of twelve to the woman of twenty.

"My little Rachel! My Shelly . . ."

I was hugging his thin shoulders so hard I feared I might hurt those brittle bones, but though he winced, his arms did not release their hold on me. His proud, lined face and pain-glazed gray eyes broke into happiness that made him look years younger.

"It's your Shelly," I murmured. "The Frenchies couldn't destroy your Shelly, Father."

He ran nervous, palsied fingers over my cheeks, my neck and throat. "I thought—they said you were to die on the guillotine."

"I've a tough neck, Father. You see?"

Neither of us mentioned my mother. I had no notion whether he was still embittered by her desertion, and the way she had taken his only child with her. And as for me, I had loved my mother and shared too much of her sufferings to deny her now. Perhaps he suspected this, I thought, and like me preferred not to mention her.

"Excellency," cut in Mira Teotochi's voice with all the authority she commanded in the sickroom, "you must not sit up too long. You must rest before receiving the Secretary from the Palazzo Correra. That will be tiring."

I released his hands reluctantly, patting them. I knew my eyes were blinded by tears and I was ashamed of them. Long ago I had learned how useless they were. Now, above all, I wanted to cheer my father, to get him well.

"I'm sorry, Father. I'll leave you now to rest. Are they a great ordeal, these meeting with your embassy staff?"

He shrugged, grimaced at the pain the gesture cost him, and looked at the housekeeper, hesitant. It hurt me to see how much he depended upon this woman whom I instinctively mistrusted. Signora Teotochi nodded, and I, observing her with deepest interest, was less than pleased to note the grace of her movements. There was no question about it. She deliberately called attention to her least attractive physical qualities, possibly in order to retain her post. I supposed there might be some prejudice against a beautiful house-keeper, some feeling that she would not devote proper time to her post. But it should really be no concern of mine.

"I shall hope to see you later, Father. When you are in good case to—to entertain one special visitor: your loving daughter." I kissed him on the forehead. Yet, I found it odd. Not like the old days, when father had been so dominant, so vigorous. He had fallen very low, almost helpless, and now I must furnish the strength for the family. Perhaps, after I learned about his post and its responsibilities, I could assist him in some small way. I would discover how when Father was able to see me for a longer period.

Signora Teotochi walked with me to the siting room door. I looked back at Father over her head and saw that his gaze had shifted from me to her. There was no doubt in my mind, painful as it might be to admit, that he found her of far greater interest than his daughter. Or maybe it was simply that I recognized in that look the sort of feeling he had had for mother and which may have made me jealous when I was young. I did not know. I could not remember having been jealous of his attention to my mother. But surely, I excused myself—surely a daughter newly returned from the dead, must touch him. He had been a loving father, between the enormous pressures of his diplomatic posts. And today, during our very brief meeting, he had shown me an unques-tionable devotion. I could not mistake the love and care I had seen in his heavily lined face, his eyes now so pale, that had once been so vivid and alive, and his arms as we em-braced. . . . Or had I mistaken it, after all.

I was so overset by this realization that I hurried out, nearly treading upon the excited Dacey's toes. The door closed behind Signora Teotochi and me, at least so I thought, until I remarked on Dacey's expression and heard her acid tone: "She closed herself in with His Excellency."

"Very true. Good heavens! Dacey, I believe I am jealous. Well, let us go out and enjoy this mad, floating city."

But first it was necessary for Dacey and me to return to our rooms and fetch our bonnets and reticules. Since I had only just come out of mourning, my lilac bonnet had no plumes but only the wide taffeta ribbons by which I formed a bow under my right cheek. Dacey being good enough to say I was "in exceptional looks," I felt more lively and con-fident than I had in years. Had I dwelt upon my father's deteriorated health, I might revert to gloom, but this was impossible in Adelaide Dace's company. Her blonde curls, worn very much as they had been arranged in her childhood, I daresay, bobbed out around her pink bonnet like bubbles from champagne and were just as contagious in spreading their cheerful aura. She wore clothing perhaps more suited to a young female, but then Dacey's outlook was permanently youthful, and her acquaintances were the better for it.

We passed the shaven-headed Turk on the ground floor. Dacey whispered that he could not be about anything good, but in point of fact, he was scrubbing the torchieres in the large vestibule and I acquitted him of criminal intent—in all but the look with which he favored us. That was unquestionably sinister, though it may have been the mere cast of his unusual, flat, larger-than-life features.

Out on the steps we realized that it would be necessary to begin our trek to St. Mark's in the opposite direction unless we crossed the larger canal over the bridge and walked along the narrow quai on the north side of the canal. We found it childishly exciting to cross over the little bridge, watching gondolas and an occasional small barge move under it at the same time. Truly, I thought, a remarkable city! Very like a dream world and, if one believed the stories told throughout Europe, a nightmare world as well.

As we stepped onto the quai at the opposite end of the bridge, I remembered the spy I had seen last night, watching our palazzo across the canal. It would have provided him with an excellent vantage point to watch my chamber and those others on the front of the building. I decided not to think about it. Instead, I would enjoy the morning beauty of Venice. I started along the quai, in the direction of the campanile and Byzantine towers of St. Mark's Cathedral.

Dacey was still staring around at the scene behind us and I called to her. "Come along, Dacey. Aren't you anxious to see the square Captain Dandolo thinks is so splendid?"

Dacey giggled. "I shall leave the noble Captain to you, dear. I declare, if there isn't the most attractive young rogue flirting with me in that gondola beyond the bridge! I have always adored dark eyes . . ."

Laughing, I turned and glimpsed the dark-eyed lean young rogue in the gondola. And then I realized: "But I know that fellow."

Dacey had suddenly lost interest in her flirtation and was studying the facade of Father's palazzo across the canal;

when she realized I had spoken, she only said vaguely, "My dear. How could you know him?"

Feeling more and more confused, I pieced together several astonishing suspicions. "But he is not wearing his ghastly spectacles. . . . He is your friend, the Snirp."

Now Dacey gasped, and I stared at her. "What in heaven's name is the matter?"

She was still staring at the palazzo, not at our Snirp. "Well, I never! I would not have credited it. His Excellency is white-haired now, and much, much older?"

"Certainly. It has been eight years, and he has suffered two terrible illnesses."

"Yes, but—is that your dear father, standing before the long windows on the first storey of the palazzo?"

I followed her stare. Had it not been so extremely unlikely, in fact impossible to him in his present condition, I should have said it was my father embracing Mira Teotochi, just behind the double glass doors of the salon on the first storey.

"Don't stare," I said after a moment or two in a tight voice unlike myself. "Pretend you do not see."

CHAPTER FOUR

"IT CAN'T HAVE BEEN His Excellency," Dacey repeated, with less assurance. "Can it? And kissing a housekeeper!"

"Certainly not. My father could scarcely rise from his bed. It is another man with gray hair. Someone employed about the palazzo. Come along. We don't want them to see us."

But though we followed the quai to the next little humped bridge and started across, always headed, as we hoped, toward the square of San Marco, Dacey was still puzzled.

"I do not think I understand you," she complained. "Where did you meet my dashing gondola gallant before this moment? And what has that young man to do with a—a snirp?"

I considered going into details about the man with the odd, disguising spectacles at the gaming casino, and how he persisted in popping up all over Venice, but I said nothing. The truth was that, in spite of my attempts to forget what Dacey and I had seen at the window of Father's palazzo, it invaded all my thoughts.

"Let us think of pleasant things. Just for now, I would like to think about beauty and sunlight and simply living. Without thoughts of death."

"My dearest Rachel, I could not agree with you more. And you must never think of death again. I trust your interview with your dear Papa this morning has not overcome you. Was he not delighted to see his daughter alive and well?"

I assured her that he was, and then explained his weakness, the effort it had taken for him to embrace me and speak to me. "So he cannot have been the man at the window. He is so very ill. You cannot conceive how ill."

"Then who was the tall, gray-haired man? He did not look to be a servant."

I had been thinking. "Some friend of Teotochi's, obviously. Someone, perhaps, who . . . I don't know."

"Friend!" She sniffed. "Likely friend, indeed! Let us hope the rascal carried off that mistress of his. Between us, you and I can make all comfortable for His Excellency." But I noted that she was looking with great concentration along the canal as we crossed the bridge over a pungent-smelling little basin where gondolas were gathered before the wave-washed steps of a busy inn.

I laughed, reminding her, "You will be much too busy with your flirt. Do you see him yet?"

She tried not to look excessively conscious. "No. Nor am I like to see him. Not with all these endless little alleys of dirty water and cats."

"Dacey!" I teased her. "You are no romantic. You should not notice such mundane matters as dirty canal waters."

"But only consider, washing one's, er, inner garments in such waters!"

We found ourselves busy making our way along an incredibly narrow alley between the tall, unbroken walls of several buildings, and I did not trouble to remind her that it had not yet become absolutely necessary to wash one's inner garments in the canals. The alley was occupied, very possessively, by several lean and belligerent cats. Before my quick, cat-loving sympathies could be aroused, my thoughts reverted to Adelaide's romance, her Snirp, and I began to wonder if it was merely my vivid imagination, or if the bespectacled young man, minus his spectacles, had stood on the bridge last night watching the palazzo. If so, then his appearance in the gondola today had been far from coincidental. I was more than ever convinced that, for all his attractions, the man was sinister.

"Mercy! They are wearing masks. The ladies are actually wearing masks by daylight," Dacey remarked, staring wildly at the crowds passing by the arcade ahead of us. We had seemed to be alone in this dirty, sewage-littered passage but once we passed under the arcade and into the great Piazza San Marco, we were nearly trodden into the cobblestones by the endless stream of elegant strollers along the arcades that lined the long and short sides of the Piazza. A few of the women were dressed in the new Paris fashion, bonnets, slim skirts, tight spencers partially concealing—and outlining—the bosom. But a preponderance of the females wore great, plumed hats and elaborate panniered gowns, the hems sweeping the damp, dirty cobbles. Over all, and blowing in the wind, were their huge cloaks. These women wore teasing little masks, mere bejeweled trifles that scarcely did more than outline the eager, darting eyes. Fans, too, were fluttering everywhere, for the most part elegant, with beautifully carved ivory sticks. It was as if we were still far back in the eighteenth century and not within three years of the nineteenth.

Dacey began to retreat, slowly. "What shall we do, dear? The gentlemen are looking at us very oddly."

"Walk. Keep walking. Do not let them frighten us. I have seen things a good deal more terrifying that these well-breeched fops and dandies."

Dacey looked as though she didn't believe me, but she raised her chin and did her best to brave what was actually a march against the tide of strollers. Having glimpsed the Piazzetta, the short quai opening on the lagoon across the square, and remembering Captain Dandolo's remarks about the beauty of the cathedral, we turned and looked back at the great ornamental basilica which, with the neighboring Doges' Palace, bordered the near end of the Square and the Piazzetta. Though I had seen paintings and even a miniature of St. Mark's, I was vastly disappointed at my first real view of this overdecorated, fantastic example of what appeared to be a Byzantine mosque. I was to learn that St. Mark's looked its best to me under special lighting, such as a blazing sunset, or in the blue shadows of dawn.

A fellow in cape and bauta, a little the worse for a night in the gaming hells, bumped into Dacey and me, trying to go between us, under the alcoholic delusion that he might be more sylphlike than in fact he was. Dacey screamed, but I was too busy trying to release us both from the fellow's silver lace cuffs and his anachronistic gentleman's sword.

When I had finally broken free from his enormous cuff, and was at work lifting his scabbard out of Dacey's shawl, he rolled his large eyes at me absurdly and murmured with some difficulty, "Signorina . . . a kiss?"

"Not today, Messire. Another time."

"Another time? You p-promise?"

"Yes, yes. Go along. Or you will be late."

He had a broad, heavy-jowled young face that would run to fat when he was older, but there was some quality, a likable, vague grin perhaps, that made me sympathetic and my remark, thrown out at random, must have struck its mark.

His eyes opened wide. "You th-think she will f-forgive me?"

Whoever "she" might be, I answered, "Be brave. Try. You will see."

"Sapristi! It is worth a try." And away he went, having torn Dacey's shawl in jerking hard away from her.

Our little contretemps had aroused the interest of surrounding strollers, and as Dacey and I started away from the cathedral, walking along the Piazza toward the delightful outdoor café, I noticed many of the pretentious masquers of both sexes watching us. Not with admiration, I daresay. Doubtless they felt that every female in the square who was gowned in the French fashion must be "fast." But though Dacey pinched my sleeve anxiously, I was resolved not to yield to these ridiculous pressures. At the same time I was surprised at my own obstinacy. I had only newly come from Revolutionary France, assuming I fled from all I hated; yet from my very first meeting with the Reactionary Venetians last night, I had found myself completely alien to this antique world.

We reached the café and were assailed by the pungent odor of coffee. Only one or two tables were vacant and I believe if we had not been so challenged by the dandies of the square, I should have suggested that we continue to stroll under the arcade, forgetting the all-too-popular café. Across the Piazza was another café, equally crowded, but its patrons included a number dressed in the French style. It seemed much more suited to us.

"Shall we?" Dacey ventured, indicating it with a nervous nod of the head.

We had passed the café on our side of the square and when I looked back at all the busy little tables, the morning sunlight made the scene immensely attractive. Just so had looked the Paris cafés during those frightening, yet strangely stirring days of the Terror. My mother and I had often sat at the tables of La Régence, across the Rue St. Honore from the Palais-Royal. When the daily tumbrels passed on their way to the guillotine set up in the Place Louis Quinze, which we were instructed to call the Place de la Révolution, Mother and I always looked away. Later, after our own release from the Conciergerie, thanks to the events dated the Ninth and Tenth Thermidor which saw the end of Citizen Robespierre, Mother and I took our morning coffee and afternoon aperitif in the Café Procope of our poorer district, the district of Danton and Desmoulins. But always, there had been the cafés. Just such as this one catching the glorious Venetian sunlight today.

"Come. Let us sit here." I made the decision suddenly and poor Dacey, uneasy over our situation, promptly sat down at the nearest vacant table. I took the little seat opposite her and we received our coffee almost at once. I knew, as did Dacey, that we were the synosure of eyes near us, but we made a pretense of ignoring both the gentlemen and the flirtatiously masked women. The coffee we received occupied our more immediate attention. It was served in tiny cups and was as black as coal. We were afraid to drink it and exchanged uneasy glances.

Dacey leaned across the table, whispering, "I have heard that the Ottoman Empire recruits females for the Sultan's harem by feeding likely females very strong coffee. It drives them quite mad. A dangerous beverage."

I took leave to doubt this, but Dacey was looking so alarmed I felt I must make good my denial. I sipped the peculiar black potion. Whatever its ultimate effect, it was enormously vitalizing. Eventually Dacey was led to imitate me, in spite of the beginnings of comment and insinuation from the male at the next table. The man was unattractive at best, seeming effete and overperfumed so strongly we could smell his scent, yet his features were overlaid with rouge and a delicately placed black patch as a kind of beauty mark. He was not the only painted male in the Square, but the nearest at the moment. I had not seen anything like him since the second year of the Revolution, when the emigrés took flight.

Dacey murmured, "Is he speaking to us?"

"Ignore him," I said, but although I hated myself for my cowardice, I saw my fingers shake as they brought my cup to my lips again. I tried to pretend the shakiness was due to the strength of the vicious black brew we drank. The fellow grew more insolent. A pair of young gentlemen with a masked female between at the table beyond began to giggle at our discomfiture. Yet, as I was determined not to be outfaced by these scurvy fellows, there seemed little to be done but to pretend we were deaf.

Quite suddenly, over Dacey's perturbed face came an expression first of puzzlement, then of relief. A shadow crossed between us and the morning sunlight and, of all things, Dacey's young gallant of the gondola pulled out the third chair at our table. His keen dark eyes were again blurred by the spectacles whose silver rims caught the light, giving him a hideous, peering look which, I could see, was totally false.

"Madonna Rachel—Madama Dace, you have been forced to wait, and on the Austrian side of the Square. How remiss of me! I had no notion!" He beamed an enchanting smile upon both of us and had the effrontery to sit down, explaining, "On this side of the Square gather the remnants of the Old Regime in Europe. It is not too popular with the true Venetians, who prefer to seat themselves with the less Reactionary groups, upon the side of the Caffé Florian, across the Square. No matter! We will try their coffee."

Since we were now respectably accompanied by a male and, from his cut, a gentleman, our neighbors now sought elsewhere for their prey.

Dacey was, meanwhile, taken with the riddle he had set us. "Are you in truth the gentleman in the antechamber of that gaming casino last night, Sir?"

"The same," he agreed, speaking now in English with scarcely a trace of an accent. What that accent was, I could not be sure. It might have been Italian. Behind those absurd and disfiguring spectacles, I could see that he was amused and in a teasing mood. Resolved to get our own back at him after his highly mysterious conduct, I hoped to discomfort him by the abrupt question, "Are you acquainted with the red-haired lady to whom you loaned the ducats last night?"

"I have a very large acquaintance," he assured me blandly, so blandly he tried my temper to a great degree. But my question had only served to put me in the wrong with Dacey, my mentor.

"Rachel, my child, it is very bad manners to make so intimate an enquiry of a gentleman we scarcely know."

Dacey's "child" was half a head taller than she, and I was forced to laugh, catching the gentleman's too-grave assurance, "A very correct observation, Miss Dace."

I was privately wondering how he knew our names and apparently everything about us, but I did not again show my interest by pursuing the matter at the moment. Dacey, bless her heart, was now highly puffed up in her own conceit and archly asked the young man, "May we know the name of our preserver, Sir? You speak English so well; yet I do not think . . ."

"Livio."

The name may have appeared Italian, as with the easy stripling movements, the olive complexion, and the very "speaking" dark eyes that he so carefully disguised; but from some nameless fear, I suspected him of dissimulation.

"And now, Ladies, where may I escort you? I am very much at your service."

Dacey looked her relief. "I should think—forgive my making the suggestion, Rachel, that we might go to your papa's chambers in the Palazzo Correra and pay a courtesy call upon that dear little man who was used to dandle you upon his knee. He was your father's Secretary, or some such title. A very worthy man. Peregrine . . . oh, dear . . . Peregrine . . ."

"Watlink," I said suddenly, not having thought of the poor fellow in the last eight years.

"Dandled you on his knee?" repeated our friend Livio in the most odiously insinuating manner.

Huffily, I corrected his apparent misconception. "I was a deal younger then. Five or six. He did not do so when I saw him last at the age of twelve."

"Ah! I am greatly relieved."

"Not," I said rudely, "that it is any concern of yours, I am sure."

"Rachel, dear, your language . . . most unbecoming."

"Oh, tush!" I said, but seeing that I merely provided "Livio" with amusement, I subsided. Then too, it was becoming rapidly clear that Dacey and I could not continue to walk about Venice unaccompanied or unchaperoned. If, as I suspected, Livio was a Venetian agent, sent to see what deviltry that I, a woman with a French passport, was up to, then he would soon learn. I hadn't fallen into his trap when he praised the "Revolutionary patrons" of the Caffé Florian, and my business in Venice was precisely what I had stated: a visit with my father. To oblige his own masters, Livio might even assist Dacey and me in unraveling the mystery that surrounded my father's lovely palace.

"Well then," Messire Livio suggested, making as if to rise. "Shall I escort you to this dear old dandler of young females?"

Dacey twittered uneasily. "I, I daresay we should not—that is to say—we scarcely know you, and if—"

Ashamed of a slight irritation with Dacey's missish ways, I cut in, "Certainly, Messire Livio. How do we reach the Palazzo Correra most handily?"

Dacey was still feebly protesting when we all got up and without actually delegating to Livio the duties of guide and escort, we allowed ourselves to be swept across the square with a brief glance at the palace of Doge Ludovico Manin.

Dacey murmured, "How grand to be a Doge and to live there!"

Messire Livio laughed. "Poor Manin! A prisoner of his own position. He is quite helpless to do anything constructive, unless he will bestir himself to overrule the Ten."

It was a puzzling remark from a man I supposed to be a spy of the Ten. Unless he was trying to rouse us to incautious remarks that he could report. We headed toward the gondolas bobbing at the quai of the piazzetta.

"What interesting pillars!" Dacey exclaimed as we walked between them.

Livio said innocently, "Ah yes. The pillars. Between those pillars the executioner sets his blocks. And when the Ten condemns a few wretches, they are occasionally strung up by the foot between the two pillars. After death, of course. Spies and lesser traitors are quietly garroted in the dungeons beneath the Council Chambers. It is conducive to obedience, I am told."

I frowned at him unbecomingly but he took care not to look my way. Dacey swallowed rapidly and after that was in no case to enjoy the gondola ride into and through the Grand Canal, past palaces with facades of lacy splendor, and interiors that I made no doubt were as uncomfortable and eerie as Father's palazzo. Fourteenth- and fifteenth-century architecture captivated me. The sixteenth century I found less interesting. But I was at least wise enough to know that none of them would contain eighteenth-century comforts.

Our gondola slapped up against a mooring pole striped in pale blue and white while, before us, loomed an imposing but modernized building with all lacy decor and baroque additions removed and which proved to be the British Embassy's temporary headquarters, the Palazzo Correra. Even without Messire Livio we should have known it by the British banner outside and by the busy quai itself, much wider than those opening upon the inner canals of the city.

Here, we saw what appeared to be a perfect procession of wigged and powdered gentlemen, very much in the old style, coming and going through the dark, water marked portals on the ground floor.

From the amount of impudence Messire Livio demonstrated, I had thought he would enter with us, but bethinking himself of his gentlemanly estate—if any—he informed us that he would happily await us in a coffee house on the quai nearby. I thanked him, all smiles, but I privately promised myself not to search for him when we came out. Dacey may have found him irresistible, as I could plainly see, but I did not trust him an iota. A thoroughgoing rogue, was my diagnosis. Unfortunately, he had about him a certain something, a quality of charm or whatever, that made him pop into my mind much oftener than I would have liked during the next half-hour.

Had he come with us through those fierce, forbidding doors, he, I am certain, would have known how to answer the challenge of the Venetian soldier just outside the doors. He demanded our names, our purpose, situation, and address in Venice. It became rapidly clear to me that anyone not possessed of a "palazzo" address might turn about and depart forthwith. There was nothing democratic about the Venetian Republic, nor its relations with the British Embassy. I suspected the two countries' interest in each other was purely selfish. The British Fleet, cruising Mediterranean waters, might yet be sent to aid the Republic of Venice in case of attack by Austria or France.

Curiously enough, and most unsettling to me, this fellow at the door did not immediately recognize my name. Perhaps, though, it was all due to my pronunciation of Italian. I tried again, explaining that I was the daughter of Ambassador Carewe.

An English usher came down the dark, water-marked stone steps at the back of this prisonlike vestibule and motioned for us to follow him. He managed to bow politely as he went ahead, and Dacey whispered to me, "You note what correct manners we English display. Far superior to those wretched Venetians."

In defense of the Venetian doorkeeper, I could not help asking her, "In what case should we be if some French or Austrian fanatic burst in here to murder the British Ambassador?"

Dacey's reminder was either very simple or very subtle.

"But then, my dear, he should not find your good father here at all."

I called to the usher going before us, "We wish to see Mr. Watlink, if you please. The First Secretary. Then he will introduce us to the Ambassador's staff."

The usher had just tapped with his staff on a pair of doors opening off the stair landing. As the door opened, the usher must have been confused; for he looked first at me, then at the bright light pouring from the canal windows up on the first floor.

"I beg pardon, Mistress Carewe? You said . . . a Mr. Watlink? In this department?"

"My father's First Secretary, Peregrine Watlink."

He was perplexed and looked at the young adjutant who came across the parquetry floor, paused, and also looked around. "The First Secretary will be with you very shortly, Madam," the adjutant assured me, and snapping his fingers he watched the usher lead us to a little chamber, a kind of miniature book room, at the side of the imposing first floor vestibule.

Dacey waited until our usher had moved away from us, out of this chamber and across the vestibule. Then she peeked out of our door which he had left ajar. "There are several Venetians in the salon across the vestibule. Very important, I daresay. In red robes. There! A fellow in a robe as crimson as—"

"Blood?"

"Oh, my, no! I was about to say crimson as wine. Not a churchman, though. Surely not, with that cruel face!"

"One of the three Inquisitors for the Council of Ten, I should think."

"Inquisitors! Heavens!"

"Prosecutors. Have a care, Dacey. Should you commit what these people conceive to be a crime, you may meet him. In a businesslike way."

"Rachel, your imagination!"

I laughed, but I was sorry for having given her pleasant observations this little remembrance of cruelty. I suppose my mind had been conditioned by events in my own life and I hoped to blur these horrors by a quiet life with my father in Venice. Thus far, I had failed. There seemed to be no running away from life. One had to face it. All the same, though I had teased Dacey, I did wonder what business brought the Council's Red Inquisitor to the British Embassy.

I was familiar with the laws of Venice which forbade contacts between the Doge himself and the officials of any foreign government, except in danger of war, and I supposed the suspicious and highly secretive nature of the Serenissima would likewise make it awkward for the Council or the Inquisitor to be seen with English officials. Were they discussing plans of defense against the onrushing French Army? Or against the menace of grasping Austria which had once held half of Northern Italy in its power? Thus far, there had been all too much fraternizing between the French and the people of Italy, anxious to throw off the repressive Austrian yoke. When Father improved in health, I intended to impress upon him the dangerous contagion of the democratic French.

"He is coming," Dacey murmured, "Yes. This way. But . . . it isn't Mr. Watlink. Someone to bring us to Mr. Watlink, I should imagine."

I had one of those little insights into the immediate future which are always disquieting. "No. I do not think so." But I stood up, hopeful that my premonition had been wide of the mark.

An elegant gentleman, somewhat under forty, minced across the vestibule, in and out of the sunlight pouring through the leaded windows. He was gorgeous in his fine satins and silk hose, and his striped waistcoat that was like a mooring pole, I thought. Why, then, did I suspect that his thin lips, his rouge and his pale eyes concealed an ability and a brain not always found behind such an innocuous facade?

"Miss Carewe? Your servant, Ma'am. Gerald Fortman-Truscott." He bowed over my hand and bestowed a pretense of a kiss somewhere just above my fingertips. "And yours, Ma'am." Dacey was inordinately pleased, but I wondered at the curious, narrow-eyed look he gave me over Dacey's hand.

"Now, then . . . Miss Carewe?

I did not like the manner in which his voice trailed up questioningly over my name.

"I am Miss Carewe."

"I was of the impression that His Excellency had but one daughter, unhappily lost to the guillotine in '94."

"He has one daughter. Myself. As you see, I was not lost to the guillotine."

He bit one thin, bloodless lip in thought, an exaggerated perplexity, it seemed to me. "Astonishing."

"May I ask why?"

"One would never have suspected it. Forgive me, but I recall Miss Carewe as a child. A round little face. Masses of unruly dark hair. An ingenuous smile. I recall Rachel Carewe very well."

It was a blow that left me breathless for a few seconds. I then said coolly, "The guillotine you mention is remarkable for erasing ingenuous smiles and round little faces."

Dacey recovered her tongue as well. "I do not know who you are, Master—Master Twitchett, but—"

"Truscott, Ma'am. Fortman-Truscott."

"But I have been acquainted with Miss Carewe since time out of mind, and you may rest assured, this is she. Will you be so good as to show us in to the First Secretary."

Silently, I thanked Dacey for her staunch defense of me. Truth to tell, I had been stunned by this man's peculiar implication that I was not the woman I knew myself to be. Then came the second blow.

"Frankly, Ma'am," said Fortman-Truscott. "I am the First Secretary. I take it that your—that His Excellency is in good spirits? How may I assist you?"

Dacey and I exchanged glances. I said, voicing our alarm, "Where is Mr. Peregrine Watlink? When the Ambassador arrived to take his post with the Serenissima, Mr. Watlink was First Secretary."

Fortman-Truscott motioned to the interested usher stationed outside the tall, paneled doors which were partially open. The usher signaled to someone across the vestibule.

"Were they expecting us?" Dacey whispered.

"Nothing would surprise me, at this point."

Fortman-Truscott glanced at us. I suspect he heard our exchange. Then he extended his hand, received a ledger of some age and decrepitude and examined it. "There seem to have been no recent employees of that name. Are you entirely certain, Ma'am?"

"Heavens!" Dacey exclaimed. "What can have happened to him?"

But I did not feel we should be so easily fobbed off. "You will not find Mr. Watlink's name among your smaller ledger employees. His post was your own, as I have stated."

"I wonder . . ." I almost saw the clockworks operating in Fortman-Truscott's head. He had known all along who Peregrine Watlink was and had been either playing with us or attempting to delay us while he decided what to say. The really important question became: Why?

Fortman-Truscott finished his little performance. He turned and signaled to a clerical-looking young man coming into the vestibule from the flight of steps we had taken.

"Amworthy! My predecessor's name, if you please."

"Yes, Sir Hawkins. William Hallidey Hawkins. That will be Sir William Hawkins, M.P. for a district in the west counties now."

"Before that," I cut in, forgetting myself.

Young Amworthy stared, but at Truscott's nod, he took a few steps toward us as we stood now in the doorway, Dacey and I suddenly tense, expectant. "Well, Sir, and . . . Ma'am, the First Secretary when Sir Maitland first presented his credentials—that would be Peregrine Watlink. He came over before Sir Maitland, to make all right for him."

"Peregrine Watlink," Truscott repeated; and to me, "that was the name you enquired about, Miss Carewe?"

"You know perfectly—" I began, and then, recalling myself, I added on a less violent note, "that is the man. Where is he now? Not in Venice, I take it. He was seconded to another post?"

"I fear not, Ma'am." The young man looked uncertain and frightened. "If the gentleman you were enquiring about is the same, then I regret to say, he was set upon by footpads one night on his way to his lodging in the Rio San Jacopo. His body was rolled down into the canal . . . It washed between some pilings and was recovered the following day. There were—ah—stab wounds, one at the nape of the neck, and one in the back . . . Between the shoulders. You see, Sir, it was most unpleasant. My first experience with a body recovered from these waters. I trust Mr. Watlink was not closely related to the ladies. It did occur years ago, Ma'am."

I could not discuss the matter with these men. I was not hypocritical enough to pretend poor Mr. Watlink had been closely related to me. And I knew it to be a selfish thought, but it was present all the same: The information about my old friend was one more cord tightening around me since my arrival in Venice.

CHAPTER FIVE

WHEN DACEY AND I stepped out onto the quai, we found Messire Livio awaiting us while cozily bobbing about in a gondola at the mooring pole. Nonetheless, as we were escorted across the quai by the pale young man who had known Mr. Watlink, I noted a little fuss and excitement in a gondola just sweeping out into the Grand Canal. Seated comfortably among cushions was the man in crimson robes, the Grand Inquisitor of the Venetian Republic. In one instant I was certain I caught an exchange of looks between our obliging escort, Messire Livio, and the Grand Inquisitor. In despite of all I had observed and learned today, this seeming corroboration of my suspicions most troubled me. Dacey and I must be exceedingly careful with Livio. Undoubtedly, anything he heard between Dacey and me, or any imprudence on my part, would be reported at once to the Council of Ten whose reputation for secretiveness and sinister machinations I was beginning to understand.

But how did this affect my father? He had always been a friend to the Venetian Republic. Perhaps my suspicions of Messire Livio could be put to some use. I must dissemble and let Livio know whatever I wished the Venetian government to know. As our gondolier shipped us out into midstream, I remarked with a partial hypocrisy I loathed, "How wonderfully they seem to deal with political affairs here! The Venetians know this is the only way to stop the French or the Austrians, by their cooperation with the embassy."

I had expected Livio to leap into an agreement like a true Venetian. He surprised me instead by asking, *"The embassy, Miss Carewe?"*

"Of course. The British Embassy."

I was seated beside him, and the sunlight struck us from directly overhead. For a minute before he turned to me, I saw his profile and the expression around his eyes, the keen, alert look so easily masked by those absurd square spectacles. He became aware of my intense scrutiny—or suspicion?—and looked at me. His infectious smile, I felt sure, was often used in just this way, to make us and others think things quite unrelated to the truth.

"But Miss Carewe, the embassy is, I should think, wherever your illustrious father presides."

"Thank you. I trust the Serenissima feels as you do."

This was jarring. He paused so brief a time it may not have been noticed by anyone else. But I was on the watch. Then he said smoothly, "I trust that it does. Unhappily, I am not in a position to know. The Serenissima does not give its confidence to me."

"I understand perfectly," I lied. For the truth is, I was of two minds over everything he said. I was silent after that.

When the small talk between Dacey and Livio drifted into silence, our gondolier asked how we were to reach my father's palace.

"By the swiftest means," I said, too curtly. Everyone looked at me and I was sure Dacey thought me cruel to her new-found friend, Messire Livio.

"By the Rio del Cavallo," Livio said, and very soon after we turned sharply out of the Grand Canal into a narrow canal already shadowed, crushed as it was between high, palatial buildings with few, if any, breaks in the walls for windows. There was an eerie blue cast to the walls themselves and the very air, which should have been sunny and golden as I had found the Grand Canal.

"What an odd thing for that gentleman to say!" murmured Dacey presently.

This unexpected remark naturally puzzled me and intrigued Messire Livio who looked from one to the other of us.

"What can you be talking about, Dacey?" I asked, partly because it was so obvious that our self-appointed guide had become interested.

"Mr. Fortman-Truscott. He seemed absurdly doubtful about you."

"Absurdly, indeed. The man undoubtedly never saw me in his life before today. And at all events, how should he possibly judge me from my looks as a child?"

Dacey frowned at an inquisitive cat our gondola passed. The cat was pawing the water that lapped the lowest step where he crouched. I knew that Dacey did not dislike cats. Certainly she was too tenderhearted to object to them as they tried to assuage their hunger; so the frown was obviously for my words. "Yet how very odd," said Dacey, "so disquieting to think that they all believed you dead. I myself was astounded when I received the news about you, dear. Astounded and delighted, I mean to say."

I did not like the way Livio was listening to this absurd discussion, nor, to be frank, did I like the odd little afterthought which Dacey had added because she assumed I might be hurt. She need not have troubled. An addendum, so to speak, was worse than none at all.

Livio obligingly had his gondolier bring us up to the mooring pole in front of Father's palazzo, where we disembarked, thanked Livio, and I very nearly spoke aloud my private suspicions: "And where are you bound now? To the Chamber for Spy Reports in the Doges' Palace?" Instead, however, I listened cynically to his charming farewells and felt an undeniable thrill at his attention, absurd in the circumstances; for I did not, in the least, believe his protestations. I felt he must have some special, perhaps sinister, interest in Dacey and me—why else would he have persisted in our lives from the moment I first saw him, offering gaming money into the hands of Father's astonishingly elegant housekeeper?

I said suddenly, surprising myself, "Are you acquainted with my father, Ambassador Carewe?"

I think Livio was also surprised at the abruptness of the question. "Slightly, Miss Carewe. Like many other Venetians, I am a great admirer of your father."

"And is the Council of Ten an admirer of my father?"

He was not to be entrapped a second time. He looked up at me where I stood on the palazzo step. The early afternoon sun glittered on his spectacles, blinding the onlooker to his eyes. He was perfectly bland. "I fear I cannot speak for the Council of Ten. Farewell for the moment, Miss Carewe."

I said flatly, "Good bye," but unfortunately, when I glanced back as Dacey applied the knocker, Livio was still looking up, watching me. I probably flushed a little in my embarrassment at being caught staring at him, but there was no help for it.

The Turkish mute opened the door to us. He looked me up and down insolently but I pretended not to notice and went rapidly through the imposing, striped vestibule to the staircase door with Dacey following, a trifle more dignified. As I placed my foot upon the bottom step, I heard the first-storey door open above me. A man's booted step rang upon the stone floor of the landing.

"The next dispatches from London should arrive by sea, Mistress Mira," he called, obviously to father's red-haired housekeeper. "They will be delivered at once. Prime Minister Pitt is most concerned to have the good will of the Serenissima in case Venice is needed to aid us against Bonaparte's Armies."

"Just so, Colonel. His Excellency would not be remiss, in despite of his condition." That would be Mira Teotochi's voice, elegant, surprisingly so for the housekeeper she professed to be. "But stay! His Excellency desires—" her voice faded; then, as I remained in shadow below and the English Colonel waited above my head, she reappeared on the landing. "Two more dispatches which required his signature. Here you are. Good luck to you."

"You are very good, Ma'am." The uniformed officer saluted her. "Traveling by sea we shall avoid both the Austrian and French Armies. Gad's life, Ma'am! I know not which of the two to lay my wager upon. Before last year who had ever heard of that little French upstart?"

"Corsican upstart," Mira Teotochi corrected him crisply, but he only shrugged.

"French? Corsican? Italian? It is all one, after all. Mr. Pitt, however, says one can deal with the Austrians. They will bargain and yield, if necessary. Whereas, there is simply no dealing with *canaille* like those French Republicans, damn them!—pardon, Ma'am."

"Not at all, Colonel. I could not have expressed it more happily myself. But to fear an Army without shoes! We are told they bind their bloody feet with rags. And these against the full might of the Austrian Empire!"

By this time I felt it incumbent upon me to make an appearance, lest I should startle the English Colonel who was rattling down the steps, threatening to stride clear over me. I called up to the housekeeper.

"It is I, Rachel Carewe, Signora. Is my father up and about?"

She leaned over the balustrade and looked down at me. "He is laid down again at the moment, Signorina. If you wish, I will inform him of your return when he awakens."

The Colonel, meanwhile, had come to an abrupt halt in front of me, saluted and with a pleasant, slightly flirtatious attitude, remarked, "So you are a daughter of Maitland Carewe, Ma'am! Delighted! I had supposed there was only one, your unfortunate sister who died on the guillotine."

"I am that daughter. Happily resurrected," I said, returning his smile.

He was a good deal surprised, repeating that remark I was now growing heartily sick of: "But one would never have guessed! I knew you as a child, Miss Carewe. You have changed beyond all knowing you."

"Nonsense!" I said. "I am very much as I always was. Allowing for my present age."

"A prodigious age, to be sure," he teased me, and then, with another smile and salute, he left me, passing Dacey and going into the vestibule.

It was curious, I thought, how the Italian, Mira Teotochi, had spoken with an almost proprietary interest in the Imperial Austrian Army which had ravaged Northern Italy for years. There was no figuring the woman.

Dacey hurried up beside me with those mincing little steps that sometimes annoyed me, for they put me too much in mind of the exquisitely coiffed ladies of the Ancien Regime in the early days of the Revolution. These ladies had been blind to every change, every danger; to every step however moderate that was breaking down the incredible privileges that had enchained France since the tenth century.

"My dear," Dacey murmured breathlessly in my ear, "What a very odd thing, to be sure! Why did that charming Colonel not recognize you? How very provoking!"

"To express it mildly—yes! It is provoking." All the same, though I laughed and made an elaborate pretense of finding these persistent mistakes in my identity amusing, I was more than a trifle uneasy. I longed to reach a mirror and peer into it, just to assure myself that I was truly Rachel Genève Carewe.

When we passed Mira Teotochi, it seemed for an instant as if she would avoid me and scurry off, but something, some expression or unconscious gesture of mine made her pause. I said, "Will you be so good as to tell me at once—at once—when the Ambassador is awake?"

"But—naturally, Signorina Carewe." Could I be wrong, or was there a slight nervousness about her, an attempt to placate me? "You will understand, the Ambassador finds it tiring. These many papers. The signatures. The individual consideration . . . He is still truly the Ambassador, not one of those who pretend. He is very useful to the English Prime Minister."

"I am sure he is. And particularly now, with war so near."

Mira Teotochi turned to me. Her slanting eyes crinkled in an odd way, as if they might smile, though her lips were solemn enough. "Very true, Signorina. Your French are very near to us. Very dangerous. We must all be upon our guard."

How silly and how anticlimactic I felt as I replied indignantly, "They are not *my* French. You are mistaken, Signora Teotochi."

She sketched a faint, ever-so-slight curtsey. "Quite so. I had, for the moment, forgotten. It was only that His Excellency insists . . . he is not young, you understand. His mind occasionally misgives him when he speaks of you and he calls you 'une vraie Française.' "

I felt my fingers clench to fists. "That is a lie!" I said, and then, recovering common sense, I raised my gloved fist to my lips and stopped this bad-mannered outburst. "I beg your pardon." I made as if to pass her.

She stood aside. "It is entirely understandable, in the circumstances, Signorina."

I did not know how to accept that and was uncharacteristically afraid to find out. I passed her, turned and went out to the steps and on up to my bedchamber. Dacey followed, confused by my ill-temper and bad manners. We separated in the wide hall outside our rooms. I had scarcely entered my own chamber when I discovered from slight signs that the room had been inspected by someone. Very probably the person who made up my bed and cleaned after me. I went about the large room examining objects whose exact position I remembered all too well. My experiences in Paris during the last six years had made me keenly aware of spies and those paid informers who would search one's belongings, one's wretched, simple lodgings, in the hope of trapping some shred of evidence that could be used to gain a few devalued paper assignats for the informer.

As I searched the room and my meager possessions I wondered what could possibly be used against me. It would be absurd. Yet, having so much experience, I knew at once when my things were moved. Even in the armoire the garments I had hung on the wooden pegs were not replaced in precisely the correct order. A much worn but favorite black spencer of mine was hung so that the lining stretched noticeably below the wrist. My best pelisse had fallen and caught upon a sleeve button. What in heaven's name was the reason for the search? The searchers had seemed extraordinarily interested in linings.

And then, as I turned away from this upsetting invasion of my private bedchamber, I suddenly associated the search and the curiosity motivating it with the developments that had shocked me this morning: someone was trying to discover who I really was. If I was not Rachel Carewe, miraculously resurrected daughter of His Excellency, the Ambassador, then what did they think my purpose might be in this house?

Considering the situation of Venice at the moment, it seemed logical that someone—perhaps more than one—suspected I might be an agent of the French Revolutionary government, sent here to take the place of the executed Rachel Carewe. It would have been a clever plan, had it been true. A surreptitious knock and Dacey's loud but confidential whisper relieved me enormously. Dacey, at least, saw my true identity.

"Rachel, may I see you?"

I crossed the room, unbolted the door. She came in with a secretive and conspiratorial manner that would have amused me in former times, but now after my discovery, I shared her fears. I locked the door behind her.

She said quickly. "That man we saw embracing Miss Tokay? Remember?"

"Teotochi. I remember. Too well."

"I've been thinking. Couldn't it have been that Colonel we met on the steps?"

I considered, but I was certain the man at the window had not been in uniform. Of course, I was not so innocent as to imagine the man remained in uniform during his romantic moments. I wanted very much to believe I had been mistaken about the identity of the two lovers, but I could not forget the height, the head, the poise of the man with La Teotochi in his arms. So like Father. But that was impossible.

Dacey prowled around the room, muttering. Plainly, she noticed, as I had, the fact that my things were not in correct order. She echoed my question. "But why, Rachel? What have you that they wish to see, or to steal? Or is it footpads? Cutpurses?"

"Not likely. They probably are searching for something that will prove me a French agent—a spy for General Bonaparte's Army."

Dacey gasped, covered her mouth nervously.

"But they won't find anything like that . . . will they?"

It was a ghastly little moment.

"No," I said with a coolness I was far from feeling, "I think I may safely promise you I am not a representative of the Directoire Française, nor of Bonaparte."

"I'm certain you are not." She recovered with an effort. "But then, I could never doubt you, dear."

God of heaven! She was lying, this second mother, this dear soul I looked to for comfort, companionship, for moral support—now, even she was beginning to doubt. Well then, I needed no one. I had come through worse than this. Besides, I had my father.

"It's of no consequence," I said finally, my voice sounding much too brisk, as sharp as broken glass. "I believe I will take a stroll."

"A stroll? But, Rachel, we've only just returned—"

"A stroll through this house. Father's silent tomb of a palace. The place is haunted by his condition. Why has Father never been replaced by Mr. Pitt? One would think the Prime Minister needs the sharpest English wits at work in Venice today."

"But he has, dear. Your father."

"You don't know. You simply cannot imagine how feeble he is now. Or—" I recalled the brief vision we had seen at the window, "—in any case, he seems feeble. And at a time when England needs all her wits to stop Bonaparte. If we are not careful, we will have a Tree of Liberty planted in St. Mark's Square."

Wistfully, Dacey murmured, "Would that be so very bad? I often wonder . . ." At my horrified exclamation, she flushed. "I beg your pardon. After all you have suffered at the hands of these French savages."

"Do not think about it. I am half French, after all. Now, I am going to look at this tomb we are sharing. See what and who inhabit it besides ourselves."

She looked around. "Are you troubled about the person who spied upon your room?"

"Why? There is nothing that can be found. I have nothing to hide. Come along if you like."

We went out into the wide, grimly furnished hall which was the equivalent of the gallery on the floor below. Dacey shivered. Trying to cheer her, I laughed and made a light joke. "You have been reading *Castle of Otranto* again. You know perfectly well you will not discover some ghastly visitant solemnly dripping blood. Not in this house. Whatever is here, is real."

She made a brave attempt to smile. "I shouldn't be in the least surprised. Where shall we start?"

I was suddenly aware that if we meant to investigate the palazzo we must open every one of those forbidding and secretive doors. And we had little excuse, other than mere curiosity. No matter. It must be done. I was determined to find out what dangers and mysteries surrounded my father in this place. That man embracing Mira Teotochi, the man who resembled Father, for instance—where did he fit into the web being spun around my father and me? And web it was! From the very beginning they had been surprised to see me. Obviously I was unwanted. Perhaps I would interfere with . . . what? Some plan.

"I have thought of something," Dacey announced with some trepidation as I tried the door next to mine. "What shall we do if some of the doors are locked?"

"We shall take note, and when we see Mrs. Teotochi, we will ask her to unlock those mysteries and show them to us."

"Rachel! Are you sure—?"

I opened the door after a good, solid push and looked inside. The large, gloomy room offered nothing significant or exciting. Its north wall was the same that ran behind my great, curtained bed. As I looked around the chamber I saw that it appeared to be at least partially furnished with odds and ends, old trunks, a denuded bedstead and, surprising to me, a great pile of women's garments draped over a table. The objects in the room had a very unsettled, "hasty" look, as if they had been piled together and dropped into this unused room. There were half a dozen modern pairs of neat, feminine shoes dropped on the floor in a pile below the hems of the garments. It was mysterious. The clothing, when I examined the various gowns, looked sophisticated; modern in the Venetian style rather than the neat, slim fashion of Paris.

"Could there be a woman we haven't seen here in the palace?" Dacey asked, almost hopefully. I knew she was locked in dreams of her favorite *Castle* romance by Mr. Walpole.

"There may be, but I suspect what we are seeing is the wardrobe of our modestly dressed housekeeper, La Teotochi. See this? Is it not a pinafore such as she might wear when giving orders and supervising the kitchens?"

It was of no account, actually, the mere fact that Mira Teotochi had hastily dropped her clothing in this room. But once again came one query whose answer just might be important; why?

I thought I knew.

Dacey picked up one of the shoes with its old-style but still fashionable carved high heel. "I should think this might fit that woman. You think she was here? But why should she keep these things here?"

I considered those garments, neither old nor dusty. They had been tossed there hurriedly, within the last day or so—certainly no more. And I remembered the equally fresh condition of the chamber assigned to me. Surely the bed would have been dusty, the hangings impossible, if the room had been unused. "I wonder if my arrival last night did not cause Mrs. Teotochi some hardship," I said, as I studied the wall between the rooms.

"How so? I don't believe I understand you, dear."

"She must have been told my identity at the Casino last night. Do not ask me who told her. Or she may even have heard our conversation with Captain Dandolo and hurried home to the palazzo by some back-alley canal to prepare. My father certainly has portraits of me. Or even if she did not know me, she knew that chamber next door was the only one decent enough to provide for the daughter of the Ambassador or his guest."

"Yes, but—"

"She was staying in that bedchamber, don't you see? And it is obviously one of the finest chambers in the palace. Certainly it is not the room for a housekeeper; so she quickly removed her possessions to this room and ran down to admit us in her role as a humble servant of the house. Look at these clothes—surely these are the lovely satin and taffetas she wore last evening at the gaming casino."

"But why should she pretend to be a housekeeper? Would not your dear father know if she weren't what she appears?"

"Not if he loves her."

"Rachel!"

"What else am I to think?" All the same, after a brief further examination of the room and finding nothing, we left the chamber. Dacey wondered if Mira Teotochi had slept in it, but I thought not. It was just some handy place to drop her things when she saw me arriving and realized she must remove herself from that front chamber if she was to keep her carefully constructed role as housekeeper. "I wish I understood her purpose in this masquerade."

Dacey shook her head. "She seems most efficient. An excellent housekeeper. How can it be a masquerade?"

The hall was shadowed. She looked toward the long window over the canal. I followed her glance. It was a north window and as the afternoon advanced I found the atmosphere tightening around us; the strangeness of our situation and Father's case nagging at me.

"Poor Father! He would never have allowed such a thing to happen in the old days. No one ever controlled him as this woman seems to control him now."

"She is very beautiful," Dacey admitted.

I tried to deny it, but my tongue tripped on the words. Of course, the woman was beautiful, with that same porcelain-skinned fairness I had seen in Austrian women in Northern Italy. She had undoubtedly used that beauty to win over my father. He had never been susceptible, except to my mother's charm. But since it had happened once with her, why couldn't it be repeated with Mira Teotochi? It was a painful thought.

We peered into other rooms in a gingerly way, knocking first, waiting breathlessly, then finding them almost empty, furnished with a few pieces in the heavy, depressing style of the early Renaissance, dusty, clearly unused. Occasionally we came across the exquisite furniture of the present century that Dacey ached to rescue from this dank, shadowy oblivion. But we learned nothing we had not known before, until we reached a small chamber we at first mistook for a powdering closet.

"What is it?" Dacey asked, her voice shaking.

"Boots!"

"What in heaven's name—!" She followed me in, across the

narrow, coffinlike confines of the closet to the far corner under a small, high window. Piled in a bed coverlet whose corners had apparently been tied together at one time, were several pairs of gentleman's boots of English make, very like those my father was used to wear. Those reversible-top boots, the walking boots and other footgear in a style worn by men of my father's generation; the low, buckled shoes, the half-boots.

"And only partially used," I discovered, holding them up one after the other to the slivers of light cutting through the warped shutter. "This is well worn, but this pair is scarcely used at all. And the London maker. My father patronized him."

Dacey murmured, "How very odd!" But neither of us really understood the significance of the discovery.

There were a few other items but none identifiable as anything but the usual household discard, scraps and torn, well-used kitchen or stillroom items, to be found in any attic. We left the room, found the last two chambers locked, and went down to the gallery on the first storey above the canal floor. Dacey was certain that something sinister was hidden behind the locked doors, but I thought it highly probable they merely concealed more discarded household items. I could not accuse Signora Teotochi of chicanery upon the slim evidence of some old British footgear and the female garments left in that bedchamber next to mine.

Dacey, who had gone ahead of me, started back suddenly with a little cry of surprise. The Turkish mute had loomed up before her and was motioning us to follow him. I confess that though he might be the soul of innocence, he was huge and terrifying enough to overawe anyone. Dutifully, we hurried after him through the gallery to a small room at the back under Dacey's chamber above. Mira Teotochi was standing at a large table brushing the lengths of two crimson velvet window draperies. She looked over her shoulder, turned and curtseyed. I suspected that she had been schooled—by my father, I hoped—to a greater politeness, a more careful courtesy.

"Ah, a pleasant day, I trust, Signorina." A slightly less enthusiastic addition, "And Signora. His Excellency asked me to convey his invitation to dine together."

I did not want him to overestimate his strength. He had seemed very frail that morning. If, of course, he was not the man we had seen at the long canal window. I said quickly, "Is he well enough? If not, I might visit him for an hour instead. I would not wish to try him beyond his powers."

"That need not concern you, Signorina. His Excellency is aware of his powers. But he insists upon dining with you. No matter what—what difficulties it costs. It has been such a long time, he says."

I felt a quick emotional tightening of my throat and could only thank her, asking her to be certain my father was in condition to join us.

She nodded. Then she reached under the velvet hanging and brought out a folded paper sealed with the Winged Lion of St. Mark. "This was delivered some minutes ago, by an Officer of the Port. For you, Signorina."

I took the paper. My fingers were stiff with tension as they broke the seal. For some reason, perhaps a compounding of the hints expressed against me today, I feared that I was about to be arrested and charged with being a French agent. The matter was quite otherwise, however:

Is it possible the Madonna Rachel will do me the honor of accepting my escort to a Masque at the Casino Bartolini this evening? My gondolier will await your reply. You will gratify Venice by your acceptance.
                    Your servant,
                    Pietro Dandolo, Captain of the Port.

Dacey asked anxiously, "What is it, dear? It looks excessively important with that seal."

"Ridiculous. That is what it is. As though I would make an engagement with a gentleman I scarcely know! Even a Masque."

"Where are you going? Rachel!"

Forgetting that in Venice servants were utilized for such purposes, I said, "To dismiss the Captain's gondolier. It is a great piece of nonsense." I started to the stairs, then I reminded the housekeeper, "Please tell my father that I am delighted at his invitation, if it is certain than he will not risk his health in coming to dine."

Mira Teotochi shrugged. "I am sure he will feel it necessary to make an appearance. I believe—that is, he informs me that he will question you very closely before the ball."

"The ball? What ball?"

"To welcome you to the Serenissima, of course, though that

was not our original intention. Sir Maitland had another and
even more delicate ceremony he wished to celebrate." She
smiled, a smile that seemed to sneer at me, though I could
not guess why. "You see, your father has asked—but let
him tell you. In any case, the ball has been planned for
some time now, and your arrival merely creates an added,
and charming, cause for celebration."

All this was very mysterious. And worse. I felt that she
was somehow creating obstacles between me and my father.
"He wishes to ask me questions? About what?"

"About your experiences, perhaps. But I am not in a
position to know what his thoughts may be upon the subject.
You must ask His Excellency."

"I see." I went on to the steps and down. I did not see. I
was furious and I was frightened. I had a strong sense that
the housekeeper had been at work upon Father's thoughts,
turning them into doubts and suspicions. The further I
walked, the more angry I became.

I walked through the vestibule, passing a plain careworn
female on her knees scrubbing the beautiful parquet floor.
Then I was at the great canal doors. I did not know what
reply I would make until I reached Captain Dandolo's
gondolier in his cockle-shell boat. Quite suddenly I knew.
I had a friend in Captain Dandolo. Perhaps he could help
me. "Yes," I said. "You may ask Captain Dandolo to call
upon me this evening."

CHAPTER SIX

I REGRETTED MY impulsive acceptance only minutes later, but the thing must be carried through tonight, a dull engagement to gamble, and masked. As though nothing had happened to the world in the last ten years! Had Venice any conception of all the earth-shaking events that swept away such petty vices as masquerades, ridottos, useless aristocrats and the ancient injustices of Privilege?

However, by the time I reached Dacey who came down to meet me, I was female enough to see that there might be pleasure in the masquerade at the gaming house. The invitation was improper. A young lady of Venice still required a duenna whenever she left her father's household, just as had been the case in France before 1789. But—I raised my chin and reminded myself firmly—I was a product of that Revolution, much as I might hate it. I was one of the New Females of Paris. If I chose to accept an invitation to supper at a gaming casino, properly masked and disguised, I was old enough and modern enough not to need a duenna. Poor Mother! She was used to say that this lowering of moral standards was a far greater calamity than the work of the guillotine.

"My dear! I saw from the gallery window. Isn't that the

gondola from the Examiners of the Port?"

"I am attending some sort of gaming casino rout tonight with Captain Dandolo. I must ask the housekeeper for a mask."

Dacey was all aquiver. "But you will not go alone! These events may be all the thing in Paris, but such an undertaking is in the worst of *ton* here in Venice. They are very proper, very formal, you know."

"Nevertheless, I am going. The Captain may be useful to me. I intend to speak to him of my problem."

She followed me, still protesting that I would ruin my name, my reputation forever. "And no one will marry you. Then how will you feel?"

"I will not care in the least," I said recklessly, adding the cruel idea I was immediately ashamed of, "I shall marry whomever I choose—perhaps your gallant friend Livio." I was just about to apologize quickly when Dacey, eyes shining seized my arms and cried,

"I believe you would find him a delightful young man. He only lurks about me in order to be near you, you know."

"Dacey dear!" I hugged her, feeling all the guilt of my bad temper. "That is not true, at all. He could not help liking you. Dark young men always like blondes, you know."

She turned pink with pleasure, but denied vigorously, "Never. I'm—I'm older. You are so much prettier. I mean to say, well, my dear, in my youth I was considered—but now!" She was giggling and laughing. "Do I sound entirely too puffed up in my own conceit?"

"Not even a tiny bit. So if you wish to go to some gaming hell in Messire Livio's company, you must do so."

Very much in charity with each other, we returned to the first storey where Mira Teotochi's curious stare stopped me. I was reminded that she might assist me, and in that thought I pretensed to myself that her animosity was mere concern for my father's best interests.

And so I asked her, "I wonder if I might obtain a mask from you, Signora, to wear to a ridotto this evening."

The woman said, "Nothing easier." I wondered why I had the impression she was relieved to hear it.

"You wish, in fact, to appear in masquerade. A *bauta*. Nothing easier. And may I assist in any other way?"

"A mask will be quite sufficient. Please inform me when my father wishes my presence at his dinner."

"Very well, Signorina." A graceful curtsey punctuated this.

But when Dacey and I had returned to the second storey, my friend said confidentially, "You have touched that dreadful woman at a sore point. Did you notice? She had been used to playing mistress of the house. She is not at all fond of anyone who usurps her place with His Excellency, as hostess of the palazzo."

I agreed; then I asked her, "What did she do when I left you and went down to speak with the Captain's gondolier?"

Dacey walked with me to my bedchamber where, lowering her voice, she confided to me, "The woman made a pretense of seeing to the cleaning of that front chamber. The one where we saw her embracing your—that gentleman. She excused herself to me and went into that room—she said the cleaning wench might not clean the bric-a-brac on the mantel properly. I went after her. But I think Mrs. Teotochi wanted to watch you and the gondolier. She said, 'Why, it is a gondolier of the Serenissima!' Then she came out and waited for you."

I brought her into my bedchamber, bolted the door, and said to her that I would much appreciate knowing if Teotochi spent the evening in my father's company while I was at the Masque with Captain Dandolo.

Her eyes seemed to grow wide with her enthusiasm.

"Yes, yes. I shall be your agent, your spy."

I found it necessary to calm and reassure her. "Ah, but we must be circumspect at all costs. If you were to let the woman know our suspicions, we would be lost. I only suggest that you might find an excuse to visit Papa this evening, unexpectedly, and to discover if the woman is with him." I was considering and planning as I spoke. "While you are here, I will question the Captain. And after that—another day, perhaps—we will question your bespectacled friend, Messire Livio."

The notion of playing the spy had obviously brightened Dacey's prospects for the evening. "That would be splendid beyond anything. Do you think the invitation to dine with His Excellency was meant to include me?"

"I certainly thought so." I was looking through the armoire for garments to be worn tonight. "I believe it will be early. I will attend Papa's dinner before I leave with Captain Dandolo." But I was wondering what questions my father would ask me at dinner. I was certain the idea of mistrusting my identity had not originated with him.

"What a pity we discovered nothing from our investigation of the chambers of this storey!" Dacey sighed as she was leaving the room. "I so hoped we might find . . ." Her voice trailed off.

I could not forbear teasing her. "A chamber full of horrors, I make no doubt."

"You may laugh, but I do not like this place, all the same. Especially at night."

I stopped her in the doorway. "At night? What happens then? Were you also troubled by dreams?"

She walked along the hall, reluctant as a child. Then she looked back over her shoulder. "You may laugh, but it is excessively like the *Castle of Otranto* where the suit of armor dripped blood, and the—"

"Adelaide Dace! And you once taught me not to use my imagination so freely!"

"Well, dear," she had the last word, "I was wrong." And she went on to her own chamber at the end of the hall.

I had attempted to dismiss her fears, yet had by no means dismissed my own. I washed and began to dress for the early dinner with Father and the gaming casino later. The maid sent up to assist me by Signora Teotochi knew nothing of dressing the hair, but I had become accustomed to this task myself and managed a creditable Grecian headdress with a jeweled headband and matching jeweled comb. My hair thus appeared to fall in careless curls over the band. I wore one of the new silver lace sheath gowns with the sash just under my bosom and the train of my sleek, full skirt tossed carelessly over my arm. This revealed my clocked silk stockings and more of my limbs than was considered proper, but it was *all the crack* with ladies in Paris. My arms were bare and required long white gloves. My slippers were of white silk and flat-heeled. Fortunately, I am of at least average height. I carried my reticule in my white silk muff and over the whole of my toilette I draped a silver gauze scarf "carelessly," as was proper, but with a carelessness not easily achieved. This was my crowning elegance in my wardrobe. If I were invited twice, I could not again put forth much effort. Nothing else in my wardrobe could match it.

Dacey was a trifle shocked, being used to the fashions of London which were usually far behind, like those of anachronistic Venice, but when the Turk led us to the first-storey dining salon, an elegant, long chamber, high-roofed and imposing in red and gold, his rolling eyes clearly informed me that he found Paris styles not unattractive.

Mira Teotochi, superintending the dining salon service, equally clearly did not like my appearance. "Your pardon, Signorina," she added to the mischief of her elaborately surprised glance. "I had not seen—how very—original!"

Although I am quite certain there were angry red spots in the center of my cheeks, I managed a fairly convincing indifference as I was ushered to my chair at the right hand of Papa, who came in with difficulty, leaning upon the arm of a thin, forbidding individual whom he introduced as Ridgen, his valet. The valet bowed to me and retired from the room while I bent toward Papa with anxiety for his frail appearance. It was inconceivable, I thought, that this pitifully shaking man with his almost transparent flesh and pale eyes could still be vigorous enough to satisfy his master, Mr. William Pitt, and serve Britain in the highest degree.

"Are you feeling more the thing now, Father?" I asked gently, as he patted my hand in a gesture so weak it brought tears to my eyes.

"Much better. Do not concern yourself, my dear Rachel. You yourself are in excellent looks tonight."

"With your permission, Sir, I am being escorted to a ridotto."

In spite of the strangeness, the terrible ravages of illness and age, he managed to smile and assure me tenderly, "It is time you enjoyed your youth, child. Your life has held too much tragedy."

"And you, Sir. Will you be comfortable here alone in this great, empty house? If you grow lonely or would wish Dacey to read to you, I am persuaded she would oblige."

Eagerly, Dacey insisted, "With the greatest of pleasure, Sir. Nothing, in fact, would please me more."

But he waved aside the offer. "No, no. Poor Miss Dace has quite enough to play duenna to you, my dear. As she was used to do. Do you remember those long strolls down the green banks off the Thames above Richmond? What an energetic child you were! Indeed, on Guy Fawkes Day your mother and I thought you had lost your hand. What scars that made when you cut yourself with my old rapier!"

He and Dacey and even Signora Teotochi who was supervising the thin-faced kitchen maid as the latter served a tureen of vegetables, all studied my left hand expectantly. Until this moment I had quite forgotten the silly business of Papa's sword, which I had borrowed, needless to say, without permission. I glanced down at my hand, raised and stared at it. I could no longer find any sign of that long-forgotten double scar that had run across the thumb just beneath the nail, and up into my forefinger.

I showed them all my hand, amused at their interest. "Quite pristine. Free of scars."

Father caught his breath in a wheezing, painful little gasp. "But my dear Rachel, that is not possible. I remember those two scars most distinctly. They bled for hours. We found it necessary to send for a surgeon to staunch the blood."

"It wasn't actually two scars, Papa. Simply an extension of the one. I dropped the sword across my thumb and forefinger. I had no notion it was so heavy."

"Extraordinary!" Mira Teotochi stepped forward, staring at my hand. I felt remarkably conscious of everyone's attention. She murmured, "Pardon, Your Excellency, but is it not possible that your daughter's growth to maturity might result in the scar's disappearance?"

"That much is obvious, is it not?" I asked coldly.

The horrid thing was Father's long silence. Second only to that was Dacey's sudden chatter. She became a perfect rattle, much to my discomfort. But in the end, it was Dacey's chatter that turned the subject from my nonexistent scars. When I glanced at Father during these minutes after the tension had abated, I noticed his deeply troubled look and it hurt me very much. He was never used to be troubled or uncertain for long. A very positive man, he had never let trivial concerns upset me. But someone—doubtless the Teotochi—much have worked upon his frailty, his illness, and produced these uncertainties.

Gradually, the subject returned to my childhood and to our mutual memories. Fortunately, we agreed upon these occurrences.

"But yes," said my father with a bit of the old sparkle, as the bounteous second course was laid before us. "How well I recall the day you aroused the ire of the Richmond Hunt . . ."

"What? When?" I was caught unaware.

"What a naughty child you were, when you rescued that fox, a vixen, as I recall . . . And the hunt scattered over the whole of the Shire, searching!"

I laughed. I was not ashamed of that moment. I could still see, in my mind's eye, the glorious little red vixen, protecting her cubs. A few minutes later, and these little creatures would have been torn to pieces by the hounds.

"And when I caught you, my dear!" He laughed for the first time and I saw a tiny flash of the old, vigorous Maitland Carewe. The trouble was, I could not remember what had happened when Papa caught me. And yet, I knew I had been punished. As before, I caught everyone staring at me. What they were waiting to see and hear, I could not imagine.

"Rachel," Dacey nudged me conversationally. "I believe your dear Papa wishes to have you tell us more about that day when you rescued the fox."

I tried desperately to think. It must have been very long ago. I remembered that time vaguely in a confusion of childhood memories. When I attempted to single it out, this incident of the fox, it kept receding, entwining among other flashes of those days when Father and Mother lived together.

"Really," I said aloud, far more haughty and self-confident than I felt, "You are all making far more ado about this than is necessary. There were many times when I was bad, disobedient—"

Father smiled, his new, faded benign smile, as he corrected me. "Not bad, my child. Only . . . mischievous. But you gratify an old man by these memories. Pray continue."

But I had begun to feel that this bore all the symptoms of a friendly inquisition. I passed off the matter with a bright, laughing generality and hoped they would let it rest. It was, therefore, with a good deal of anger that I heard Mira Teotochi enter again to see to the removal of the enormous and scarcely touched second course, while she said, "Your Excellency has so often been gracious enough to discuss your daughter's childhood with me. Surely, the Signorina will favor you now with these memories!"

I suppose she had goaded me into this trap; for when challenged thus, I found my mind totally blank. Had I merely been allowed to ramble on idly discussing moments in my past, I should have been able to relive my entire youth. I was so angered at my own helplessness to answer this woman's challenge that I made the mistake of backing away from the challenge. I said angrily, "I find this all very boring. Too much has happened since those days. Will you give me leave, Father?"

He sighed. "Very well. We excuse you, child. Go to your revelry. You have earned pleasure. And present my compliments to this Captain of the Port. If only . . ."

I had arisen. Dacey made as if to rise with me but everyone, including myself, was held by his unfinished thought. I nearly reached the center doors and was very close to Mira Teotochi before I let my curiosity get the better of me.

"What do you mean, Father? Is there some way we may help you? If you prefer, I will not leave you tonight."

But he waved me on. "No, no. Go about your play. I only wish—but it cannot be."

"What cannot be, Father?"

"If only you were more like the girl who went away . . ."

Needless to say, that left me speechless. As I left the long salon, I looked back once with a faint hope of support from Dacey. But no. She was staring at me like Father, with that perplexed, wondering gaze which sickened me by its mistrust.

"Thank God for Captain Dandolo!" I said to myself as I went hurriedly through the gallery. "At least, he believes I am myself."

I decided to wait in the vestibule for his gondola. I could not bear to spend another second in the presence of two people I loved, who showed such doubt of my identity.

While waiting, I walked the length of the gallery and stopped before the long window over the canal. It was night, but the flicker of mooring lanterns and a lamp at either end of the little humped bridge gave a curious, hellish glow to the scene. Oddly enough, these lights only made the canal waters blacker by comparison. From my vantage point high above, they looked bottomless and I wondered what things lay just beneath the surface, driven through these narrow canals, swept to sea by unseen currents . . . Things like the body of that man I had known as a child, Mr. Watlink. I wondered precisely when Mr. Watlink had been murdered and if it was possible that his death at the hand of a bravo with a dagger had been less coincidental than it seemed.

Again I asked myself: Why?

Was it possible that the years of my close acquaintance with Revolution had made me preternaturally suspicious?

A long black gondola slipped along between the banks and quais of the canal. It was filled with masqueraders, glamorously asparkle with jeweled masks and enveloping black cloaks billowing out like wings to reveal gleaming satin small-clothes on the men and exquisite, panniered gowns on the females. Several gondolas passed and at last one came up to the mooring pole of the palazzo, carrying its grizzled gondolier and Captain Dandolo. I would not have known the Captain had he worn a mask, but fortunately his splendid almost consciously handsome face was bare and glowed in the mooring lights. He looked up, but I doubted he could see me, and I hurried to the steps.

On the ground floor in the great, empty black-and-white vestibule, the Turk met me and pantomimed the Captain's arrival. Recent events had made me so suspicious, I wondered if he was actually mute, or if this, too, was a masquerade. By the time I reached the canal steps and Captain Dandolo's obliging arms, I was aware of an accumulation of recent problems, my own uncertainties, and the growing fears that plagued me.

The Captain lifted me down into the gondola, his hands lingering rather too long over my person. He grinned as he contemplated me, a knowing grin that made me exceedingly uncomfortable. I shifted in his grasp, and belatedly he settled me in one of two gleaming, varnished black seats.

"You do me great honor, Madonna Rachel. Be assured your identity will be guarded. You have a mask?"

From my muff I took the winged little black mask and the Captain obligingly fastened its velvet strings at the back of my head, beneath the jeweled headband. As the gondolier shoved off, I looked at my escort. I smiled, but I hoped he would know that I was not playing the coy temptress.

I tried to make it clear without offending or disappointing him. "Messire Capitano, my identity may be guarded, but I am aware that no lady appears in public without a companion. However, I must tell you—"

"That you are in all things, a lady of the Quality." He grinned, and tried again. "Then I am to assume—pardon! I believe you are reminding me that His Excellency is a considerable power in this city, and this his daughter is to be treated quite as though the Ambassador were present."

At the least *he* recognized me as His Excellency's true daughter, a decided step above my father and La Teotochi! Poor Captain Dandolo! We were no sooner on our way and he had begun some preliminaries to a serious flirtation threatening to become physical, than I questioned him about the death of poor Mr. Watlink. I tried to be casual about the murder, but found it excessively difficult. The Captain leaped to the notion that the unfortunate First Secretary had been either my lover or my affianced husband. While I explained that I had known Mr. Watlink as a child and had no further interest in him except to wonder who had murdered him, the Captain destroyed my hopes of learning anything.

"I was in the field against the Austrians, at the time. But

it made quite a stir in Venice. I should think it was one of the typical dagger men who committed the crime. Look through that alley as we glide by—I'll wager you there's one of the damned villains hiding there now. Impossible to find them all. Between the strangler's cord and the headsman's ax, one would think there could not be a cutthroat left."

I shivered. Until he pointed out the huddled creature only faintly illuminated by a canal lamp at the far end of the alley, I would have supposed it to be a great heap of rubbish. I began to wish I had not been so hasty in accepting the Captain's invitation. The city was as ominous as Father's palazzo. I said this aloud and received a shocked stare from chauvinistic captain.

"Madonna! I am abroad upon the waters every night. I have not yet been attacked by a cutpurse. It is simply the foreigners. Tourists wandering foolishly across the city at night—you understand."

We bobbed out into the windswept lagoon and around toward the Piazzetta by water. I knew we should have reached St. Mark's sooner by the various alleys and bridges of the city, but aside from the danger of footpads which the Captain had just made all too clear, it would not be nearly as pleasant at night as by gondola—let alone the eternal risk of being drenched in refuse thrown out of some high window! I tried to put a good face on things, to smile, play the flirt within reason, but unfortunately, memories of that dreadful dinner with Father and Dacey intruded upon my thoughts.

Almost before I was ready to meet the aristocracy of Venice, our gondola glided through a narrow, dark canal beyond the Piazza San Marco and the shining silver teeth of the prow brought up sharp against the long, low flight of three steps leading to the quai. A black cat, all bones and teeth, glowered at us and scampered off between a windowless building and a shadowy arcade on our left, leading toward the lagoon. I started nervously at its sudden movements.

The Captain, too, seemed oddly interested in our dark surroundings, but he said briskly. "Come, Madonna. Do not be alarmed. That cat will merely locate a rat or two for his midnight supper. The rats grow gigantic around these pilings and the bases of all these palazzos. Cats have our blessing."

I tried to laugh but the sound was thin. "You fail to re-assure me with your talk of giant rats, Messire Capitano."

We left behind us the gondola and the gondolier who

squatted in the waist of the little boat and settled himself in a bored way, to await our return. I was almost sorry to leave him. He looked like an excellent guard. The Captain and I walked under a moldering archway and along a wider cobbled thoroughfare. There were few lights and those only at a distance. The moonlight only cast our way in deeper shadow.

In the distance the street was cut off by a great windowless wall which proved to be our destination. Captain Dandolo explained, "It is the Casino Bartolini. The land entrance is to the left of us, halfway to the Grand Canal. You will find everyone of any consequence at the Casino Bartolini—Austrian sympathizers, French emigrés, and the patricians of the Serenissima." Reaching for my waist as I withdrew gently but firmly, he asked, "Which do you prefer? The choice shall be yours."

I was not passionately attached to any of the three. As a Frenchwoman for eight years, I detested the Austrian enemy, knowing its history of pillage and rapine, its medieval rule in its conquered provinces, and I found the French emigrés behaving little better than traitors. "I believe I should prefer the Venetians."

"Excellent. And I too. Nevertheless, we find such places politically desirable."

Evidently others shared his taste. I saw a group of masqueraders pass under the high, forbidding wall ahead of us, toward the iron-bound door let into the wall like a kind of postern gate. A few seconds later we were once more the only human beings in this strangely desolate little street. The movement and shift of shadow beneath the arcade reminded me of the lean cat off to pursue his nightly ration of rats among the perennially wet pilings everywhere beneath our feet, even beneath this cobbled thoroughfare.

There was a sudden little gritty noise, like a shoe sole upon the cobbles. At the same time a cat, perhaps the black rat-catcher, dashed across our path, and in one swift motion, because I love cats, I knelt to pet the frightened creature. Something flashed above my head, like a streak of moonlight, and my companion, the Captain, uttered a strange little *oof!* sound, as though he had suddenly been stricken breathless.

I looked back, unsuspicious, to remark on the elusiveness of cats, and saw Captain Dandolo spin around in the most astonishing way and then drop to the cobblestones in a motionless heap.

CHAPTER SEVEN

I THOUGHT—I knew not what I thought in that dreadful second—perhaps that he had been the victim of a heart seizure. Or a sudden spell of vertigo. I cried out and knelt over him. For a horrid moment or two I believed there was no heartbeat. It took those seconds for the blood to soak through the bandolier of his uniform, and I realized that he had been wounded in the left breast. Something painful and sharp cut through the knee of my gown. I felt for and located the stained dagger that had fallen to the cobblestones under my knee. Belatedly, I became aware of the danger around us in these deep shadows beyond the moonlight.

Frantically, I tore off my mask. A breeze swept across my face from the distant canal, so quick and unexpected that I threw myself flat over the wounded man, momentarily expecting a second dagger. There was a stir under the arcade and then silence, except for the rush of the wind. I felt under the bandolier which was rapidly growing soggy with the spread of Captain Dandolo's blood. I groaned aloud, in despite of the danger around us in the cool Venetian night. I took the ridiculous and impractical lace kerchief from my muff and stuffed it under the bandolier to staunch the blood.

A minute later, becoming aware of a shadow that

loomed up between the Captain's pallid face and mine, I looked back over my shoulder. My first horrified thought was of some monstrous thing looming there, a black monolith with two gleaming eyes reflecting the moonlight. The gleaming eyes reflecting the moonlight. The gleaming eyes betrayed Messire Livio; for they were his insufferable spectacles. Behind them was only his slight, unimportant self, terrifying only, as I thought, in his usefulness as a spy to Doge Manin and the Council of Ten.

"In heaven's name, do something!" I cried, "Go fetch the police, or the Watch, whatever they are called."

"The *sbirri*," he said. "Move aside. Let me see him."

Something in his quiet voice impressed me. I obeyed, watching as he removed his spectacles and knelt to examine Captain Dandolo. "How did it happen?"

I explained that we were walking toward the Casino Bartolini when I reached down to pet a cat that had crossed our path. And when I stood up again, the Captain was falling. I pointed to the dagger where I had dropped it.

He nodded and went on examining the Captain's wound. "He is alive, at all events. Did his gondolier remain?"

"I think so. In that canal between this arcade and the end of the Piazza. Shall I go and fetch him?"

He looked up at me curiously and with something else in his luminous, dark eyes. Not admiration, surely? "You are a brave woman!"

I felt a pleasant little glow of warmth. "No. Merely sensible."

He reached up, took my hand. There was blood on his fingers. "Are you aware that you may have been the target for this bravo with the dagger?"

I was stupefied. "But why? He is an authority, a—kind of policeman. A natural target."

He shrugged off his cloak and bundled it tightly around the Captain's slack body. "I have seen men die of shock in these cases. He should be kept warm until he can be removed to a *Hôtel Dieu*."

It was the name that I, a Parisienne, used for a hospital and I thought nothing of his use of it. Besides, we were both too concerned to care about trifles. He got to his feet and after one of those quick, encompassing glances of his, said, "We will fetch up his gondolier first. These fellows are long tested in their loyalty to the Serenissima."

Although my companion had said there was no more

danger, I was obliged to him for the care with which he shielded me from the dangerous arcade. It was only a minute or two before we reached the canal. The gondola floated gently on the swaying black waters, but it was empty.

Livio, still keeping his body between me and the gathering dark, went up on the bridge and gave an odd, long drawn-out call. No gondolier replied or appeared on either side of the bridge, but in the distance, from the direction of the Piazza, we heard pounding feet, and another gondolier, big and impressively muscular, came hurrying toward us.

Livio waved him forward. Obviously, he was Livio's own gondolier. "Gino, Captain Dandolo has been wounded. We must get him to treatment."

The gondolier hurried down the bridge and along the cobbles. Livio followed with me, not quite so rapidly. He pulled me to him, looking into my face in a most possessive way. "How are you feeling? Are you quite all right?"

"Of course, I am. Don't be silly. That poor man! Do you think he will live?"

"I imagine so. He is a healthy fellow. You look very pale. Your hands are like ice."

Crossly, I pointed out that I was not the one who had been stabbed and prayed him to see to the injured man.

"To all intents and purposes, you are the injured one. And you are not wearing a stiff, heavy bandolier. That dagger would have killed you."

"But why would anyone wish to kill me? I had nothing worth robbing. Only a few *scudi* in my muff. So why would anyone—?"

I broke off. The absurd, yet frightful thing was that this man, this unknown named Livio, had appeared out of no-where, soundless, silent, only a minute or two after the attack upon Captain Dandolo. And he was the only person I had actually seen or heard. Further, he was trying very hard to make me believe I was the target, and not the obvious victim, the Captain.

"How did you happen to be here?" I asked him, trying to make the suspicious question sound more innocent than it was.

"I, too, was headed toward the Casino Bartolini. I heard something. I came through the arcade and saw you bending over this poor devil."

"Where is the Captain's gondolier?" Livio's big friend asked as he began to raise the wounded man's limp body. "Fled in terror, like these other heroes?"

"Quiet!" Livio commanded, while I puzzled over this censored conversation.

I had occasion afterward to wonder what would have happened to me—if, indeed, this Livio was the assassin—if the little street had not suddenly become crowded with reveling masqueraders ascending from their gondola and heading toward the gaming palace.

One of them, a lean male, dressed in the quiet elegance of black and silver, lingered behind the others.

"Is it Miss Carewe? Jove! But it is. What has happened?"

The man was no pleasure to see; for he was the icy, doubting Fortman-Truscott of the embassy staff.

I said abruptly, "The Captain was attacked by a footpad. We were rescued by this gentleman." I do not know why I added this. I was by no means free of my suspicions.

Fortman-Truscott made noises of shock and consolation, and waved on his little group of revelers, though two of the men remained behind to watch the scene.

"You must let me aid you in any way possible," he announced with one of his tight smiles that evaded his chill, gray eyes.

"Thank you. You are too kind, but it is quite unnecessary," I began, and then Livio took upon himself the disposal of my time and person.

"You may be of service to His Excellency, the British Ambassador, Messire, if you will be good enough to escort Madonna Carewe to the palace of His Excellency."

"As it happens, I do not wish to leave until I am assured as to Captain Dandolo's condition," I protested.

I might have guessed how it would be. The two men ignored my objections and discussed things in a most businesslike way, even deciding the degree of danger to the poor Captain, now tight-wrapped and in the huge arms of Livio's gondolier.

I said, "Is no one going to ask what has happened to the Captain's gondolier?"

Fortman-Truscott did not answer. He was busy discussing the Captain's wound with Livio's big friend and making suggestions about how best and most painlessly to carry the wounded man.

I was startled when Livio murmured for my ears only,

"Do not pursue the matter. The missing gondolier may be our assassin." I gasped, and he added, "Or—he may be dead in that canal."

"But we must do something . . . see to it . . ."

"Leave the matter to me."

Oddly enough, I did so. Recent events had so vigorously crowded in upon me that I found my usual determination and strength of will badly weakened. I was trembling when Fortman-Truscott took my arm to lead me away.

I looked back. I felt helpless, deserted. "No. I do not wish to go."

"But you cannot disappoint the gallant Signore Truscott."

"Fortman-Truscott," said that gentleman.

"To be sure. We envy you your task, Signore. You will escort Madonna Rachel safely to His Excellency's palazzo." This effusiveness seemed a trifle warm, and even more odd was Livio's next action when he spoke louder than was his custom, so that his gondolier and Truscott's friends were all witness to a perfectly pointless remark: "How fortunate you are, Signore Fortman-Truscott! You, and you alone are responsible for the safe restoration of the lovely Madonna to her father. All of us, Signore, who see you depart, envy you."

I still persisted, "You must tell me how he goes on. Give me your word." And Livio promised.

When I left with Fortman-Truscott I looked back and saw that Livio and his gondolier were not leaving alone with Captain Dandolo. Two of Fortman-Truscott's friends went with them. It relieved me a little.

As for myself, I must have been very dense that night. It was not until I was carefully deposited upon my father's doorstep that I understood the meaning of Livio's absurd and loudly proclaimed statement. It had been his way of providing witnesses to my safe return. So I could trust Livio; surely, I could trust him, at least!

Fortman-Truscott provided a distinctly subdued and boring escort, as I was myself. Boring, and thoughtful. He had little to say and I had less to reply as we were swept from the lagoon toward the small canal and Father's palazzo. I was busy thinking over the events of the evening.

How had Livio happened to arrive on the scene so silently and unobtrusively after the attack on Captain Dandolo? Now that I had convinced myself of his innocence, I had to find other reasons for his arrival. As a representative of the

Council of Ten he probably felt it his duty to protect the guests of the Serenissima. His heavy-handed gondolier friend might be one of the Serenissima's stranglers, judging by the size of those hands.

Much to my surprise, Mira Teotochi came rushing out of the great canal doors of the palace, demanding to know what had happened and why I returned home so soon. Before I could open my mouth, Fortman-Truscott was explaining. At that instant, as I heard him describe how the dagger struck the Captain as I stooped to touch the cat, I saw her slanting eyes as she glanced my way without turning her handsome head.

She is thinking I might have been the victim, I told myself, *and she regrets the error.*

I was very tired but still wary enough to be cautious; so I smiled upon her fatuously, thanked the First Secretary for his escort home, and went into the great, chilly house, wondering if Mira Teotochi and the First Secretary exchanged any interesting secrets concerning me.

Apparently not; for when I reached my bedchamber and went directly to the balcony windows, I saw that Fortman-Truscott, his gondola and silent, unobtrusive gondolier were already under the bridge and heading rapidly away.

I stood there for some little time, pressing my face against the cool glass and shivering. . . . *Father. If I could talk with you, confide in you the way it was when I was young! But there is an entire world between us . . . If only we could go back, be what we once were . . . But you have been sheltered. You will never know that real world, the world of the nineteenth century that I am beginning to glimpse. So I can't talk to you. And no one else understands.*

Something flashed through my mind. Just a flash. An instant between Messire Livio and myself. A single look; yet in that instant I had thought: *He sees what I see. He looks with my eyes. He has been through the Revolution, the eerie presence of the guillotine, the war, as I have been . . .*

And then the absurd notion faded. Livio was a Venetian spy. His chief duty undoubtedly was to deliver unsuspecting victims to the Grand Inquisitor and the Strangler's cord. The only thing our eyes saw in unison was the public execution!

. . . So I am back to the truth. I am alone . . .

Angry with myself over this groveling self-pity, I turned from the window, bolted the door and prepared for bed. A large ewer of water still vaguely warm, plus several towels, served for my bath and I welcomed the comfort of the big bed. In despite of all the events of the evening, I should have slept immediately; for I had been so stiff with tension and fright during the past few hours that I welcomed the relaxation of all my muscles and even my bones.

However, it was not to be. Almost at once someone rapped in a gingerly way upon my door. I pretended not to hear, but it was all in vain. Dacey's voice pursued me in one of those piercing whispers which are sure to attract the attention of the very persons she tried to evade.

"Rachel! Are you asleep? Rachel!"

There was no help for it. I yawned, got out of the big bed and stumbled across the room. I shot back the bolt, and motioned her in, yawning and shivering at the same time. I was less than overjoyed to see her. Something of my bitterness still remained from the disastrous dinner in which I had clearly read doubt in her eyes, as in those of my father.

"Yes?" I prompted her in my coolest voice.

A flicker of concern crossed her face. "Rachel, dear," she began again in a small, half-swallowed voice, "Did you notice . . . That is, did you have a delightful time at the Casino? Oh—you must have lost!"

"I did not lose. Nor did I win. I did not gamble. In point of fact, we did not reach the Casino."

"Rachel! Was that nice Captain a bit too intimate? Oh, I knew it—he had the look!"

She was so upset I abandoned all my intentions of treating her coolly. "Dacey, you are quite incorrigible. Do come in and bolt the door. I cannot bear for you to think that unfortunate young man behaved in an ungentlemanly manner."

When she was seated on my bed in her night-rail and dressing sacque and frilled night-bonnet, I crawled in under the covers and sat propped against the pillows. We found ourselves exactly in the gossipy position that had given us to much pleasure during my childhood, and I said in partial explanation for the memory loss at dinner, "It is like the old days; isn't it, Dacey?"

She clapped her hands. "Oh, my dear, you do remember!"

This annoyed me secretly but I tried not to let it show in my manner. "Of course. But I don't feel that I need to justify my adult status to my own father."

"Naturally not, Rachel. No such thought ever entered our —my head."

"Dacey . . ."

She looked exceedingly conscious. "Yes. It must have seemed that way, but you see, I was so shocked. That is, I am persuaded your dear Papa felt a similar—"

"What?"

She looked at me uneasily, like a child pleading a case which she herself felt was not too complete. "I mean—we all remembered the little, charming things you did as a child, and we merely enjoyed recalling them. Then, you seemed so angry! Out of all proportion to the cause. That Mrs. Teotochi remarked . . . well, never mind."

"I am sure I know what Mrs. Teotochi remarked. Dacey! I know she is my enemy. Don't you know that by this time? And if you are my friend, then she may be your enemy as well."

Dacey behaved very oddly. She began to pleat the coverlet under her fingers and to color up in a girlish way. She avoided my eyes. "I wonder if you—if we might have been wrong about Mrs. Teotochi." I caught my breath and she rushed on. "Really, it is only Christian of us to give her the benefit of our doubt. After you had rushed away from the table as you did, we all felt quite dreadful. Poor Mrs. Teotochi accused herself, claiming the fault was hers—that she should never have urged your dear Papa to talk so much about you, for it only hurt him later, when you denied him."

"I denied him?"

"Well, that is how she put it, dear. And you did refuse to speak with him of all those tender little memories."

I laughed. It was that or weep or tear the sheets in a rage. What an odious, contemptible trick of that Teotochi female, to try and turn away the affections of the only two people left to me! But my sharp little laugh was the worst possible re-action, for it managed to add to the damage already done by Father's housekeeper.

Dacey looked at me in a hurt, offended way. "You have changed, Rachel. You never would have laughed at me in the old days. You are—different. Not the sweet, endearing child you were when you left for France."

Hardening myself at this added wound, I reminded her, "I was a child then. As you said, I am a woman now. Things have happened. I can never go back and be that English child again, ignorant of my fellow man, ignorant even of the absolute necessity to survive in a deadly world. I am quite a different woman from that silly child, and neither you nor my father can expect me to remain eleven-and-a-half years old forever."

Dacey's soft mouth trembled and stiffened. She got up from the bed. "No," she said, "we cannot expect that." Her warm smile flashed briefly, unexpectedly. "It may be that I can help you, more than you know, dear." The smile was gone. She, too, seemed suddenly like a different woman, one who was trying to tell me something that the others should not guess. Yet, in another moment she spoke as one who salaamed to Father and Mrs. Teotochi as though she believed every lie the woman spread: "Mrs. Teotochi was so right, as your dear father agreed—we would never have known you. I'll say good night now."

By the time she reached the door I was over my silly miff and got out of bed to follow her. She seemed to be behaving very oddly, her mood so changeful. "Dacey . . .?"

The door closed and I stopped in the middle of the floor, telling myself that this was nothing but a ridiculous little disagreement brought about by the lateness of the hour. Yes, it had been a bad day, bad above all in this sinister new influence on Father and Dacey, exerted by Mira Teotochi. And the entire business made it no easier for me to go back to bed and to sleep. I walked up and down the big bedchamber, hugging my arms against the imaginary cold. When I approached the balcony, I glanced out at the canal and the little bridge. I could not see anyone and assumed Livio was too busy caring for Captain Dandolo to worry about reporting the doings of my father's palazzo to the Venetian government.

I asked myself if there was any hope for a future as my father's companion here in the palazzo. Would there ever again be the old, dear relationship between us? It was not my father's fault that I had changed, grown a hard shield against hurt. He had not wished my mother and me to desert him. The fault was ours. And he couldn't know how it felt, or that I understood his confusion, and his doubts about me. For I had been too stubborn and too proud to tell him.

I walked back and forth with a nervous energy I could not control. Minutes passed while I tried to reassure myself that all would be made clear tomorrow when I saw my father. But what of tonight? Was my father suffering at this very minute from his doubts of my love and my devotion, even of my identity? Perhaps he, too, could not sleep.

And so, by this persistent and nervous consideration of my

father's feelings and mine, I decided to do my best to reassure him tonight, if he was still awake. I went and got out a light summer cloak, threw it around my shoulders, stepped into a pair of flat-soled day slippers, and went to the door. I fancied that when I shot back the bolt, its echo reverberated through the wide second-storey hall. In a gingerly way I peered out, to be greeted by the usual creaks and cracking noises of an ancient house settling during the night. Then, suddenly angered at my own cowardice, I strode out into the center of the hall and walked toward the door which opened on the three circling flights of stone steps.

I saw nothing untoward. All my conceptions of danger on the previous night seemed absurd now. The single light illuminating the hall was a tall and fresh candle set in a bed-candlestick on the side table halfway between my bedchamber and Dacey's at the opposite end of the hall. Aside from the natural flickering lights and shadows, nothing moved. Whatever my fears, they were obviously imaginary. I reached the steps, looked around and below, found the three flights lighted by a kind of storm lamp, the candle protected by its glass walls. This lamp swung from a ring let into the wall. As there was a rising wind sweeping across the Venetian waters, I found a considerable draft running through the steps from the open roof. No matter. I was warmly dressed, and such weather was not nearly so alarming in my experience as the actions of human beings.

On the gallery floor I looked around, keenly aware of the pursuing gaze of all those fifteenth- and sixteenth-century portraits. All were illuminated in varying degrees by another of those wholly inadequate bedcandles. There was no possibility of silence. Everywhere in this great stone monolith built upon piles driven into the water there must be wooden additions, warped and expanding or contracting—whatever they did in abruptly cooling weather. The sudden snap! the slower, agonizing creak! Each startled me more than I would have admitted to any but myself.

I had just touched the door of Father's sitting room when one of those sounds made me jump. The door opened abruptly under my unexpected shove. Making my way through the shadowed sitting room, I had no intention of startling Father and so I called out very softly, "Father? Are you awake?"

Belatedly, I remembered how Dacey's similar greeting had annoyed me earlier; but if I was to talk with my father in

private, and especially without the interference of Mira Teotochi, I had to use the tactics of a thief in the night.

There was no response to my call and I did not like to
awaken Father if he had gone off to sleep. I moved quietly
across the room to the bedchamber door, which was ajar.
The pleasant pink glow of a lamp inside it softened the heavy,
forbidding furniture, which greatly resembled that of the
Jacobean style in the England of my birth. The room was
paneled and the bed curtains, which were pushed apart,
revealed the huge, dark bed. It was empty. I was both
relieved and disappointed, my relief being due to the fact
that Father must obviously be feeling more himself, since
he had been used to remain up very late in the old days.

I turned back, then heard voices in the gallery. I could
not make out the words but there was no mistaking the embrace I witnessed in the sitting room doorway. Mira Teotochi
and Father, still in the clothing they had worn at dinner,
kissed in the quick, affectionate way of longtime lovers, so
familiar they were almost without passion.

It was Mira Teotochi who saw me first over Father's
shoulder. She drew back, her face suddenly drained of color.
"You!"

Father swung around. I was happy to note that though he
was surprised, he did not seem shocked. He even smiled, a
tired smile but as genial as in the old days. With considerable effort he limped toward me.

I couldn't bear to see him exert himself in this painful way,
and hurried to meet him. "Father! I am intruding, I know.
But I did not wish to go to sleep without asking your pardon
for my conduct at dinner."

"My child, no!" He held out his arms. They were shaking,
wavering, but they were only dearer to me for that. I went
into his arms, then rested my cheek against his, remembering
other times, other years when I had been far too small to
touch his cheek.

"I did not mean to intrude," I said again. "Please forgive
me. I only wanted to talk to you, to explain why I have difficulty remembering the old days."

"I know. Let me explain as well. You see, Rachel, I want
you and Mira to become great friends. I am glad you saw
us a moment since. I do not wish to have secrets from my
little girl."

"I—I don't understand. I shouldn't have come in without

making my presence known. But you see, I expected to find you alone."

"Rachel . . ." He took me by the shoulders, looking firmly into my face. "I am a man and human. Mira has been very good to me during my illnesses. And—in short—I have learned to love her. I intend that she shall be my wife. Some days ago runners from the embassy were sent out with the invitations. The ceremony will take place here. Mira has made arrangements. She is so very—er—useful. And now it will serve the double purpose of presenting you, my daughter, to Venice. Then, my dear Mira will be the mother you need." As he saw my face, he added urgently, "She will take care of you, be a good mother to you, and look after you with exactly the supervision you must have. Give yourself time, Rachel. You will find Mira indispensable, as I do. Embrace her now—there's my good girl."

I wished to oblige him, but I was so stunned I could only stand there motionless as the woman moved across the floor with all that surprising grace and beauty I had first observed in quite a different context, at the Casino when she had taken the ducats from Livio. Her arms went around me like slender steel threads, leaving me weak, defeated. Her breath faintly brushed my face as we "kissed" by touching cheeks. I wondered if my touch affected her with as much revulsion as I felt in her close presence.

I must learn to accept her, I thought, *and even to like her.* But I had this dreadful sense of her malevolence as she flashed upon me her warm-lipped smile while her slanting eyes glittered as they regarded me.

CHAPTER EIGHT

THAT WAS A NIGHT for considerable soul-searching on my part. Once I returned to my chamber, I could not immediately sleep; so I spent some time in thought, the while I tried to wash out the stains of Captain Dandolo's blood from my best ballgown. The task was hopeless. The gown could never be worn again, but I did accomplish something, in that I decided I had been most unfair to my father. I would be the last to deny the attractions of Mira Teotochi; and besides, she was certainly a most useful woman, conducting the affairs of this household with all the aplomb of its mistress.

And when she married Father, she would indeed be the mistress of the house!

Could I ever grow to like her, to live under the same roof with this woman who looked at me in that glittering, almost reptilian way? I was sure she hated me, but was it only for fear lest my arrival would influence Papa against her? If so, there might be some hope for our future relations, since I would begin at once to demonstrate my willingness to accept her as my father's affianced wife.

But if there were more to her hatred than mere jealousy and fear for her position, what then? Whom outside could I trust? Captain Dandolo was wounded, perhaps dying; and

Messire Livio knew a great deal more about my family and Mira than he should know if he were not a spy. Was it not Livio who had loaned the ducats to her for her gambling money only two nights ago? Perhaps he, too, was a part of some conspiracy against me.

Had he been the dagger man of last night? But if so, why had he not killed me during those minutes when I knelt over the Captain's body? He had ample time, and no witnesses. What was it he had told me: "But for your sudden movement, you would have received that dagger. And you wore no bandolier to deflect the blow. You would have died."

Was that the warning of an assassin?

I found myself hoping he had my best interests at heart. It was amazing how much more attractive he was when he removed those absurd spectacles. Yes, I thought, as I finally climbed back into bed, the worst that could be said of Livio was that he spied for the Serenissima. His paymaster was the Venetian Republic and it did not serve their purpose to allow the daughter of the British Ambassador to fall victim to a cutthroat in the public alleys of Venice.

All the same, my dreams were full of faceless assassins, stealthy footsteps, pools of blood, and a recurrence of the nightmare in which my father called out to me for help. Help from what? Was it this appalling marriage? Or was the marriage, indeed, only appalling to me?

After such a night of unquiet slumber, daylight was welcome. In my confusion the previous night I had not quite closed the portieres over the long windows that opened upon the balcony, and the sunlight poured in, reflected off the pale, cream-colored surface of the building across the canal. My first inclination was to close them tightly, shutting out the sun, but I heard the rattle of a cup and saucer on a tray set by my door in the hall and that, combined with the welcome warmth of the sunlight, caused me instead to draw the portieres open wide and to look out at the rust-red rooftops of Venice from the balcony.

A morning barge moved past and I started back into my room, aware of my bedgown and robe fluttering around me, but I was arrested by a hail from someone on the little quai below. It was Livio, his dark hair tousled and windblown, making him look oddly young as he waved to me.

"All serene," he said. He was waving his square spectacles and I realized again how careful he was in general, to hide what were, if not perfectly handsome features, at least quite prepossessing good looks. Though he smiled, he did not have that vacuous, easy charm of the Venetian gallants. His compassionate eyes were those of a man who has experienced many things, and perhaps suffering was among them.

"The Captain?" I asked.

"He will be receiving lovely visitors at the Port Customs before noon. Shall I escort you?"

"Thank you. I would appreciate it."

"Masked," he reminded me.

"What? By daylight?"

"This is Venice. Do you want people to think I have seduced the Ambassador's daughter?"

"Or vice versa," I told him, and laughed; for he looked exceedingly harmless by sunlight.

Suddenly he fastened on his glasses, masking those extraordinarily fine dark eyes, and a second or two later, I saw Mira Teotochi come out upon the scummed step. She said something to him which I could not hear, and he shrugged, pointing upward to my balcony. I backed into the room, belatedly conscious of my bedrobes. Their conversation must have gone on for another couple of minutes, after which I saw him stride off toward the little bridge where he crossed the canal. He did not look back. I thought it a pity.

One fact I hugged to myself in the hour following. For Mira he carefully masked himself with those spectacles. But he let me see him as he really was. That must count for something. I think it was sincerity and belief in me that I sought now above everything. Thus far, only Captain Dandolo and Messire Livio seemed to meet this qualification. The Captain's dreadful wound therefore seemed doubly important to me, and I wanted to assure myself that he was recovering.

Livio believed, or said he believed, that the dagger had been meant for me. In such case, I was doubly in debt to poor Pietro Dandolo. But if Livio was correct, who, then, was my enemy? Was it truly Mira Teotochi? Yet no one else had reason to fear or dislike me; I could think of no other people with similar motives for my death.

I went finally to the door and brought in my tray of chocolate left by the young chambermaid. It was a welcome sight, still warm, still foaming and rich when I poured it. I drank it at the table by the balcony windows. It was calming, reassuring, and I was grateful for the custom. Afterward, I dressed hurriedly, hoping to spend some time with Father during which we could renew the old, dear relationship and, at all events, renew his shaken belief in me. As for my quarrel with Dacey, much as I regretted it, I felt that my father must be of the first concern to me.

All the same, when I left my bedchamber half an hour later, I looked at Dacey's door several times, aware that I would be a good deal more easy in my mind if Dacey were to appear suddenly in her usual good humor, to tell me that our quarrel was at an end. But I could not go to her and say that I had been wrong. It was a matter of my own identity. Dacey was half of the opinion that I might be a fraud. The quarrel had begun by her own making—and Mira Teotochi's, of course. Surely, it had begun with her hints to my father!

Reassured of my own stand but by no means happy over it, I went down to the gallery floor, resolved not to leave until I could see my father. If Mira or her mute servant interfered, I would simply wait for the appropriate time. Perhaps I could learn to deal with Mira herself. It would not be the first time I had found it necessary, for my own safety and survival, to pretend a feeling I did not possess. If Mira Teotochi was innocent, then my pretense of friendship would not matter. If she was guilty of intriguing against me, it might buy me time.

It was fortunate that I had not too many hopes of reaching Father at this hour. I had scarcely stepped into the gallery when I heard a door open at the back of the gallery, and Mira Teotochi appeared, quietly dressed in black as usual, and equally as usual, looking her beautiful self. She was with the tired cleaning maid I had seen on the ground floor yesterday and had apparently been issuing the day's orders. Seeing me now, she sent the maid on her way to the quarters below.

Whatever else she might be, there was no doubt that she was remarkably efficient at her tasks. I ventured a hesitant smile, as if anxious to make up any misunderstanding that might exist between us. I said, "Good morning, Signora. I have been hoping I might see you."

Her frigid manner thawed slightly. She was understandably surprised after my previous and all-too-obvious suspicions of her. I thought I read doubt in her flawless, marblelike face.

She blinked and then smiled, with an effort. "The Signorina is too kind. May I ask—are your quarters satisfactory? Were you perhaps seeking me to make new arrangements?"

"No, no. Everything is quite satisfactory." Feeling very

like an actress with the *Comédie Française,* I ventured timidly, like the obedient daughter my father apparently wanted and expected, "It is only that I am concerned for Papa's happiness, and when he told me of your plans for marriage, I was surprised. I am sure Papa will forgive me, but a beautiful young woman like yourself—you will understand?" I thought it would be more convincing if I played upon a half-truth: her beauty and the difference in their ages.

Evidently what she conceived to be my frankness swayed her to a belief in my sincerity. Her features now definitely softened. "You are very kind . . . Rachel. I may call you Rachel? Your father has discussed you so often and so lovingly, that I had long felt the great tragedy of your death."

Was she going to begin again on the eerie subject of my identity? Or was she testing me? It seemed to me that the safest course was frankness. Within reason.

I said, in a hurt tone. "But that is what I particularly resented, Miss—Mira. You and my father seemed to imply I am an imposter." Yes. It was the correct approach. I allowed my indignation to recede under her quick apology.

"You could not be more mistaken, Rachel. As I told your dear Papa the night you arrived, if you permitted, nothing would make me happier than to be a mother to his motherless daughter. You see—" her smile was dazzling "—I am older than you think. Quite old enough to be devoted to your dear father . . . and to you, if you permit."

I allowed myself to be persuaded. I said ingenuously, "I think I can understand that. Father is a very attractive person. I know he is a little, a trifle ill now, but I'm sure he will soon be well again and then—then you can marry him and bring him the happiness he once knew with Mother." I couldn't resist that, but she didn't allow herself to be angered by the reference to my mother. In fact, she used it very cleverly.

Her voice became subdued, even wistful. "But your dear mother deserted Maitland, did she not?"

I started to deny this, but of course, there could be no denial. So I played out my charade, angrily saying, "That isn't true!" Then, as if recollecting the truth and regretting it, I added with proper shame, "I beg your pardon. I suppose it would seem that way to someone who truly loves Father." I put out my hand. "I do believe you love him. When he is well, I shall be happy to witness your wedding."

She was jarred by this, and contradicted me quickly. "Oh, no! We cannot wait so long. You see, we cannot bear to remain apart." She must think me naive enough to believe they had been apart thus far. "He needs me," she added. "It is for this reason, we have planned to be married at once, and your arrival—your resurrection, if I may say so—is most timely." As I caught my breath, she patted my hand. "Will you do us the honor of appearing as an English witness at that time?"

I was shocked and revolted but did not dare to show it. I allowed myself to protest vaguely that it was so soon, but if I wanted to throw off her suspicions, I had to have her good will. So I yielded after reasonable hesitation: "Well, if it is going to make Papa happy . . ."

"It will!" How odiously sure she was. But I ended by convincing her of the truth; I did indeed want my father's happiness. The difference was that I did not believe his happiness could be assured by Mira Teotochi.

As if anxious to keep her precarious hold upon me, she asked if I would share my father's breakfast. I agreed, hoping to speak alone with him, but unfortunately, Mira herself joined us. I was relieved by Papa's manner toward me. He acted as if nothing had happened the previous night, as though the wedding was understood and agreed to by all of us. But he acted, too, as if he had never been prey to any doubts of my identity. That, at least, cheered me greatly, though it showed me how far his old, stern will had depreciated; for in former days he would have had the matter out, not hesitating to open the quarrel once more if necessary to have it settled once and for all. But he looked so tired now! Worn and frail and doubtless glad of peace between those he loved.

We all ate at a table in Father's sitting room, with Father comfortably bundled in a cushioned chair. Since I was not used to eating a large meal before noon, I shared Papa's sweet, honeyed cakes and the strong black coffee that he drank and which I found made me inordinately nervous. Or perhaps it was simply that I had become so much aware of Mira's eyes watching my every move, thoughtful and doubtless wondering if my conversation was sincere.

Since I suspected that Mira had seen Livio this morning and doubtless heard us making plans to visit Captain Dandolo, I made no pretense of hiding the fact. At the same time I felt that it would be well if Mira thought my interest in the dashing Captain was greater than my interest in Livio.

Her connection with Livio still puzzled and intrigued me. I found it surprisingly distasteful.

At my news about going to visit the Port Customs offices, Father raised his head slowly, looking troubled.

"Only with Miss Dace, my dear. And masked. Otherwise, it would not be the thing at all."

"But Dacey is out-of-reason cross with me, Papa, for my behavior last evening. I hate to ask her. Naturally, I would not venture into the gentleman's bedchamber except in the company of the Port Commander and Messire Livio."

"Messire Livio?" asked Father, glancing at Mira with a puzzled air. "What sort of—have I not heard that name before?"

Breathless, I waited for her reply, trying not to seem that I waited. She waved her hands indifferently. "A singularly ill-favored young wastrel with too much money. I suspect—I have no proof, but the gossip is that he is in the pay of the Serenissima. Possibly the Grand Inquisitor."

So my suspicions on that score had been correct! Well, no matter. I did not threaten the *Most Serene* Republic.

Father smiled and reached for my hand. "Then perhaps, it will do no harm. Always providing he is—as you say—singularly ill-favored."

"Hideous!" I said firmly, for Mira's benefit. "He stares at one with those horrid spectacles that magnify his eyes until, I dare swear, you would take him for a toad."

Although I was not looking directly at Mira, I was keenly aware of her reactions. She seemed in no way surprised at my description; so I guessed that he must strike her in very much that light. I hoped she would always think of him as an ugly toad.

And then the breakfast was over and Father, answering my unspoken prayer, said gently to Mira Teotochi, "My little girl will be leaving shortly on this excursion to the Port Customs. I should like to be with her alone . . . for a few minutes."

"Of course, Messire. At once, Messire." But as the woman left us she looked back. I had an unpleasant notion that she could read our minds, guess whatever was to be said, and perhaps even guide it. I wondered if I must be careful and guard my tongue, even from my father.

"Ah, Father, how nice it is to have a little talk like this, how like the old days!" I reached for his hand which shook with the slight palsy.

"Like the old days, Daughter," he murmured in a voice so hoarse and weak it made tears start in my eyes. How many years had passed since Father and I sat together! And how different we were from the lively, hopeful little girl, and that strong, vigorous, unconquerable man in the prime of life!

We could never return to those days, I knew, with a pain in my throat so great I could not speak for a moment . . . But we would accept second-best, the relationship that the years and Father's illness had left to us.

"Now then," he said with an assumption of vigor that was a shadow of himself, "you are going to be much sought after in Venice, and my girl must be prepared to refine her judgment, to choose carefully."

I smiled. I felt a great tenderness for him in spite of the enormous changes in us, in our lives and our relationship. Now it was I who felt protective, even if that dear, young hope and trust in him vanished. "Yes, Papa. I will choose carefully. In any case, I don't intend to marry for a very long time. Perhaps never. Was that what you wanted to tell me?"

He looked around the room vaguely. I had an uncomfortable feeling that he had forgotten what he was about to say. I tried to recover that wonderful mind that had once been his. "You wanted to tell me something, Father? About . . . our life here?"

"That. Yes. I want you to be happy. And I believe you will be, with someone to look out for you. I—alas—I am no longer what I hoped to be to you. But my dear Mira can be mother and sister and confidante. All that your mother and I can no longer be."

"I understand," I said quickly, to avoid the subject. "But you forget—I am well grown now. I have lived without mother or sister, or confidante, and can continue to do so. And, of course," I added in haste, "I have you, my dear Papa."

"But Mira can be such a help. She has so many excellent qualities! And you will remember, Rachel, that under the law you are placed in my care, and that of my wife. You are not permitted to conduct your own life. You are a female and unmarried."

Uneasy at this turn in the conversation, I tried to calm him, to contradict his appalling statement without upsetting him. "Father, I am in your charge, I know. But you must not joke about placing my conduct, my very life, in the hands of a woman I do not know. You will see, when you think of it, how impossible that would be."

I expected him to smile, to soothe me. Instead, he shook his head and his pale eyes regarded me soberly. "It is the law. And it is for your own good. A young woman like you would be helpless without an adult, a married woman to have the charge of you . . ." I started to say something but he cut me off. "We are to be married tomorrow. All the Venetian friends of the embassy have been invited. After tomorrow, you will be in my dear wife's hands. You must look to Mira as your mentor. Your mother, if you will."

I won't! The words flew to my mind, although I could see that Mira Teotochi might have the law with her . . . Aloud, I said, "Is that all, Father?"

He stared at me, blinking rapidly. "Yes, my child, I think that is all."

As I left him he looked crushed, as if he expected me to curtsey and kiss him on the cheek as in the old days. But too much had happened since those years. And now, to be told my life was in the hands of a woman I instinctively recognized as an enemy! It was too much. I went out rapidly, not looking back.

I thought I would try to make up the quarrel with Dacey before I left, but when I went up to her door and knocked, the cleaning maid came to meet me and reported that Miss Adelaide Dace was with Mira Teotochi at the moment, being shown the kitchens and stillrooms of the palace. This gave me a few painful thoughts. It seemed more than slightly possible that Mira was separating me first from my father and now from Dacey. I had an impulse to burst into tears but conquered that childish notion, went up to my chamber and made some last minute additions to my gown and spencer, wearing my prettiest emerald-green bonnet and the slippers that best displayed my ankles.

After the painful scene with my father, I looked too pale, so I used just a suggestion of rouge upon my lips and cheeks. The green silk bonnet did a great deal to bring out the darkness of my eyes and lashes, so I felt my best. I could only hope both Messire Livio and Captain Dandolo would share this opinion. It would cheer my spirits immensely, and I was badly in need of friends.

From the balcony I watched for Livio's gondola. Several others moved past in the meanwhile and when he did arrive in the vanguard of a whole armada of barges, I nearly missed him. It was Mira, naturally, who went out to the steps and greeted him. I was happy to note that as he talked with her he did not remove his spectacles. It was the one fancy I clung to, that made me feel he was not on her side but upon mine. I tried to hear what they were saying but understood only snatches of their rapid Italian.

"Very well, I understand," he said several times. And a little later, "I did not intend to seduce her, Ambassador's daughter or no. But the Serenissima likes to know the thoughts and entertainments of its visitors."

"You damnable spy! Always your duty!" Mira's voice was harsh, uncontrolled. Almost hysterical, I thought. "Well then, go your way with the girl. But if she turns out to be a French spy, by all means inform her father and me. It would be of importance that the British Embassy know it has an enemy agent in its midst."

I had always imagined Livio to be in the pay of the Venetian Republic even before Mira confirmed my suspicions, but the curious thing was that thus far, whenever we were together, he made no attempt in any way to trick me into a betrayal of my political opinions. I wondered if it was Mira and not I who was his real prey.

Mira came herself to fetch me, playing my "second mother" with a remarkably convincing performance. I paid little heed to that, accepting her new role politely and without fuss, but it was secretly upsetting to note Adelaide Dace in the background, hovering in her wake. When I greeted Dacey without reserve, hoping she had decided to accept our old relationship, I could see that Mira had accomplished more damage than I had at first supposed.

A trifle stiffly Dacey said to me, as I passed her in the hall, "I am happy to see you have accepted the situation, my dear. You are wise not to make trouble for someone who has your best interests at heart."

I was more shocked than angry; so I merely nodded, waved good bye to her and went below to join Messire Livio. I found him standing in the high-roofed vestibule, studying the black and white walls through his spectacles, looking nearsighted and somewhat absurd. Certainly, he appeared to be a different person from the dark, romantic young man who had spoken to me on the balcony earlier in the morning. I wondered how many people, if any, knew the real Livio.

He swung around as I approached, peered at me and bowed elaborately over my hand. By this time I was beginning to recognize his pretenses and as I curtseyed slightly, I suspected that we were performing for the benefit of an unseen audience. When we were near enough for whispers, I asked him in a low, amused voice, "Are we performing for someone?"

"But of course. Your well-loved parents."

"My—" I nearly turned around but his pressure on my wrist stopped me and we went out to the quai together. Once we had reached his gondola, I asked incredulously, "Did you mean both my—that is, my father as well?"

"Naturally. They wonder what I am about with you."

He lifted me down into the waist of the gondola, making no attempt at familiarities as had the dashing Captain Dandolo; yet I was intensely aware of his hands about my waist.

I could not resist looking up into his face with elaborate innocence, asking, "And what are you about with me, Messire?"

But he was ready for me. "If I told you, there would be no suspense in our relationship."

I laughed. His reply reminded me of so many young Frenchmen I had known during the Paris years. Looking back to them now, it seemed to me that nearly every one I found attractive ended either as an emigré or on the guillotine. There had been years when I had not dared to love, fearing always that my affection was death to any youth of my acquaintance. And so I had reached the age of twenty unmarried and considered myself "on the shelf," with very little likelihood of ever marrying. But I could joke with this crafty and mysterious spy, feeling that he was more than able to take care of himself if threatened by the Serenissima's equivalent of the guillotine.

"How serious was the Captain's wound?" I asked then, partly to take my mind off a queer malaise that struck me, once we were on the water. I bit my lip and tried very hard to concentrate upon the beauty of the morning and of the palaces along the quai, each with its own special facade, a different tracework of lace carved from stone.

Livio assured me easily that the Captain would soon be his gallant self again. "With his left arm in a blue satin sling. Nothing could be more admirable for his purpose in life."

With an effort I played up to his teasing. "And a satin sling would somehow contribute to his abilities as a captain of the port?"

"His abilities as the gallant pursuer of Ambassadors' beautiful daughters."

I tried not to show my pleasure at this sally.

"What nonsense you talk! I daresay the Captain might take lessons from Messire Livio's School for Gallants." He only looked amused. I was glad of that. "But the wound laid him unconscious. I was afraid he would bleed to death."

"Yes. The loss of blood seems to have been the most serious problem. And then, too, the surgeon bled the poor devil, which in my opinion, did not help matters, except to give him a pallor I've no doubt you will find romantic."

I muttered something, trying not to think of blood. The subject only made my stomach seem to turn over. It was extraordinary, and unaccountable, this sudden sickness of mine.

Our gondolier was bent forward with his big sweep, carrying us out into the lagoon, and Livio had been saying something amusing about the Captain and me when he broke off. The sudden stillness made me look up. This motion itself was an effort and further complicated by the intensity of his gaze; for there was no laughter in his eyes or behind those stupid glasses now. He had taken them off to look at me with great concentration.

"W-why did you stop speaking?" I asked, confusedly trying to make out his face as he bent over me, but it was blurred and unreal.

"What is it?" he asked me sharply. "What is wrong?"

"I think I am—seasick."

"Don't be a little silly! Of course you are not seasick!" His voice was worried, angrily worried.

"Well, in any case—I—am sick."

The blur of his face dissolved into darkness.

CHAPTER NINE

I COULD NOT REMEMBER where I was, or why I was there. I had gone to sleep in my own bed. Had I not? But what bed? In Paris? No. It was later now. I was in Father's Venetian palace. When I awoke, I would see the closed portieres across the room and know that beyond them was the balcony. Beyond that was the sunny canal.

None of these fancies proved to be fact. After repeatedly dreaming of Messire Livio's dark eyes watching me with great care, and dreaming too of horrid doses of warm, salted water and the immediate revolt of my sorely tried stomach, I finally opened my eyes to find myself in a bedchamber that was totally foreign to me. This gave me such a shock I sat straight up in the bed and stared around in such panic as I have seldom known.

It was evening. Just after dark. Beside the plain, four-postered bed, which lacked both curtains and tester, was a long window looking out upon a wide body of water. The working offices of the British Embassy faced upon this water which, I realized, must be the Grand Canal. The arching Rialto Bridge, top-heavy with shacks built upon it, was off to my right. The room belonged to a male. So much was obvious. And at last I realized that these must be the lodgings of Messire Livio.

"What is wrong with me? What has happened?"

I put one foot over the side of the bed, and then, looking down, I saw that my new, slim-skirted round gown of sprigged green muslin had been removed. Horrified, I stared at my ribbon-trimmed petticoat. But common sense came to my aid. Obviously, I had been ill, and there seemed no point to my tossing and turning in my fresh new gown. But to be partially disrobed by a male who was not my husband—it was the outside of enough!

How long had I been here? Since morning. But was this the night of that day?

Still dizzy and shaking, I got out of bed and staggered to the window. I leaned my cheek and forehead against the cool glass. Gradually, I borrowed some of that coolness and felt better. Best of all, my stomach had settled, although it felt as though someone had stamped on it. I gazed out at the canal view and sleepily watched the occasional gondola lights, the choppy black waters, and the faceless, masked creatures passing on their way to their eternal masquerade, their nightly carnival.

A door opened quietly across the room. A candle flared smokily. Conscious of my disheveled petticoats, I ran for the bed, but was still trying to burrow under the coverlet when Livio came into the room, looking oddly formal in a white shirt, black breeches, and no jacket or proper white stock about his bare throat. I was not used to seeing males in this state of careless undress and I remember how my pulse beat rapidly, though I felt more uneasy than frightened.

"I was sick, wasn't I?"

"And you are yourself again. Good."

I was relieved when the candle flame showed me his face looking calm, reasonably interested in me, but neither sinister nor lascivious, I thought. As he approached the bed, however, I became exceedingly conscious of his eyes fixed upon me. There was about them a power and warmth that disturbed me more than I cared to admit.

"What happened to me? Please tell me."

He smiled and said lightly, "You told me you were seasick." But he had raised the candle over my head and was studying me with considerable thought.

Indignant, I contradicted him. "I have never been seasick in my life. It must be something I ate."

"And what have you eaten today?"

Was it only today? "Nothing at all. Nothing that Papa did not eat."

I thought of that and anxiously considered the possible danger to my frail father. "Oh! But perhaps he also became ill."

"He did not. I spoke to one of the servants from the palazzo this afternoon."

"But they must be worried about me. I must go home."

Livio set down the candle and leaned against one of the tall bed posts, watching me. "Is that ugly place home for you then?"

I resented this and said so, explaining what he should have guessed, that my father was the only relation left to me and where he was must be my home.

"And when he marries his—the Teotochi? What then?"

"He will need me more." I was sure that she was marrying him for his fortune, his position, for many reasons far from love. But I could not tell a stranger.

Livio sighed, and moved away from the bed post. He looked toward the window. Masqueraders must be sailing by. I could hear the laughter and the music of mandolins. I was reminded of my difficult position, here in this man's lodgings, impossibly compromised. Neither Father nor anyone else must ever know what had happened to me today.

"Messire, I know you mean well," I began, careful to be very dignified.

He turned back. I had a recurrence of the uneasy feeling that he was secretly laughing at me. "How can you know I mean well? I wonder."

As I started to make some indignant demand, he said hastily, "I know. I know. You want to return to that mausoleum you share with the Teotochi. Well then, you shall. But not now. And I suggest we do not mention where you have been, unless, of course—" his eyes glinted with amusement, "—unless you insist upon boasting of it."

"Very likely!" I said with a caustic air that did not seem to trouble him. "May I have my gown and my bonnet and spencer?"

"Later. Later. But we had best agree upon our story. And also an explanation for what ailed you today. Aren't you curious?"

Actually, now that I felt so much better, it was easy to dismiss the morning's illness as a nervous reaction after my long and nerve-wracking trip from Paris. It could be nothing else, in spite of Livio's unsettling hints; for I had eaten nothing but my father's food and if it had not affected him, it could hardly have done me harm. My imagination pictured Mira Teotochi sneaking about, poisoning my food and hoping to destroy her lover's daughter, but the evidence in no way supported this suspicion.

"Why did you bring me here? I assume these are your lodgings. But why did you not remove me to a hospital here in Venice? Or take me back to my father's home?"

He gazed at me steadily. "I think you know why I did not bring you back to the Ambassador's palace. Strange things have been occurring there, and I was not altogether sure your illness did not have its origin in that place. As to the hospitals in Venice, I had as lief take you to the Cemetery of San Michele and be done with it. So—" He shrugged. "You seemed more comfortable here. No one recognized you, if you are concerned for your reputation."

I laughed abruptly at that. "If one word of this, even a suspicion becomes known, I am ruined, as you must be aware."

"Knowing society in Venice, I am inclined to agree. But it seems to me that your life is of more importance than your reputation. You cannot return to that place until you are quite recovered. And then it may be necessary to put up a fight for your life." Studying me thoughtfully, he sat down on the edge of the bed; as I drew back with instinctive caution, away from him, he smiled and got up. "Or are you more afraid of me?"

Feeling ashamed of my ingratitude, I said rapidly, "No. I am not in the least afraid of you. It is only that Papa will be worried, fretting over my long absence. . . . You see, I believe we—you were wrong to suspect my illness was induced by—by someone. I ate and drank nothing that my father did not touch."

He moved away from the bed, still thoughtful, as if making plans or analyzing the entire affair, and I said in sudden realization, "You have some other motive for your interest in my father and his palazzo. You may have been kind to me—and I do not deny it for a moment—but that was not your original motive. You have been watching the palace. That was your duty, I suppose, but—"

"My duty?" He swung around, his face tense, a little pale in the candlelight.

I was surprised at his reaction and hastened to explain how I knew. "From your friend Mira Teotochi."

"Ah, yes." But he did not look any easier. "And what does she say?"

"That you are a—that you work for the Serenissima, the Republic of Venice. Naturally, they would want to know what the British Ambassador is about. And the French and Austrian Ambassadors, when it comes to that."

Was I mistaken or had he relaxed at this revelation of his true motives?

"In any case, we need not immediately decide whom or what to suspect," he said, turning the matter aside. "You must get more sleep, unless you are hungry." He came back to me. I could not avoid the warmth in his eyes, the actual concern. However political his interest in me might be, I could not mistake this intimate cord of warmth between us. Considering our present situation, the vibrant moment between us was dangerous. And even more dangerous was his interest in my petticoat, or rather, my bosom in my petticoat.

"I must go," I said. We looked at each other silently. He must have understood, but he said after that brief, unspoken exchange, "I wish you would not." He tried to make his request light, uncomplicated. "Aren't you curious to know what the Ambassador and La Teotochi will do when you do not return?"

"Do! But they will be—he will be worried. He will think something dreadful has happened. And you! They will hold you responsible."

He smiled and shrugged. "But I can lie to them. It will not be my first lie, I assure you."

"That I haven't the least doubt. May I be alone now, to dress?"

"I wish you would not leave. Please wait." But he was across the room, away from me. I supposed he must have given in to my request but still hoped to delay me, for some reason of his own. A political reason, doubtless.

I tried to make my refusal a gentle one, but he was now in the doorway. He ignored what I said and reminded me, "So long as you are here, you cannot be poisoned. Shall I see to some kind of meal? Tea? Broth? And something pleasanter afterward . . . that won't make you seasick?"

He had not answered me about my departure, and this sounded very much as though I was to be kept here to suit his own convenience. Worst of all, my presence probably had nothing to do with his personal desires. I was sure he wanted to keep me here for some political scheme of his. I had been shocked to find how much his presence affected me. Until today—no, surely it was that first night in the Casino!—I had thought I was done with the heartbreak of love and loss. This man, with his disreputable post as some kind of spy, was just another possible love to be worried about and wept over when his job finally cost him his life.

I had better not let him use me in his spying business, and I would certainly do better not to remain here under the influence of those warm, dark eyes. "You will not let me go, Messire?"

He hesitated. For an instant I thought he was going to yield. Then he reminded me with a little gleam of humor, "You must trust me to know what is safe for you, and much as I might desire to make you feel unsafe with me, that must wait for a more suitable occasion."

I should have left the matter, which was a dangerous subject at best, but I could not resist answering that humorous look in his eyes and I laughed. "I should think no time would be more suitable— Never mind!"

He looked as though he might change his mind; but I sobered instantly. "You will let me leave now?"

With his hand on the door latch, he considered, but briefly. "We will talk about it later."

"With your spectacles on or off?"

He laughed and was gone.

I went quickly to the door. He had locked it from the outside. I returned to the window, looked around and gave thought to climbing out. We were less than one storey above the steps of the quai. Providing no one saw me—and the quai was deserted at this dinner hour—I thought I might simply drop down to the cobblestones and make hire of a public gondola that would bring me back to Father's palazzo. I knew there would be shocked "cluckings" from everyone over my mysterious absence. A female sitting alone in the waist of a gondola, masked or not, was sure to shock all beholders. But I could not remain here longer and depend upon the mercurial notions of Livio, who seemed charming and amenable, but doubtless had his own plans that would, in the end, be to the advantage of his Venetian employers and against my poor father whose position was precarious enough considering his ill health. There was no doubt of it. I simply must reach my father's home this evening. A night away from the palazzo and there would be no possible explanation acceptable to decent people.

While considering my escape, I recalled the long days my mother and I spent in the Abbaye Prison in Paris before we were removed to the Conciergerie for our trials. I reflected cynically that Messire Livio could take lessons from the Abbaye and the Conciergerie. One did not escape from them so easily!

Meanwhile, there was the matter of my clothing. I went over to the dark armoire at the opposite end of the room. Hanging beside the neat, slightly raffish garments that suited his trim body, I found my Paris round gown and above it, on a shelf, my green silk bonnet, my slippers, and—good Heavens—my white silk stockings. So he had removed them, too! I had simply not noticed their absence. As I sat in the nearest chair, putting them on, I pictured Messire Livio removing them. I felt decidedly hot at the thought and hurried through my dressing.

By the time I was ready to leave, only minutes later, I will admit I did so with a haunting little moment of regret. What a pity there were still such things as "genteel conduct" for females of good family! I sighed but I found my mask and held it dangling from my fingers so that I might fasten it under the back ruffle of my bonnet. Meanwhile, I found the long window easily opened outward. I squeezed through and looked down. The cobblestones seemed further away than I had bargained for, thanks to the evening darkness. The moon had not yet risen, and only the starlight illuminated the scene. I held tight to the heavy iron rail, thankful for the slimness of my skirts, and let myself down. Though the drop to the cobbles was scarcely the length of my body, I dropped hard upon the soles of my feet, stinging them and giving my right ankle a twist that took several minutes for the pain to subside.

On the Grand Canal a gondola slipped by on its way toward a sixteenth-century palace across the dark, choppy waters. The lacy front was lighted by torches and a number of hooded lanterns. There were several gondolas moored outside the palace. Otherwise, I could not find one in sight. I had not thought of this possibility. I looked around, glanced back at the thin, aged house in which Livio was lodged, and saw a light flickering through the broken shutters at the back of the building. Was Livio there in a kitchen or stillroom, perhaps assisted by a servant, busy preparing a tray of food for me? I regretted having to disappoint him. He had been kind to me. And I was certainly not immune to his charm.

Then two gentlemen strolled along the quai toward me. They were tipsy already and it could not be late in the evening. I backed into the shadow of Livio's house. Nervously, I waited until they had gone by, but one of them looked back. I held my breath. He muttered something indistinctly but, thank heaven, his companion did not understand him. When they had passed from my sight around a jutting terra-cotta palazzo, I hurried in the opposite direction, toward the Rialto Bridge. There was still the eternal commotion of trade, bargaining, and even fishmongers among the more elegant traders passing over the arching bridge, and I knew I would never be able to enter that crowd without marring my reputation forever.

I avoided it, turning aside into the widest of several narrow, dark *calles* leading in the general direction of the canal that ran past Father's palazzo. It would be a very bad business, walking into the house as I was, unescorted, and at night. Much better if I could find a conveyance. I would pay the gondolier well, for—"What a fool I am! I cannot pay anyone. I left my reticule in Livio's room. I have no money. Nothing."

Of course, I could be taken to Father's palace and have the servants pay. But I doubted if any gondolier would listen to me in the first place, without even a *scudo*. And if I ran, I might reach home within ten minutes or so by the short cut through the alleys and over the bridges. I wished I had eaten or drunk something tonight! If only a few bites to give me the energy I needed.

No matter. The longer I stood here on a corner, irresolute, like some waiting whore, the more danger surrounded me. Already I heard booted footsteps crossing the cobbles behind me. Perhaps the soldiers had seen me. I hurried along through the alley, between those enormous, windowless walls that had stood for nearly five centuries.

Shortly afterward, the alley narrowed. The only light hung above the water-washed steps leading to a tiny canal a short distance away, on my left. The area in which I found myself was like a series of tunnels, surrounded by the silence of a tomb. I heard my footsteps far too clearly in the night. But this direct passage failed me all too soon. I found myself suddenly stepping out onto a narrow quai, my path cut off by a deep and very dark canal.

"Now, which way?" I looked up, grateful for the first pallid rays of the moon. There was a bridge in the distance on my right, but a man was huddled on a canal step, looking very drunk, and managing to be entirely in my way. I considered him carefully, decided I might pass beyond his reach if I hugged the walls of a building whose canal doors were securely barred and forbidding. Somewhat to my surprise, and my great relief, the drunken man had no interest in me whatever. He did not even raise his head. I hurried toward the bridge.

There were sounds now, the rumble of crowds and laughter and music somewhere coming across the night and the waters. But I had no idea how to reach them. The perfectly innocent encounter with the drunken man had affected me far more than it should have. I was now terrified, and for no precise reason. Perhaps it was the faint lap of water so near my feet . . . The gradually reviving memory of that dagger which had struck down Captain Dandolo . . .

I hadn't gotten to see him, after all. Had he been struck down by mistake for me, as Livio thought? It did not make this walk any easier. I began to take account: "First the dagger, then my upset stomach. If only I could connect them both in some way with my *bête noir*, Mira Teotochi!" It was unfair, but my instincts persisted in their distrust of Father's affianced bride.

I found the next bridge and hurried over. Along the quai on the further side a figure detached itself from the darkness and began to stride toward the alley beyond. I thought at first that it was a woman. Then I realized it was a priest taking big strides with his cassock whipping against his legs. I was considerably relieved, but at the same time I saw at the end of this new passage another canal and this looked familiar. I was headed toward the little bridge that I could see from my window in Father's palace.

I began to run, with very little thought for the night-walking priest behind me. I began to glimpse the red stucco corner of the palazzo and the dim but welcome mooring lights. As I slowed briefly to consider what story I would tell, I heard the running footsteps behind me, and then their sudden silence. I stepped out upon the bridge. The steps behind me began again. . . . But a priest?

I rushed over the bridge and down along the water-marked quai, reminding myself that a cassock does not make a priest. Hurry! Hurry! By the time I was rattling the knocker on the ancient palazzo door my pursuer was striding rapidly over the bridge. I turned once but could not make out the features. He had already passed beyond the bridge lantern and was on this side of the quai.

The door opened under my incessant pounding and I was face to face with Mira Teotochi. I laughed and I felt hysterically amused. "Good evening . . . *Mother*. I see you are inside the house, so you could not possibly have been pursuing me!"

"You are not yourself, Rachel. What has happened to you? Do you know how worried your father has been?" She glanced out at the canal, then closed the great door. It swung to with a force that shook me out of my laughter. "There is no one out there but a Man of God. Is that what you are afraid of? *You are sicker than we thought.*"

CHAPTER TEN

I COULD SEE that already today Mira and the servants had been busy decorating the vestibule and the great salons on the canal floor. From the high, beamed ceilings hung faded banners of past Venetian glory. The furniture was newly polished. Great piles of greenery were set around in casks of cool water, awaiting the morning when they would provide wedding garlands. All these preparations made me shudder.

Hungry, frightened, and angry, I knew I was no match for Mira Teotochi who had, doubtless, been awaiting this chance to put me into my correct place in the palazzo. The place which appeared to be that of a perennial child in the life-and-death control of its parents. And in the most legal manner Mira was to become the person who controlled my destiny! I could scarcely count upon Father in his present feeble condition.

Always remembering my experiences in Paris, particularly the Law of Suspects which made it necessary to keep to myself all my opinions and thoughts, I knew I was better equipped than might have been some women, ignorant of the world and its evil. I looked soulfully at my Father's mistress and pleaded, "I have had a very bad day. I became dreadfully seasick. Messire Livio left me with the nuns in a little hospital on the Giudecca. A dreadful place. They wanted to keep me the night, but I ran away. So—please forgive me!"

The woman's eyelids flickered. Suspicion warred with an inclination to believe me. I could read it all there in her basilisk eyes. She had put out her hand to lead me somewhere when we heard slippered footsteps, hesitant and heavy.

I swung around and ran across the wide vestibule to the old man who put his arms out shakily, enfolding me. "We were so worried, my child. You cannot conceive how worried we were. Why, Mira was terrified that something had happened to you! She kept saying that something dreadful— She cares a great deal for my little girl."

So Mira had prepared Father for bad news! And what part had she played in seeing that her prophecy came true? The fact that festivities were planned for the morrow would incline Venice to a belief in her innocence. "Surely," they might say, "a wedding would never be planned for the day after the daughter was murdered! They cannot be responsible!" Mira must have been shocked to see my bedraggled person on the doorstep tonight. I gave her full credit for turning her surprise and shock into "maternal" anger.

"I know, Father," I lied, and felt his trembling body relax as I hugged him. "I'll go to my room now. I've had a terrible day of it. And then, as I came to this canal I was chased by someone."

Mira Teotochi had come to join us and at this comment she cut in with her odious sympathy. "Rachel was frightened by a priest, poor child. I think we should not be selfish and keep her here shivering when she will be feeling more herself after a night's sleep. I have some laudanum. It will be excellent to give the rest you need. I'll go and fetch it."

"No!" I cried, unable to carry through that pretense. "No. I don't wish to take a drug."

Father patted me consolingly as one would pat a child. "Rachel, Rachel, you are not well. Anyone may see that. Mira is only thinking of your good health. See how nervous you are even now, my poor little girl! You must allow that Mira knows what is best for you. Think what she has done for me. I am able to walk now. I have improved out of all knowing. So much so that I can walk to my wedding tomorrow. Isn't that fine? So let her give you a few drops of laudanum to rest you after your—dear me!—after your seasickness, and you will awaken just in time for the wedding." He raised my chin with his forefinger. "Go to bed now and dream lovely dreams of weddings. I believe young ladies like to dream of weddings; do they not?"

Good God! I thought, I shall be sick for certain . . . I lied with frantic haste, "You are very kind, Father, to think of it, but—"

"But your future mother thought of it," he reminded me with a little shake of his finger.

Mira assumed an expression as close to maternal as was possible for her, and took my arm. "Come along, my dear. I'll see to your rest. Exactly what you need; a comfortable, long rest."

I shuddered, though I was stiffly determined not to reveal my fear and suspicions, and of course, she felt my reaction. To cover this, I explained, as she looked at me narrowly, "I think I've gotten a chill, wandering across the half of Venice. I'll go to my room now. You stay with Father. You must have a great deal to talk about, so close to your— wedding."

I kissed Father's cheek and left him, but I could not shake off the woman's grip. She had a surprising strength.

"Good girl," said Father approvingly. "Go with Mira. You want to be at your best tomorrow at noon."

So the wedding was to take place at noon! And afterward, they both imagined I would be entirely in their power. The ghastly truth was that I could not at the moment find a way to thwart the woman's plans. Father's fortune was her object, of course. But he was still the guardian of Mother's English properties which were considerable, and these would be mine and my husband's, should I marry. Providing, however, that I outlived my father. An interesting proviso. I wondered if Mira Teotochi knew this. It would hardly endear me to her, but it would certainly explain any effort to poison me. Did Livio know these details?

There is no gainsaying the fact that I was terrified of the possibility of poisoning. But I could see no way in which I had been poisoned today unless Father was poisoned as well, and he seemed in good spirits. This fact, however, need not prevent me from being poisoned in future, and laudanum was an excellent start. No matter how often it was utilized by sleepless people to give them a restful night, I was well aware of the fact that a mere few drops extra would put me to sleep forever. I could think of no eventuality that would make me accept laudanum at the hands of Mira Teotochi.

I was enormously relieved when, as Mira and I entered

the wide hall of the second story, Adelaide Dace rushed out in her fluttering nightrobe to greet us.

"Oh, Miss Tocki, you have found her. Bless you, my dear! How good you are! Now then, Rachel, you bad girl, where have you been until this hour?"

I felt like a five-year-old being chided for running away from home, but I accepted the opportunity offered to get out of Mira's clutches.

"Dacey! You must come with me. Father needs Mira . . . It's quite all right if Dacey comes to help me. I think I shall retire almost at once. I am deadly tired."

While Mira looked at us with her slanting eyes thoughtful, Dacey said enthusiastically, "Just so, dear. I'll help you to undress and you must tell me all about your naughty day."

Since I was on the verge of starvation, I was anxious to get Dacey alone and see if, between us, something safe might be contrived for me to eat; so I continued to behave angelically. I even apologized again to Mira for my unfortunate manner as I entered tonight. The result was all I could have hoped for. Mira Teotochi swallowed my lies, accepted Dacey as her substitute wardress and departed, promising to return with a few drops of laudanum. "I shall trust you, Miss Dace, to persuade our young Rachel of the efficacy of laudanum. It will give her a comfortable night's rest. You and I understand these things, Miss Dace; as a woman with experience in such matters, I trust you do agree."

Poor Dacey, completely taken in, indeed agreed that if Mira would send up the laudanum, she would certainly persuade me to take it. I reserved my own opinion.

When we were alone, I bolted the door and, taking Dacey by the shoulders, embraced her. "All forgiven?"

She sniffed and returned my embrace with tears dotting my shoulders. "Nothing—nothing would please me more, Rachel. I was so worried about you today when you did not return at luncheon. And then, all this long afternoon . . . You cannot imagine, my dear. I even thought—" She said loudly, suddenly, "They do care so very much about you."

"Do they?" I asked.

She looked around nervously. Was she afraid of being overheard? Or, for some reason, did she expect to be overheard? "But they do. That Miss Tocki, she was so jumpy. Every sound, every gondola that passed, she was actually as worried as your Papa."

I had no doubt she was. If, somehow, she had managed to

poison me, she had reason to be jumpy. What a shock when I came walking in tonight reasonably safe and reasonably unpoisoned! Small wonder she was so ill-natured!

"I promise to tell you all about it—" *Within limits,* I added silently. "But I must tell you that I have never been so hungry. Do you suppose there is some way that I might be served a small supper while we are having a cozy chat?"

Astonished and concerned, she suggested, "But you should have told Miss Tocki. Wait! I'll fetch her up. She can't have gone far." And here she was, bustling off with every good intention in the world.

By some breathless effort I got between her and the door, laughing, making a desperate pretense of feeling light and happy. "No, no! Please, Dacey! Poor Mira wants to be with Father. This is the night before their wedding. We must not disturb them, on my account. You must promise me."

Understandably confused by my vehemence, Dacey assured me that she would not dream of calling upon Father's bride if I wished it so. "And I will say, Rachel, I am very pleased that you no longer feel that unhealthy prejudice against your Papa's happiness."

"Certainly not," I agreed, showing my teeth.

"I am proud of you. You are going to accept the beautiful thing that has happened between your bereaved Father and a woman who has his welfare genuinely at heart. Just think of the long years your poor father spent alone while you and your mama—" I straightened rapidly and she colored and added in a flustered voice, "—so many years alone! And then, in his illness, who took care of him? And saved his life. You do see how much your dear Papa owes to—" She looked over her shoulder again in that odd way and added the cryptic remark, "My Dear, do not let anyone hear you say anything else. It is necessary to—"

I said, "I have an idea! Dacey, let us go down into the stillroom and the kitchen and prepare a meal for ourselves. It will be great fun."

I could see that she did not share my enthusiasm but she valiantly agreed to accompany me. I persuaded her to sit down while I changed to a comfortable gown, recalling secretly and with some excitement those moments when I had sat in my petticoats discussing my situation with Livio and been intensely aware of his gaze. Still, his interest in me must be primarily political. It was a rude setdown.

"I do think it would be simpler to call upon the servants

for a tray of supper," Dacey said, with a hopeless air.

I ignored this. When I left the chamber, however, she came after me. The halls were dimly lighted as always, but having placed no trust in those slim candles, I went armed with the full three-tapered candelabrum that had been obligingly set in my chamber. I suspect that Dacey was still obsessed by the idea that I was not myself, but she was faithful enough to see me through whatever calamities I brought down upon myself.

We started toward the door opening upon the steps with which I was already familiar, but here Dacey surprised and gratified me by suggesting that we take the servants' stairs.

"What? I had no notion they existed."

Dacey explained, "Today, when Miss Tocki became concerned about you, she was in a great hurry and used these stairs beside my bedchamber."

We had reached the unobtrusive door Dacey indicated and were making our way down the steep staircase with my candelabrum held high when it occurred to me to ask, "Why was Mira in such a fret? It seems absurd—unless she did not expect me to return alive."

"Rachel!"

"Well, what are we to think? Doesn't it seem odd to you, Dacey, that she should be so certain I was in great trouble?" Clearly, Dacey didn't; so I changed my tactics and asked, "Even if she was only guessing at my trouble, why must she be in such a hurry?"

This did strike a cord. Dacey nodded thoughtfully as we approached the stygian darkness of the ground floor.

"I did wonder. You see, she was carrying those boots of your Papa's. I daresay she intends to clean out that chamber and use if for guests, after the marriage. She was probably just cleaning. It is quite natural to a housekeeper."

Destroying the boots. Why? The reason was undoubtedly a simple one. But it was not Dacey's reason.

We made our way by one of two doors through a stillroom packed with supplies such as rice and macaroni, into the large kitchen which looked as if it might have been an additional dining hall in medieval and early Renaissance days. But now the great hearth had been divided. Pots, pans and a grill served their purposes under the old, blackened turning-spit and pot hooks. I thanked Providence that the hearth fire had not been doused and put on a kettle of tea. Dacey kept criticizing the impracticality of such an old kitchen, too large, and requiring too many steps.

No matter. It served my purpose. I found eggs and some strange sausages which Dacey thought were for the servants' meals, and made myself a delicious late supper, although Dacey kept groaning that it would be indigestible. While I ate, she questioned me about my day. Remembering her vulnerability where Mira Teotochi was concerned, I took care to repeat my story of the seasickness and how Livio had rudely left me practically on the doorstep of the little hospital run by the Sisters of the Poor.

"Then you did not see poor Captain Dandolo," Dacey murmured regretfully, to my surprise.

"No, but Messire Livio said he was doing well, and apparently parading an arm in a sling. The wound was to his left breast. It must have injured a shoulder muscle." At Dacey's warm, dreamy look, I explained, "He cannot have been too seriously hurt, else he would not be receiving female visitors so soon."

"Very true, but such a gracious young man! Much superior to that Livio person!"

This was certainly a complete turnabout. Astonished, I dropped my spoon, and stared at her as I picked it up again. I hoped the little metallic ring of the spoon on the pewter plate had not aroused anyone in the household. "But I thought you were quite attached to Messire Livio. What is this?"

"Oh—that!" She had the grace to look a trifle flustered. "But then, I had not spent time in the Captain's company. And he looked so pale, so romantically tall and handsome, you can have no notion!"

"Indeed not. When was this?"

"After noon. Miss Tocki was ordering gaming tables for the wedding party. She has a passion for gambling, you know. She must be eternally in need of money, which may explain—nothing."

"Yes, yes, but about the Captain?"

"To be sure. Well, I do not know which was the more amazed to see him, Miss Tocki or myself." Dacey poured herself tea and drank, gazing dreamily over the teacup at her new vision of romance. "He was so weak it was necessary for Miss Tocki and that Turk to help him into the palace. He was taken to a little music salon on this—the canal floor. We all made him comfortable. We thought, of course, that he had come with word about you; for Miss Tocki had servants out earlier, asking if you had been seen anywhere in the vicinity of the Port Customs. At all events, he said he had paid the call to be certain you were well after that dreadful knife attack last night. Of course, when he told us he had not seen you today, we were very concerned and your dear Papa kept saying, 'I told you so. I told you,' and Miss Tocki—" Dacey shut her small mouth firmly against that memory. I was naturally twice as curious to know what had been said between my father and the woman who clearly dominated his life.

"Dacey, don't stop now. Tell me what happened. What did she say?"

Dacey looked furtively over her shoulder into the darkness of the stillroom. "Did you hear that? I thought I heard a noise." I listened. Nothing happened and then she leaned forward over the table, toward me. "It was then I knew they were certain to marry. She sounded so like a wife. She said, 'Be quiet! We will simply have to scour Venice for her.' The Captain looked very much upset at the way she talked to your father. And when Miss Tocki saw how upset the Captain was, she remembered her place and became her pleasant self again. Poor woman. I imagine—forgive me for saying this, Rachel—but it must be very difficult for a vigorous woman her age to have the responsibility of a man your Papa's age and condition."

"She knows she need only give up her self-imposed task," I said curtly.

"But it would be such a difficult thing for you, my dear, if she did. To be responsible for a feeble, elderly man. Why, you may be married soon, and forming your own household."

I gaped at her. "What nonsense is this? I've no notion of getting married. Nor are there any candidates. If you think for one minute that Livio, in his job with the Serenissima will be permitted to—"

"Livio? Heavens, no! He is nothing but a catchpole, Miss Tocki says. A spy who reports to the Grand Inquisitor. No, no. I was thinking more of a man like that handsome Captain. Imagine his coming to visit you on the very day after he is wounded in your defense!"

"In my defense! You are grossly misinformed there. He simply was standing in the way of a footpad's dagger. As a matter of fact, if I hadn't stooped over, looking for that blessed cat, I would have been—"

"Precisely. You owe him your life."

I would not have described it so, but perhaps the Captain saw it in that light. The poor fellow had paid for being in the way. I could not deny it. When I had finished my improvised supper, I washed and replaced the dish and cups and the pan I had used, while Dacey argued in a puzzled way that it was a task for the servants. But I did not want Mira and her servant cohort to guess how I obtained my food and managed to avoid whatever she concocted for me from her Borgia blends.

Unfortunately, as we made our way past the stillroom to the servants' stairs, my candelabrum flared abruptly as if a door had opened somewhere and a draft made the candle flames curve away from the draft. I did not know whether to be relieved or terrified when a dark, gypsylike creature loomed up before us. A female, and the Turk's mother, I assumed. Her eyes were rimmed in black, and our uncertain light gleamed on her dangling metal earrings and her beaky nose. Dacey screamed and I let out a gasp myself, but the woman only grinned at our discomfiture.

"You want that I shall make the late supper? I am Jamela, cook for Madama Teotochi."

"No, thank you." We hurried past her.

"She is sure to tell Mira," I remarked, disgruntled. "And after all my careful scheming."

Dacey disapproved as I might have expected, but very loudly. "Really, Rachel, you must not show your dislike so plainly. It will only be dangerous for you."

I said furiously as we climbed the stairs, bringing abrupt light through the creaking darkness, "You are not about to deny my identity again, I trust."

"No. But it does seem that your stay in that heathen country has not improved you in any way. You are very reckless."

I laughed because I was trying hard not to lose my temper with her again. Nor did it improve my temper when she reminded me, "Get a good sleep, Rachel. Tomorrow is an important day, and we must all be on our toes. One never knows what will happen. Weddings should be festive, of course. But this one . . ."

"Good night." I said it abruptly at her door and walked alone along the hall toward my chamber at the far front end of the building. For some reason, probably because I had just eaten and was wide-awake, I hated to return to that bedchamber. Perhaps, too, I was dreading the night's sleep with its eerie dreams of my father calling to me. Pleading for my help?

I stopped before the door next to mine and tried the latch. The room was unlocked and I looked in. Everything was very much as it had been when Dacey and I had examined it, except that the clothing that I had assumed belonged to Mira Teotochi had been removed. Very likely Mira was moving all her property into my father's bedchamber, now that she would soon be mistress of the palazzo. And my place after she became mistress? I shuddered to think what that might be. I left the room and went on to my own door.

With no sense of the unexpected, I stepped into my big, darkly furnished bedchamber only to see a huddled figure in the chair beside the long balcony windows. The candelabrum shook and I set it down on the table beside the wretched figure.

My father was in a heavy brocaded nightrobe and padded slippers with a Near-Eastern design in semiprecious stones. He looked up at me, his pale eyes watering in the sudden light from the candles. Had he made his way here to sit in the darkness until I returned? He put out one shaking arm to take my hand.

"My child, must you remain here? I am greatly troubled about you. I suppose . . . a return to Paris is out of the question?"

I said stiffly, "Without a sponsor, certainly. They will think I have returned to spy on them."

"And the other possibilities . . . Have you considered marriage? You might be very happy. A companion for life. A loved one who thinks always of your welfare, takes care of you and your life and property. We—that is to say, I think I have just the man for you. He went to great pains to visit us today, only to see you."

I weighed every cruel word that I spoke. "You are determined to rob me of every *scudo*, are you not? First, this marriage. That is your affair. Your fortune is your own. But now you want to marry me off so that Grandmother's fortune, which you promised to hold for me, would go to some man, doubtless related to Mira Teotochi." That was a stab in the dark and Father was able to deny it indignantly.

"If that were all, my dear, you might be dead, and the money and properties would be mine. And my wife's. So you see . . . Your poor nerves are betraying you into these dreadful suspicions." He got up with an effort. I helped him and he gave me a tender smile. "I do believe you must confess, my child, that the young Rachel I once knew could never say such cruel things to her old father. You would have done well today to remain safe in that hospital with the good nuns. This illness of yours requires care and watchfulness. Else you will do yourself, and others, serious harm."

"I'll take you back to your room now," I said, as though he had not spoken. His words were mere rambling nonsense. But, poor man, he did not realize the sickness was his, not mine. I meant him no harm. And there were none that could prove I did.

CHAPTER ELEVEN

I DID NOT DREAM about Father that night, perhaps because I was so tired, but I am glad I did not dream of weddings, either. I had those hours of pleasant peace that were destroyed the next morning when I opened my eyes and remembered that on this day my life would be placed, legally, in the hands of a woman who, I did not doubt, was my enemy. But as I lay there thinking over the future and the possible ways of defeating her, only one thing seemed clear. I must pretend once more to be won over, and this time, I must not betray my true feelings, even to Father. Father's visit to me proved last night that in every way he was under Mira's influence. I had no doubt whatever that his talk of my "illness" came from Mira, as did the dream of marrying me off.

Or was the marriage idea a lie, so that I would not suspect her the next time she tried to poison me? I was terribly confused. I sat up in bed and promised myself not to persist in betraying my real feelings. They might be the death of me. In her odd way, Dacey was right about that.

I had scarcely finished dressing when a knock on the door announced that the usual morning tray of chocolate was waiting. It was while I was on my way to the door, and in this brief second or two, that I realized how I must have been poisoned the day before . . . All that delicious, foaming chocolate I had drunk before breakfast. It had been the only food I ate, or drank, which was not shared by others. I had been incredibly slow in recalling the danger. And now, were they attempting it again?

They? Not Father! Dear God, not Father, too!

I threw the bolt back and opened the door. Considering my suspicions, I was somewhat jolted at seeing Mira Teotochi with the young chambermaid who carried my tray.

"You!" I greeted them discourteously.

Mira smiled. I could see in that slow, seductive smile how she won people like Father and, perhaps, Dacey.

"I thought this day, which means so much to me, should begin pleasantly for my new daughter as well." She indicated the tray in the girl's hands. I wondered if Mira meant to feed me forcibly and felt myself grow stiff with tension and resistance. I said, "You expect me to drink that?"

Had she been quite innocent, I thought, she should be astonished at my rudeness. Instead, flashing that warm look of understanding and sympathy, Mira motioned the girl ahead of her and they came into my room. In spite of my determination to challenge her, I found myself backing away before Mira and before what I supposed must be that deadly tray.

"I don't want it. Do you understand me?"

The girl's hands shook on the tray but Mira said in this new, soothing voice, "I thought, if you permit, I would drink with you. A little ritual, you might call it." The girl set the tray down and Mira motioned her to leave. With a backward glance at us, she did so.

In amazement I asked Mira, "You will drink that?"

"Certainly. I thought it might be a peace offering. I believe your companion, Miss Dace, will be joining us shortly."

It was difficult to remain suspicious and warlike under these blandishments. I decided that she had only begun to demonstrate this new personality because everything else had failed her. I could almost pity the woman. How she must hate me for having come back suddenly into my father's life, just a few days before she married not only his fortune but that of his "dead" daughter, as well!

And was Father also disappointed? . . . I would not think of that. Besides, he was too feeble to be blamed for hoping his little world remained peaceful, even at the cost of his daughter's life, or her freedom. I must depend solely upon myself. And my unexpected friend Livio? He was a dubious

ally. After all, I had first met him giving money to Mira,
bribing her and encouraging what appeared to be a gaming
fever!

Mira was removing the little chocolate pitchers from the
tray, setting our cups and saucers at our places, arranging
sugar and warm sweet cakes. She explained with that new-
found friendliness, "I thought you would not object to the
informality, since we are all females. I do not like to see your
father until the ceremony, you understand. It is said to bring
ill-fortune to a marriage."

"Have you been married before?" I asked suddenly, curious about this for the first time.

Her eyelids flickered. I imagined I saw fire hidden by
those eyelids, but if she was angry, she contained her feelings
with great skill and murmured with nostalgic sadness, "When
I was very young, as is the custom in Venice for young ladies
of good family. The Teotochis are one of the Serenissima's
oldest, but not—alas!—a moneyed family. When I was
widowed many years since, I found it necessary to take just
such posts as this with the Ambassador."

I had discovered that the Teotochis, this "oldest of Venetian families" were her husband's family. I still knew nothing
of her own name and past. Dacey arrived to cut short these
romantic, if theatrical, reminiscences. She was all aflutter
over the bride and playfully desired to know if Mira was
beset by bridal nerves, and also what was the style of her
gown. Mira got around this question with her usual finesse.

"At my age, Miss Dace, the only matter of importance is
a deep, abiding concern for the person who fills one's life."

She went on carefully setting the little table while Dacey
looked at me and, edging nearer, whispered audibly, "You
see? It is a pure, unselfish concern. She does not even care
about a wedding gown." It was extraordinarily naïve, even for
Dacey. Was she actually trying to show Mira that she was
blind to her plans?

In exasperation, I knew that Mira had heard this and
further, that she had meant Dacey to be impressed by her unselfish little dismissal of the customary wedding gown. But
there was nothing to be gained by letting Dacey know my
cynicism, and there might be time gained for me if I let
both women suppose I believed this tale of selfless love.

Meanwhile, we sat down to her chocolate, and while I
tried to keep an innocent face upon the little pitchers and
cups, I watched intently as Mira reached for one of the

pitchers. However, she was thoroughly prepared for my suspicion. With great care she poured chocolate into each cup.
One third of each of us, including herself. Dacey looked at
the cups in a puzzled way. Meanwhile, Mira took up the
second pitcher and poured. There could be no question. We
all shared the chocolate.

When she offered us sweet cakes, she managed to have a
spoon in her hand. To Dacey and me, she said, "I seem to
have my hands full. Would you be kind enough to put a
cake on my plate?"

Dacey and I exchanged glances. Haphazardly, she took one
of the cakes and dropped it before Mira. I played with mine,
taking a well-baked crust and put it to my lips, but there
could be no doubt. Mira was rapidly devouring hers, with
the aid of the cup of chocolate. Dacey and I followed her
gestures.

At all events, if we were to be poisoned, it would be the
three of us, and a highly questionable wedding . . .

But the calamity did not occur. When we had completed
our breakfast, Dacey asked Mira if she could help her to
prepare for the wedding and I, less practical, asked for mere
facts. "Where is the wedding to be?"

"In the great vestibule on the canal floor. It would make an
excellent *sala,* as you may have observed. The decorations
and the altar are being prepared now. A small affair, to be
sure, but one we had dreamed of for many months. We felt
it would not be appropriate until my dear Maitland could
stand and even walk. It is a miracle, his recovery."

"Thanks to you, I believe," Dacey put in, with a coy smile.
I could say nothing. For aught I knew, Dacey could be right.

Mira dismissed Dacey's claim with a modest smile. "That
is as may be. I would appreciate your help, Miss Dace. And—
Rachel, if you are feeling yourself again, might you play
the hostess and greet our guests? They will be chiefly from
the embassy."

With an effort I ignored the remark about being myself,
and agreed to play hostess to my father's wedding. It might
give me a chance to grow better acquainted with the embassy personnel, and in the end they must know if any
undue influence were used upon Father in his ambassadorial
duties. Aside from his fortune and Mother's, his important
political office could conceivably be a motive for Mira's determined interest in him.

Mira and Dacey went off together, Dacey after a brief

apology to me for her "desertion," and Mira announcing, "I will send to you when you are needed to greet the first of our guests."

"That will not be necessary," I assured her with equal friendliness. "I shall be up and about. I may take a brief stroll, and, of course, I shall be interested in the wedding decorations."

But the current award for generosity went to the prospective bride. "Perhaps you will be good enough to speak with your dear Papa this morning, my dear. He will be so happy to have a little private visit with you before the wedding."

I hoped the irony did not show when I replied, "You are too kind."

I decided not to be in a great hurry to obey her suggestion, however. The time seemed contrived in some way. Perhaps she had prompted Father, prepared him in some way, for my "little private visit" with him. Anyway, I hoped to encounter Livio somewhere in San Marco or even nearer the palazzo. He was usually around here, up to his spying tricks. And he must be at least a trifle curious over what had happened to me when I ran away from his lodgings last night. When I looked out of my balcony windows onto the canal and the little bridge, I saw no sign of him, but I supposed he must sleep some time. Still, it would be disappointing if I did not see him today. Despite of his money dealings with Mira Teotochi, doubtless building her up to depend upon him for funds, I could not but feel that he was her enemy in some way.

I left my room shortly after, determined to enjoy the sunny Venetian morning, even if I did shock the natives by walking unescorted. On my way past the gallery floor I was arrested by the sight of a visitor far too early for the wedding. He was the Embassy First Secretary, Fortman-Truscott, and he had stepped into Father's sitting room, leaving the door ajar. I do not think I would have remarked the oddity of his conduct but for his astonishingly rude way of addressing his superior, my father.

". . . You are a fool not to have counted upon the worst. Bonaparte and that gang of French ruffians will be fighting Austria at the Serenissima's borders within a fortnight. I tell you, that weeping Doge will do anything to keep the peace. There is talk he wants to make a treaty of alliance with the French—to restore Venice as a democracy. A democracy, mind you! Citizen-rule!"

"Nonsense. The Doge has no power. It is just talk."

"He has one thing—treaty power. If he signs with that upstart, Bonaparte, the French will come to the rescue of Venice if she is attacked. And you know what that will mean to Austria, and to our plans."

It was bad enough to call my Father a fool. Perhaps his age and physical condition laid him open to insult. But why should Fortman-Truscott care what happened to the Austrians? He must be mad. Or a traitor to his own country. Could he be in the pay of Venice? But Venice was England's ally. And he was obviously not in the pay of the French. That left the only other enemy currently in Italy, the Imperial Austrian Army which had held Northern Italy in bondage for so many years that most Italians outside the Venetian sphere of influence regarded the French Republican Army as their savior. Even I, with my ambivalent ties to Britain and France and Venice, felt that the only common enemy was not the French under General Bonaparte, but the Austrian invaders.

And here in the house of the English Ambassador a man was talking in a way that could only be pro-Austrian, even at the price of condemning the English. I could believe much accidental evil of my father, considering his feeble health and long illness, but never that he would betray his trust. What was happening in this house? What had happened to Maitland Carewe? He scarcely seemed like the man I had known and loved as a child.

I heard his dim, faded voice, with all the old power gone, saying, "I have done everything you demand. All the changes. No official dispatches go to Prime Minister Pitt without having been evaluated for their use to us . . ."

Us? Who were these men whom my father called *us?* Clearly, if he was withholding information or even falsifying the dispatches going to the Prime Minister, he had sold out his country.

"It is not enough," said Fortman-Truscott sharply. "That Corsican ogre needs but one more victory and we are done. No chance then of the rewards we have gone to bloody lengths to earn. If the Austrians are defeated, there'll not be a ducat in it for any of us. You have got to see that Pitt enters the war with troops on our side. Let it be 'to preserve Venetian independence.' That is always a popular cry."

Father said something in a low voice.

Fortman-Truscott cut into this. "You are not so blind as

to imagine that damned French democracy is preferable to the Imperial rule. For us it will be a disaster."

Imperial. That would be Imperial Austria, which had managed to get itself hated and despised by the people of Italy. And my Father had sold out to this hopelessly anti-quated despotism!

"And, furthermore—" Fortman-Truscott went on as he reached the door. I dropped back, terrified, but he was merely closing the door tightly.

I hurried to the steps and went down to the canal floor. The big hall with its austere black and white motif had sud-denly come alive with workmen, several of them chattering in English. Obviously, they were from the embassy. They, along with the Italian house servants I had heretofore only glimpsed, were busy festooning the walls and high windows with flowers and greenery. They had already placed what appeared to be the altar made from intensely polished black chests from faraway China. Above them was the great cruci-fix. I knew myself to be a dog in the manger, so suspicious of my poor Father's last grasp at happiness, but this latest ghastly discovery had put the entire marriage into the realm of treason. Somehow, Mira Teotochi, with her not incon-siderable wiles, had made a traitor out of a man of heretofore unimpeachable integrity.

I would never have believed my Father capable of such actions as I had overheard. Yet, what do we know of other human beings, save by their actions? Father had very nearly been led to deny my own identity, because I had so greatly changed after eight years in France. Yet he had changed fully as much. Small wonder that I should have failed to recognize the man he had become.

The man he has become . . .

"Pardon, Miss. These chairs go across this half the hall."

The unspoken thought slipped away. I jumped and moved away from the workmen. It seemed odd to see a dozen precious fifteenth- and sixteenth-century armchairs, made in the ancient Roman style, now scattered through this hollow, cold hall, to be used by a score of the loyal English Embassy personnel who could not know that their chief was a traitor. And not only their chief—I must remember Fortman-Trus-cott, the First Secretary.

If it were anyone but Father, I must, somehow, report his betrayal to the Foreign Office in London, or to one of Mr.

Pitt's loyal agents on the continent. But I could not betray my own father.

I went rapidly through the long, high-ceilinged vestibule to the canal doors and out onto the steps. In order to reach the Square of St. Mark's, which was west of the palazzo, it was necessary to go a few steps east to the humped bridge and then walk in a westerly direction on the opposite side of our little backwater canal. I had gone some distance before I was even aware that I was walking most improperly alone, or that people whom I passed gave me dubious looks and whispered about me behind their hands. During this time, oblivious to my surroundings, I had been puzzling over the problem of saving my father without exposing his treachery.

By the time I reached St. Mark's Square, I had decided my best hope was the man who seemed to know most about Mira Teotochi, about Father's palazzo, and doubtless about the treason that was taking place there. I walked by the great, ornate Cathedral of St. Mark's and on to the forecourt of the pale, elegant Doges' Palace. A guard in uniform challenged me. In my most precise Italian, trying to concentrate on each phrase, I asked for a Messire Livio of the Inquisitors' Office. This was probably not the title of his immediate employers, but I was flustered and kept picturing the man in the blood-red robes as something out of the Inquisition. As, indeed, he might be, from all I had heard in Venice.

But whether my Italian was bad, or the offices of all three Inquisitors were secret, or Livio really was unknown there, I got nowhere with the guard. It was just like Livio to be underfoot at every step and yet to be invisible when I wanted him. I tried again, pronouncing Livio's name so carefully there could be no doubt. This time I was sure the fellow understood me and even recognized the name, but he informed me that it was impossible to see anyone.

"But," he said, "there are the Informers' Stairs for written denunciations. Do you have a denunciation to lay before the Inquisitors of State? If so, you may enter."

Was it so easy in the Serenissima to destroy one's fellow men? And worse, by denunciations with no proof, and not even the necessity to face one's victim? In France, at least, the Law of Suspects had been repealed.

"No," I said slowly. "I have no denunciation, and certainly no proof. Thank you."

I could not betray my Father, however much I would like to see the treason in the British Embassy stopped. But still,

I must do something. I could not stand by while all Britain's relations with the Serenissima were destroyed. It was appalling to think that if I could not find Livio, I had not a single friend I could trust in Venice.

I turned away from the palace and started out into the Piazzetta. At the same time I heard myself hailed from a gondola out in the breezy water beyond it. I walked to the quai, shielding my eyes against the sun on the waters. I saw Captain Pietro Dandolo, stunning in his skintight uniform, with his cape flapping from the one arm that waved to me. He gave an order and the gondola headed in toward me.

"Ah! The beautiful young Madonna Carewe! You must ride with me to the palazzo. I am an invited guest for the wedding."

"Thank you. You seem in excellent condition," I remarked as the gondolier's free hand helped me into it. As I had been told, the Captain was romantically ensconced among pillows, with his chest wrapped and his left arm in a silk sling.

He managed with elaborate skill to kiss my hand and linger rather longer than I had expected with his smooth dark head very close to my breast. Smiling self-consciously, I drew my hand away.

"You . . . you are making a rapid recovery, Captain," I said. "That was a dreadful business. Have they discovered the person responsible?"

He shrugged and then groaned heavily at the gesture. "Would you be so good as to arrange that pillow under my wretched sling?"

"Of course." As I did so, however, I could not but sense that he was closer than I would have liked. He had moved near enough so that I could scarcely raise my head and arms again without finding myself pressing against his elegantly clad body. With considerable effort I settled back against my own cushions without crowding him, and out of the corner of my eye, caught his face in the beginnings of a frown. Was he so used to exercising his charm upon Venetian guests that my slowness, my prudish behavior, annoyed him? Or had I simply hurt his pride, his feelings? I was sorry for that.

"Captain, you have not found the assassin?"

"No." He did not seem to care greatly, probably because the reputation of Venice's alleys and canals was unsavory at best. "But upon another occasion the footpad will be found, and we shall have solved two crimes in one."

I hesitated. "You are certain that it was a simple case of a footpad who wished to rob us?"

He asked in surprise, "But what else could it have been?"

"Then why did he not rob us when you had fallen and I was alone with you?"

"But—" He stopped. I wondered what he was thinking and what had prevented him from completing this thought.

I went on hurriedly, hoping to help him out of his confusion, "I suppose it is because so many people arrived . . . almost at once."

"Precisely. I am told that several persons came to your assistance the moment I fell. I wonder who the first might have been?" He looked at me, with so direct a gaze I found myself coloring up as though I had been caught in a lie. I had a prickly feeling that I would do well to tell the truth as nearly as possible.

"I thank heaven for it, Captain. There was a gentleman calling himself Livio. I know of no other name. He and his gondolier were a great help. And almost at once there was a Mr. Fortman-Truscott of the British Embassy, with his party. They were all exceedingly kind."

"I heard something of their assistance. The man Livio is with the Inquisitorial Office." He must have seen my intense interest, for he added, with one of his big, flashing smiles, "I hope his gallantry has not prejudiced you in his favor."

My heartbeat quickened. "What do you mean? I am afraid I do not understand. He came to see me to report upon your progress. But then, when he offered to escort me to the Customs Palace, I became seasick and he—deserted me."

The Captain nodded. He put his good hand out, felt for mine, squeezed it gently.

"I fear you reposed too much confidence in the fellow. But, fortunately, no lasting harm was done. My, er, body survived, and your heart survived."

"My heart was never in danger. And if you imply that this Livio person was the man who threw that knife, surely he is not capable of so much physical exertion."

"Hardly, carissima Rachele. But he is a despicable catchpole for the Inquisitor's Office. When he is not sending French spies to the Strangler's cord, he is not above spying upon the Serenissima's guests."

I did not know whether to believe him or not. I had a curious feeling that the Captain was more vehement about Messire Livio than one might have expected. They were both, presumably serving the Serenissima. Why should he find Livio's loyalty so shameful?

As the gondolier maneuvered the gleaming silver teeth on the gondola's prow into our now familiar canal, I asked the Captain suddenly, "Did you ever discover where your own gondolier had gone that night?"

The gondolier gazed down at us. He looked like the man Livio and I had not been able to find that night in the empty gondola. Whether or not he was the same man, he certainly did not seem overfond of me.

The Captain released my hand, which felt hot and damp after its long imprisonment. He waved away the question of the man's presence. "Poor Giacomo had gone off to a taverna for a glass of wine. He missed the entire affair. He has been reprimanded, but one can find it easy to understand his desertion. Otherwise, he would have waited three or four hours while we gamed and dined."

"I see," I said, although I did not. I had thought an officer of the Venetian Republic should be able to count on the assistance of his gondolier, just as Livio had certainly made use of his own. No matter. It was not my concern. It was Captain Dandolo, and not I, who suffered from that attack. And that reminded me of something Livio had said to me.

I ventured carefully, "I imagine there can be no question but that the dagger was meant for you? Or could it, possibly, have been meant for me?"

He stared at me. We were nearing the little bridge east of Father's palazzo and I noted that our gondolier was slowing. I wondered if he understood the significance of my remark. Plainly, I had shocked or startled Captain Dandolo and he did not like it.

"You cannot be serious, Madonna."

"But I am."

"Who in heaven's name would wish to stab you? And who gave you this preposterous notion?"

I opened my mouth to reply. Something, I know not what absurd moment of doubt, made me hesitate to confide my suspicions. The gondolier was not a man I trusted. He had failed us on that night when the Captain was attacked.

"I only mean that someone might have wished to rob me."

The Captain would not stop staring at me. I found it disconcerting. "Madonna, I repeat—who suggested this horrible and I may say, utterly ridiculous idea to you?"

It was on the tip of my tongue. And then the noise of

arriving guests at the palazzo turned our thoughts to more immediate matters and we stepped out of the gondola, onto the slime-covered step. So, belatedly and reluctantly, I began to fill my position as hostess for my father's wedding.

CHAPTER TWELVE

SEVERAL OF THE WEDDING GUESTS were from the embassy, men I recognized from our visit to that palatial building on the Grand Canal. Since the Captain was clearly an invalid and leaning heavily upon my support, I found him a high-backed chair near the altar and he sank onto it with a sigh of relief. He embarrassed me, however, by making a great deal too much of my attentions to him and by lingering too long over my hand as he saluted it with a kiss. Everyone present rushed to congratulate him upon his rapid recovery, and there were many knowing glances and remarks cast my way.

One of the ladies present, the wife of the Third Secretary, coyly demanded, "When are you going to reward your gallant savior, Miss Carewe?"

Bewildered, I asked, "Reward? How so, Ma'am?"

"But it is the *on dit* of Venice, my dear, that the Captain saved your life the other night, and that an understanding has been created between your rescuer and your dearest Papa . . . Here he is now. Sir Maitland, you could do much worse than to welcome the handsome Captain into your distinguished family."

"Father!" I said sternly, forgetting that this was to be a day of great happiness for him. He had come out to the altar and was leaning there, looking frail and noble, with one arm upon the silent Turk's shoulder. "How could you spread such stories about my betrothal? They are totally false, as you know."

He looked around uneasily. "Hush, my child. They will think we are quarreling."

"And so we are!" My voice had gotten the better of my manners, but it made me out-of-reason cross to think that he would persist in this talk despite my warning to him. "I would rather—" I could not think of anything bad enough. "—I had rather do *anything* than marry where I do not love. I warn you!"

Fortunately, at that moment as I turned away from him, I spied Livio nearby in a dark corner of the great hollow vestibule. He was watching me and smiling faintly with one eyebrow raised. I pretended my object was to greet other guests, but I made my way toward him, and soon he was telling me in his low voice, "From the sounds of your quarrel, you have fully recovered from your bout with . . . seasickness."

"Do you realize I have run all over Venice looking for you today?" I demanded rudely, because the terrors seemed to be enclosing me on all sides.

"And here I am. You will allow that I am nothing if not obliging." He looked amused but I thought there was concern in his eyes as he took my fingers and brought them to his lips.

But I was not to be wheedled into a good mood by his exaggeration of the Captain's attentions and told him so.

He looked astonished. "Now, what on earth makes you think I fall in love with beautiful young termagants only to imitate our brave Captain?"

Far from dissatisfied at this news, I pretended to believe he was teasing me; but I was happy to note that the dark, serious expression remained around his eyes, and I reminded him of his missing spectacles.

"True," he agreed. "Can that be why you look beautiful to me?" But I refused to take the bait, while remaining aware that the person I was beginning to care most about in Venice was sincere to me, and whatever lies he led others to believe, with me there were no disfiguring spectacles. *With me,* I thought, *he is utterly himself. . . .*

The Captain's voice suddenly cut into our warm little moment. "And here is my rescuer, Messire Livio. How fortunate!

I can thank you in my own person."

Livio waved this aside. "It was nothing. Simply happy chance that allowed me to be there at that time."

"And what a precise moment to choose, my dear fellow! It may have been nothing to you, as you say, but my life has some value to me." All those within hearing laughed at the Captain's little pleasantry and he went on, to my discomfiture. "A happy chance, you called it, that you arrived upon the scene just then. Did you, I wonder, see anything of the attacker? It would be of immense help if you could have done so."

"I am sorry I cannot help you. It was quite dark and I saw nothing," Livio said.

I had an odd notion that while the two men exchanged these trivial remarks, they were saying something else entirely, and that a much greater emotion than a petty competition over rival gallantries was involved. There was certainly no love lost between them. I wondered at the real subject of their mutual dislike.

One of the onlookers, Fortman-Truscott, whom I now despised as a traitor, cut in to remind us all, "Still, one must confess it takes a good deal of courage to perform the Captain's functions in a city where cutthroats are hiding behind every arcade. Captain Dandolo, it is small wonder the females of Venice find you irresistible."

"I trust to find myself irresistible to but one young female." He reached out his free hand to my wrist, and I eluded his touch under the interested gaze of Livio who started to ask me something, obviously moving out of hearing of the others. But Captain Dandolo, with a quick glance in Livio's direction, said to me suddenly, "I believe our conversation was interrupted as we reached the palazzo. Do you recall what we were discussing?"

"No," I lied. "Nothing of great importance. Will you forgive me now? I have some guests to see to."

Livio remarked audibly to Fortman-Truscott, "Has not anyone located the cutthroat yet? He seemed to have taken to his heels directly after he threw that dagger. One would have thought he might at the least attempt to rob you, Miss Carewe."

"Or you?" I asked mischievously. "Perhaps you too were fortunate." I could not conceive of Livio doing something daring. He would be sensible and let his gondolier manage the physical violence.

The Captain said, "How opportunely you arrived, Messire Livio! A second before and you might have caught the assassin yourself. You did arrive through the arcade in which the assassin was hiding?"

People were looking at us but it annoyed me to hear what was very nearly an accusation, absurd but nasty in its implications, and I said angrily, "What nonsense! You all seem to to assume that the assassin's victim was to have been the Captain."

"Rachel—" Livio reminded me quietly, but I brushed aside his interruption with a quick, impatient gesture.

"Let me inform you that had I not bent to touch a stray cat, I would have received the dagger myself."

Fortman-Truscott moved closer to our little group. "But what possible reason would there be for anyone to stab you, Miss Carewe? Do you have enemies in Venice?"

I wanted to laugh hysterically, but caught Livio's eyes in time and managed to shrug off this dangerous approach to my knowledge of the treason in the household. I doubted that I would live the night through if Fortman-Truscott guessed I knew his treason and that of my father. Livio's unspoken warning told me something else that puzzled me. He must know or suspect what I had just discovered this morning—that Truscott and Father were working to bring the hated Austrian rule to Venice. Since there was no longer a hope for the Serenissima's neutrality, I was beginning to realize how preferable would be the alternative, a free democracy under the protection of the new French Republic.

Our matters began to sound unimportant, even the treason I had discovered, by comparison with the news brought by one of the young gentlemen from the embassy. A priest had stepped into the entry hall from his gondola and was rapidly surrounded by wedding guests, through whose chattering midst the boy from the embassy snaked his way. He seized Fortman-Truscott's silk brocade sleeve and shook it anxiously.

"Sir! News from beyond the Brenta. General Bonaparte and the French Republican Armies have whipped the Austrians once more, and the word is that the Austrians will demand that Venice declare war on the French."

Fortman-Truscott waved his hand eloquently. "And we already know the French offer. A Tree of Liberty in St. Mark's, and every jackal, every cutthroat and scoundrel in Venice to have the right to public elections. See how the mighty are fallen!" There was a buzz of excitement, not all agreeing with Truscott. He added cynically, "We need not hope for the protection of that French *canaille*. The Council of Ten still rules the Doge and Venice, and the Ten are unalterably opposed to a democratic rule. Come along now. We must take places for the ceremony. The bride is approaching."

I wondered if Livio had heard the Englishman's easy dismissal of public liberty. I felt it more than ever necessary to ask his advice about the treason in the embassy, and in my father's own house. Now, however, Livio took my arm and escorted me to one side of the altar so that I could be near Father and yet see the approach of the bride with a flustered, pink Dacey immediately behind her. Father was looking tense, unnerved, and I was in painful sympathy for him. Was he having second thoughts about the marriage?

"Poor Father," I whispered to Livio, who surprised and disappointed me by shaking his head.

"Do not be concerned," he murmured. "Simply pretend."

"Pretend!"

He deliberately drew my attention to the bride, remarking in audible tones, "A lovely creature, is she not?"

"Ha!"

He pinched my wrist and I recalled myself belatedly, feeling a complete hypocrite. "Lovely, to be sure," I said, and was rewarded by his quick smile and that of my father, who turned to glance at me in a gratified way. The insufferable First Secretary Fortman-Truscott stood up with the bridegroom.

The bride came through the aisle formed by the now standing guests. Dacey was behind her, like a dutiful lady-in-waiting. Mira Teotochi wore green taffeta with panniers, modest but stunning on her tall, mature figure, mature enough to look naturally elegant, with her red hair piled high. She wore jade earrings but no necklace. I suspect the earrings were not meant to be obtrusive. Unfortunately for the modest effect she probably intended, the sight of those jade earrings in no way softened my feelings. They had belonged to my mother, a heritage from her English grandmother. Nevertheless, I would have been blind to deny that she looked striking in them.

She came to stand beside Father, carefully readjusting a green and gold lace scarf over her bare arms. I expected Father to look as triumphantly happy as did the proud Mira, but at moments during the service, and particularly during the blessing, he reeled weakly. Before either Livio or I could reach him, Fortman-Truscott took him stiffly by the shoulder, and Father finished the service.

In spite of my private reservations over the marriage, I could do no less than congratulate him and wish Lady Mira Carewe all happiness. Though surrounded by well-wishers, my father seemed feebly anxious for my good opinion.

So feeble! So unlike the strong, vigorous, and above all patriotic Maitland Carewe of my childhood! He would never have clutched feebly at my good opinion or that of anyone else. He would have announced his own happiness and invited me to join him in it.

Mira smiled at my good wishes. Her teeth were flawless. And Dacey did an odd thing. Passing by me she murmured, "Trust me, my dear. Just—trust me to know what is best to do."

Absently, I agreed, but I didn't know what she was talking about. The crowds had stepped in now between my father and me and I found myself drawn away from the others toward the far end of the great vestibule. Livio said quietly, "Do not think of them."

"I must. I must! She is my father's wife now. She is part of my family."

"Nevertheless, you must now leave Venice."

I stared at him. "Impossible. I could never leave my father in the hands of creatures like Fortman-Truscott. And he can't return to England while this treachery—"

"Treachery?"

"Nothing. With the Austrians and the French battling over Italian soil, it is impossible to keep one's loyalties straight."

"Your father did not betray his country."

I tried to laugh. I did not want his sympathy when it made him tell lies like this; for Father *had* betrayed his country and his adopted country as well.

"You know nothing about it. My Father—"

His forefinger touched my lips lightly. "You are to leave Venice. Say nothing to anyone, especially to Carewe and the woman. She is a gambler. She needs your money. And if you remain, she will have it."

"Over my body," I murmured.

He did not make it easier for me. He repeated, *"Over your body.* And I will not have it so. In all else they have succeeded, but not this! Not you."

I looked at him, amazed at the sudden, low violence in his voice. "People in my profession always recognize those in the business. I have known the truth for some time, that—"

"What? All alone, beautiful Madonna Rachele?" asked the Captain, his smile glinting in Livio's direction. "Or so nearly alone as makes no matter, eh, Messire?"

Livio pretended a rueful manner that I suspected hid a great deal of anger. "I am beginning to be sorry I came to your aid that night, Captain. So you have designs upon the company of Madonna Rachel?"

"Designs, no. I would hardly describe it so." The Captain raised his silken sling rather obviously. "But as I have the best wishes of her dear Papa, that gives me the high card, I think."

I was now under no illusions as to the Captain's real interest in me. And from the way Father had pressed me to accept the Captain's attentions, I began to understand how Mira had been able to leave the gaming hell so quickly that first night, return to the palazzo before we arrived, and clear out that second storey bedchamber for me. The Captain must have informed her of my identity. What a jolt my unexpected resurrection from the dead must have given these conspirators! And since I was fresh from France, besides being half French myself, they must have thought I posed a serious threat not only to Mira's acquisition of my Mother's property, but to their conspiracy to deliver the moribund oligarchy of Venice to the mercies of the Austrian Empire.

I felt that if I told these conspirators exactly what I thought of them, I might further injure and even destroy my father. I had to move with care.

"Messire Livio was remarking about the beauty of Father's —of the bride. And I was saying that my own mother must have been a lovely bride."

"One glance at you, Madonna," said the Captain gallantly, "and one may be sure of that." The boy from the embassy had pulled on his uniform sleeve. "Yes, yes. What is it?"

The boy said in low, urgent tones, "The wine, Sir. For the toast to the bride and groom."

"Yes, thank you. Madonna Rachele, I believe your esteemed father would consider it of importance if you were beside him and Lady Carewe for the toast."

I glanced at Livio. "Later." I saw his lips form the word as I turned away. I blinked to let him know I understood. I was flanked by the Captain, who had taken my arm possessively, and by the young runner from the embassy, who murmured, "He will be pleased to have you beside him, as the

Captain says, Miss Carewe. He is not well yet, is he?"

"He is much improved," I said. "It is gratifying to see that he can stand without help now."

The boy shook his head sadly. "Paralysis is a terrible thing. I would never have known him."

The Captain, however, cut into this morbid talk. "I trust it is not French champagne. A good Italian wine is always preferable."

Or an Austrian one? I thought sardonically, but did not disagree with him. I joined my Father and the bride, was given a glass of something that proved to be champagne, after all, and drank the several toasts with the others in the wedding party.

"Father," I remarked when he leaned heavily upon his bride's shoulder for support and I was almost won by the tenderness of the gesture, "it is a pity you cannot take your bride on a visit to Barbary, or even to Rome. Several couples I knew in Paris took small journeys after their weddings."

"But I shall make my dearest husband comfortable here in this palazzo of tender memory," said the bride. "Dearest Maitland, are you happy now that we are one at last?"

Father's reply was vague but it was assumed by all witnesses to be in the affirmative.

"And now," Mira resumed gently, "my first task as the mother of this dear girl who has suffered so much will be to bridge the tragic gulf that has existed between you and my beloved Maitland. My dear Rachel, will you forgive your Papa, and in the sight of this company make me happy by promising never to bear again that—forgive me, dear—that unnatural resentment you have shown against him?"

Stunned, I could only stare at her, the hand that held my glass of champagne shaking so much, from rage and stupefaction, that I could not for a minute deny the charge. "I never—" I began finally, but Mira was already reaching for my other hand.

"Dear, do not refuse me. Swear before us all that the hatred and bitterness are gone, that you will never again make those silly, girlish threats which you do not mean, and that you will forgive your poor father and me for finding our little happiness . . . You will please me so much." The odious woman leaned over in all her thickly perfumed splendor to kiss my stiff, unyielding cheek.

I tried to draw away but there were too many around us, urging me now—all talking at once: "Kiss and forgive." . . . "Tell them you wish them well." . . . "Do be generous."

Worst of all, I saw Dacey's troubled face among those urging me not to say such wicked things against my poor Father for wanting to find a little happiness, even at his age!

They were driving me mad with their persistence when what I really wanted to do was to scream this woman's evil and treachery from the rooftops. I pushed away from them all, elbowing everyone, slapping some especially persistent hand away as I thought, *Stop it! You vicious, lying traitor! Stop it!* and I ran from them, across the wide vestibule, toward the door and the winding stone steps. I ran all the way to my bedchamber, now breathless and weeping like a stupid child.

I threw open the door, and then was terrified when a hand closed and bolted it behind me. I looked up wildly, scarcely seeing the man through my angry tears. But when I heard his voice murmuring tenderly in French, "*Chérie, chérie,* do not cry," I went into Livio's arms as naturally as though they had always awaited me.

"Lies!" I kept saying in English. "She twisted everything. Made it all seem as if I were mad—hating her, hating my Father."

"Do not think about it, dearest. You never hated your Father. You never had cause to hate him. You are coming away with me tonight. As soon as it can be arranged."

"I can't. Not yet. I'd die if, after all this, poor Papa were to be destroyed by them. It is the one thing I could not face. You see, I know things about them, and I have to get the information to the right people without hurting Father any more. He's been hurt and used so much already!"

I knew Livio's concern, both with me and with the situation I faced, but still he held me to him, safe and warm, while he stroked my tousled, disheveled hair.

"You must leave soon," he repeated. "You may not be safe here much longer."

"You mean because of the French Armies?" I asked, suddenly aware that Venice's land borders were surrounded. "I overheard something today that I shouldn't have heard. Something about the war. Not that I should be afraid of the French. I have a French passport."

"No, no, you foolish child. The Doge has made an agreement with General Bonaparte to protect the city from pillage and the Austrian Armies. And in God's name, tell no one! The Council of Ten must not hear of it yet. They would prefer anything to popular rule. They are like the French nobility. They have acquired their privileges, their own pillage, for a thousand years. We cannot expect them to surrender them willingly now."

I stared at him. Was he not employed by the Ten?

He went on, oblivious to my quick start. "There are traitors in the city who may give over Venice to sack by the Austrians if they are given their head. There is enormous profit in it for the pro-Austrians in the city, if they succeed. But the agreement will be clear. Venice shall have her freedom. France is not at war with the Serenissima."

He looked at me seriously. *"Chérie,* do you know what it will mean to have a Tree of Liberty planted in the main square? It will mean that for the first time in her history Venice will allow her own people to sit in judgment. Not the Inquisitors. It will be the end of secret denunciations, secret trials, secret stranglings. But it will take several days before the French forces arrive to protect the Doge himself from the Ten. Meanwhile, you must promise to tell me any suspicious act against you in this house. You must be gotten out of here, and soon."

I felt the enormous weight of the last few days, the last few months, beginning to lift from me. I could scarcely believe it, and yet could not doubt Livio. I tried, however, to eliminate all obstacles. "But after I leave, how can I save Papa? He has no idea of what he is doing."

"We will talk about that when the time comes."

"But the time is now—before that woman can bleed him of his fortune, his property, everything."

He smiled. I was exceedingly conscious of his gaze, of his face near mine, of his lips, and tried to take my mind from this intense awareness as he told me, "Let the man enjoy himself briefly. You must concede that they deserve each other."

Before I could reply, he kissed me. Maddeningly, I could never afterward remember my precise sensations. I was aware of my pulsebeat and his, of a suffocating warmth that was totally unlike my feelings for the young males I had known in Paris. I knew I loved him but I was afraid to say so.

"It is absurd," I murmured when he raised his head and yet kept me within the radius of his arm, very close against the breast of his black velvet coat.

He was gently amused. "I do not find it so."

"No, no. I mean—I know so little about you. I cannot conceivably feel anything for you, a stranger."

"When we have known each other a score of years, you

will not notice the strangeness. Now, my love, you have not promised yet to inform me, directly you are threatened—any suspicious thing."

I said indignantly, "That is all very well, but I tried all morning to find you and failed. I only located you in my Father's own house. Scarcely the safest place for us to have secrets."

"Then you must remember: do you know the Merceria?"

I smiled. "It was that dreadful little street I took when I escaped from your lodgings."

"You see? I was right when I asked you to remain in my protection. I do not like leaving you here, even for a few days."

"I must. Until something can be done about my Father."

"Very well. The Merceria. There is a leather-working shop, the first on the left as you enter the Merceria. You must go there—or send a message to me there—at any time. And I will come and fetch you."

I teased, because I did not really believe he could be quite so sure. "At any time? Midnight or dawn?"

"At any hour," he repeated firmly. "I am absolutely serious. I will be informed within minutes of your message. Will you remember, my darling?"

He kissed the crown of my head. "And then I promise, no more secrets. In any case, your safety should not have to be a secret."

"They would not approve of this." I nodded at his arm enclosing my shoulders. "Their intent is that I marry Captain Dandolo. But I daresay it should not be of any great concern to Papa." I laughed. I had begun to recover from my discovery of what Livio meant to me. Now I could be happy over the knowledge that he shared this overpowering emotion. "Father should be as quick to accept one Venetian as another into his family."

For a very long few seconds I felt the muscles in his arm tighten. Then he said easily, "Very true, my darling. But you must promise me not to tell him yet."

"Is it because of your work with the Inquisitor's Office? Or is that a secret?"

"I am afraid it is the worst kept secret in Venice. No. It is more complicated. But I promise to tell you the entire affair when you are free of this place."

He was just drawing me to him to kiss me again when Dacey's voice came to us excitedly from the hall and she rattled the latch. "Rachel, dear, the party is moving up to the guest chambers on the first storey. Please be careful."

"She knows you are here with me," I whispered. "Don't let them see you. It will only make more trouble."

He let me go and unlocked the door. Adelaide Dace looked at him with disapproval. Before she could speak, Livio took her hands.

"Dear Madame, will you look out for her safety?"

She raised her tawny eyebrows but was clearly swayed by his plea. "She is not in danger, I assure you, Sir, but I promise you we shall take good care of her."

"Forgive me, but you are mistaken, believe me, Madame. I care very much for Rachel's life and happiness. I cannot tell you more now, but you must believe there is a very real danger. Have I your promise?"

"Yes, yes. Certainly. Now, go, or both Rachel and I will be in difficulties. I will show you the servants' stairs, and on the first storey you can mingle with the guests. A number of them are leaving. You may go down with them."

Livio thanked her, and promised me, "I will try to see you tonight. Then tomorrow. I will never be far away. Remember." Then, pantomiming a kiss to me, he followed Dacey the length of the hall. Shortly after, when he had gone, Dacey returned to find me hugging my arms against the cold which seemed especially noticeable, since I was deprived of the warmth and protection of this man I had learned to love so suddenly but so completely.

"He is just going over that bridge now," I told her.

"Very charming, I'm sure," she said stiffly. "Now, my dear, you really must prepare yourself. A change of garments, I think, and one of your good shawls."

"Why?" I asked, bewildered at her activity.

"But you must know you owe your Father and dear Lady Carewe your very best behavior after your inexcusable conduct at the wedding. That a child reared by me should ever display herself in public—but I will say no more on that head. They wish you to have an aperitif with them. Lady Carewe tells me she has a Grecian wine that will put you in a most amiable mood."

"Amiable? Or compliant?"

Dacey stopped examining my wardrobe to ask in surprise, "Is there a difference?"

"Certainly," I said, shivering. "To be compliant I need only to be dead."

CHAPTER THIRTEEN

IN THE END I was carefully dressed in my sprigged rose muslin chemise gown with my rose shawl, my good black morocco slippers and with my hair piled high in curls over a rose velvet fillet in the new Grecian style. I felt a little like one of the ancient Roman chickens carefully brought before the Roman Senate so the auguries could be read in its entrails.

"Try and be pleasant to Lady Carewe, at least for the moment," Dacey told me, in the knowledgeable way of a busy-body who knows none of the facts.

"Oh, Dacey! For heaven's sake! How can you be so blind?" But it was a rhetorical question. Like most people, myself included, she was swayed by good treatment, I thought, by kindness and a certain pleasant deference that gave her a feeling of superiority. Mira Teotochi—pardon, Lady Carewe —was an adept at this method of winning her cohorts. I could well imagine her skill at winning my weakened father.

"Now, you look charming," Dacey decided, turning me around and surveying me from all angles. A certain match-making light appeared in her eyes. "I hope you have not given your heart entirely to that fellow. He may be a likable chap, as I would be the last to deny, but—"

For various reasons, I felt it wiser not to tell Dacey everything I knew. I did not believe she would betray me out of malice, but I had no doubt Mira could flatter her out of any information. So I lied casually. "Messire Livio is handsome enough, I daresay. But he cannot see beyond his nose without those awful spectacles. And naturally, he cannot be compared with your new friend, the Captain."

Dacey agreed, but only after a curious momentary hesitation. "Indeed not! Come along, dear."

As we went down the hall together, Dacey kept pointing out the advantages of good relations with my family. "If you are actually in danger, my dear, it is best not to trust anyone, even Messire Livio. Though it seems to me that the Captain has done nothing suspicious."

"I suppose it would matter very little if I did not love him," I murmured, pretending to think it over. "One seldom married for love in my parents' day."

This seriously interfered with Dacey's romantic dreams, as she made clear to me. "But I do not favor marriage where there is no esteem. You must know that, my dear. Yet I know you esteem Captain Dandolo. He saved your life, after all is said. And, too, one knows exactly where one stands with him. I have never been quite comfortable in my mind about Master Livio. Is he quite as harmless as he looks?"

"Does he look harmless?"

"When we first saw him, I confess I thought so. But of course your dear Papa and Lady Carewe say he is a spy for the Venetian government. Detestable creatures, spies!"

Considering the fact that my own father, with Fortman-Truscott and, I also made no doubt, Mira as well, had sold themselves to the Austrians, I thought it required a special insouciance for them to despise Livio's spying activities.

However, I pretended to believe her. "Captain Dandolo is a romantic fellow. I cannot deny it. Is he remaining this evening?" I was anxious for her to forget about Livio and the implications of his presence in my room. I was beginning to wonder how I might entice her out of the aura of this new "Lady Carewe," whose influence began to horrify me. Father was old; I could persuade him, perhaps, that Livio and I cared for his welfare. But we might have to lie to him, assuring him that Mira would also be rescued. Dacey could prove more stubborn, less amenable to our persuasions.

"The Captain has been most obliging, Rachel. You have underestimated him. I believe it is you who interest him, not your inheritance."

"Ah!" I said. "So he knows about that."

"Of course, my dear. Gentlemen do not engage to marry penniless nobodies."

We were in the first-storey gallery now and there was a deal of noise from various chambers, most of them small salons for the entertainment of the wedding guests. I gathered from the sounds and somewhat intemperate toasts that much wine was being consumed.

"I am willing to be agreeable," I promised, thinking that only thus could I eventually persuade Father to let Livio rescue him. "But do not imagine I shall beg forgiveness. That woman deliberately set out to incite me to anger before the wedding guests."

Dacey nodded slowly, then asked herself, "To what purpose?"

For this I had no answer.

She rapped upon Father's door before I could do so, and it was opened so rapidly I might have thought Mira Carewe was waiting for us with one hand upon the latch. She had changed to another green gown of satin and gauze but this was of greater décolletage and more suitable to an hour later in the day than was her wedding gown. From the wrist of her free hand swung a closed fan which she raised now with a warm smile, tapping me on the shoulder. "Come in, my naughty daughter. How charming you look! You oblige your dear Papa by your promptness in answering the summons."

Either her ideas of time were not mine, or she was being deliberately conciliatory, but I pretended to believe her.

"I think you asked me to join you and my father, Lady Carewe," I said, though the title stuck in my throat.

"Just so. Here is your Papa hoping his cross little daughter has mended her bad temper and come to pay her dutiful respects. Maitland, your daughter is here."

While she was exchanging a pleasant word of thanks with Dacey for fetching me, I went to Father in his big chair by a crackling fire on the hearth. His hands, frail and thin, were held out to the fire. He did not withdraw them as he looked around, but he smiled faintly.

"Yes, Daughter. Come here and let me see you. The light is better."

Although it was not yet sunset and the world of Venice was swathed in a deep orange glow which we could see out of the long windows, this sitting room was in shadow and candlelight, and much too warm. How my Father would have hated this, could he have foreseen it! So I thought, as I bent and kissed the side of his pale, veined temple.

In despite of all my resolutions, I could not resist dropping to my knees before him, taking oddly resistant hands, and saying, "Papa dear, I am sorry if I disturbed and made you unhappy after the wedding. I want your happiness always. You know that."

To my consternation he looked up anxiously at his wife, who had moved across the room with the sinuous sway and snap of satin and the heavy taffeta underdress. She bustled about him, rearranging the cushion behind his shoulders the while she said pleasantly, "We are vastly obliged, are we not, Maitland? I fear I was in part at fault. I merely meant to thank you for your presence which added countenance to our wedding, my dear Daughter. But I expressed myself badly. Maitland, Rachel and the good Miss Dace and I are about to try some of these delightful aperitifs so popular in the Barbary lands of the Ottoman Empire. I will fetch you your cordial first."

"Ay," said my Father in a querulous, impatient voice. "You promised it me some minutes since. Where is my cordial?"

Mira looked at me significantly, raising her eyebrows. "He is like that after a strenuous day. A pity, for the guests must be entertained tonight. We count upon you to help us, Rachel."

"Yes," I said, watching Father anxiously. "Should he not have some medicine? Or sleep, perhaps?"

"He will sleep before the entertainment this evening. Do not fear. Maitland, you will feel well enough to preside at the little gaming entertainment we have provided for tonight?"

"My cordial," Father insisted. "I want my cordial. Why do you punish me like this? You know I am always the better for it."

Mira passed the little glass with its peach-colored contents before me. "Brandy," she explained without troubling to lower her voice. "Naught but brandy."

I caught a whiff of it. She seemed to be right. It was ironic, I thought, that my Father, a connoisseur of all spirits, should now be so dependent upon a minuscule swallow of plain brandy.

He drank with greedy haste, and then held the glass lovingly in his fingers, as if he knew this would be his only pleasure of the evening. Poor Papa! It probably was.

"Come, Rachel, will you join Miss Dace and me over here?"

I looked up and saw the two women across the room, sitting opposite each other in stiff chairs with striped satin cushions, and looking so highly respectable I wondered how I could ever have suspected the one of trying to poison me, and the other of being her dupe, urging me on to various follies to please Mira Teotochi Carewe. If I was to throw them off the scent of my escape with Livio, I knew I must be a little more conciliatory· myself.

"It is warm in here, isn't it?" I remarked, trying to make small talk as a prelude to my false friendship.

"Poor Maitland gets chilled very easily." Mira poured a thick green liquid into a crystal glass and offered it to me. "Come, Rachel. You will find this—" she smiled, "not cooling, precisely, but comforting."

I reached for the glass, then my hand drew back, almost of its own volition. I hated the gesture, but I did not want this woman to know how she had terrified me, how I feared poison in every drop of wine, every bite of food.

Dacey watched us closely, looking shrewder than I would have credited. Then she said suddenly, "Rachel! How could you! Not again. My dear Lady Carewe, do give me that glass. Rachel, you may have mine."

But Lady Mira was not shocked. I saw the taunting satisfaction in her eyes as she exchanged the glasses. "Miss Dace does not understand your nervous condition, but I understand it perfectly. I am persuaded that when you are more yourself and have overcome the dreadful sufferings of your past, you will be enabled to drink a little aperitif without these qualms."

With full irony, I took Dacey's glass, but addressed Lady Mira: "Thank you. You are too kind."

The liquor was strange, tasting strongly of sweet herbs and I did not like it, but under the slanting green eyes of my father's bride, I drank it down rapidly, hoping she had not, somehow, managed to foretell both Dacey's actions and mine. I knew the woman was laughing at me secretly, but I did not, at the moment, see how I could prevent her amusement.

I could not forbear asking Dacey politely, "What is your opinion? Is that aperitif to your taste?"

Dacey was valiant in her defense of the liquor and, by implication, of her friend, Lady Carewe.

"Delightful, Rachel. Perfectly delightful. As you will discover when you know dear Lady Carewe better, her taste is exquisite."

I agreed at once. "I am sure that it is. Did she not marry Papa?"

Lady Mira and I smiled at each other. She was not drinking the green aperitif, but rather, a pale, watery liquid. I remarked upon it. "Your drink looks very weak, my lady. You have no taste for aperitifs from Turkey and the Barbary Coast?"

"This? A white wine. I acquired a taste for it as a child. Would you care to try it?"

Curiosity got the better of me. "Thank you."

She poured what appeared to be a white wine into my glass. When I had taken a few swallows, under the interested and faintly alarmed eyes of Adelaide Dace, I discovered, very much to my surprise, that it actually was wine. I had tasted just such a wine very recently, in Padua.

"Not an Italian vintage," the innkeeper had apologized, "but we have been forced to sell the Austrian wines. The Imperial Army was very firm upon the point. We hope for better luck now that the French have defeated the Austrians at Arcola and at Rivioli."

I was no authority on wines but they had been my chief beverage during the past eight years, and then, too, I was aware that Father and Fortman-Truscott, and doubtless others, were in Austrian pay. I decided to have a little fun with Lady Mira, to insinuate that I knew her secret and those of the people in this house. Only a hint. Not enough to make her sure, for then I could be absolutely certain to be poisoned!

"It does taste familiar," I murmured. I had to admire the sheer nerve of the woman. She was watching me with the faintest of smiles.

"Familiar?"

"Rather like an Alsatian wine. But it is not, of course."

"Hardly. Although there is an *esprit* between Maitland and the French Ambassador to Venice, as between all of the plenipotentiaries in an international city like Venice."

"Yes," I said, finishing the glass. "Not Alsace. A little east. I think . . . it may be an Austrian vintage." It occurred to me as I spoke that Mira's coloring, and much else about her, looked Austrian. Certainly, she did not look like a native-born Venetian.

I had startled or angered her into an indiscretion: "To be

sure. And once Venice realizes that the Imperial Army is preferable to a rule by the people, we may all be drinking Austrian wines."

I pretended to ignore that. "Now, Lady Mira, what are the plans for the evening? How do I dress? I suppose what I am wearing will not be suitable. I warn you, I did not come to Venice prepared for routs, balls, ridottos, and masques."

"It is a pity the lovely gown you wore with Captain Dandolo was so bloodstained." Lady Mira sighed romantically. "To think that after such loss of blood, the Captain was still able to seek you out the very next afternoon. He looked so pale, my dear. You cannot conceive how very pale he looked! But still he was here, to see to your health and safety. A remarkably handsome man, and with such a flattering fondness for you! I vow, I almost envy you!"

I said, with great understanding, "I can appreciate that. Poor Papa, though very distinguished, can scarcely be compared with Captain Dandolo."

I was happy to see that she bit her lip. After that, she was silent for a few minutes and I was able to leave after going over to Papa once more and kissing his perfectly indifferent cheek. Dacey followed me, after expressing to Lady Carewe her own thanks and mine. "So much nicer than afternoon tea, I think, dear Lady Carewe. And so obliging of you to include me in your invitation. We shall look forward to this evening."

She came hurrying after me, nudging me between my shoulder blades. "Rachel, your manners grow increasingly worse. You must say thank you."

I waved to Lady Carewe who stood in the doorway watching us. "Thank you, my lady," I said, and dropped a curtsey.

As we went up the steps to our rooms, Dacey shook her head. "You persist in overdoing, Rachel. That curtsey was quite unnecessary."

"You are never satisfied," I told her, and we said no more.

When I had gone to my room, I decided to investigate my wardrobe for Lady Mira's night entertainment, but found nothing suitable since my best ballgown had been ruined. I stood before the mirror on the tilt-top table and then backed away, carefully considering the figure I might present in my rose-sprigged muslin. It occurred to me that if I changed my shawl to my best white silk, and changed to my white silk-covered slippers, I might present a reasonable picture for whatever games, gambling or other entertainment Lady Mira had in mind. Thanks to Dacey's skill, my hair was beautifully arranged, and at the least, I thought, I would not be a figure of fun.

I looked out several times after darkness fell and the mooring lamps were lighted, but saw no sign of Livio. Though why I should, I could not guess. But it worried me. Was he, too, about to betray my faith in him? I felt sure he had not told me all the truth about himself, but whether the part he refrained from telling me concerned myself, I could not guess. I was forced to cling to the memory of his low, pleasant yet firm voice, the tenderness I had seen in his eyes, the wonderful, vibrant experience of his kisses, and to hope that, whatever his secrets, he was sincere in that he loved me.

Lady Mira was so obliging as to send up her maid to help me dress my hair and generally prepare for the evening, but, thanks again to Dacey's hand earlier in the day, I could send the girl on her way, with my extravagantly expressed gratitude. I was trying to play another game with my father's new wife. I would now be as overfriendly and overobliging as she was. I would play all her games, keep her puzzled and unnerved as she had so skillfully puzzled and unnerved me.

Meanwhile, however, as Dacey came to fetch me, I glanced out once more at the canal waters, black and sparkling, and then at the bridge beyond the palazzo. This time, I was sure I made out something moving in the darkness beyond the far end of the bridge. I could not expect Livio to spend his life there; yet I was much consoled by the thought that he might be so near at hand.

Dacey came in looking quite delightful in bright sky blue with panniers, an underdress of blue lace, and above the whole her white-blonde hair piled high. I was very properly enthusiastic, and clapped my hands in genuine surprise, although I realized I should not let her know I was surprised to see that she could look so lovely.

She was charming about it, however, receiving my praise with pink cheeks and modest happiness. "And you, my dear," she hastened to add, "you look exactly proper for a young lady your age. Much more appropriate than the elaborate absurdities of the rest of—that is, of the women my age."

Which was a delightful way of informing me that I must expect to look quaintly underdressed tonight.

Just as we were leaving, I decided to look out once more

to be certain I had actually seen Livio in his accustomed place.

"What in heaven's name do you find so fascinating out in the darkness, Rachel?"

"The canal. A gondola just passed."

"Ah, the canal! I adore canals." She peered over my shoulder on tiptoe. "So mysterious and romantic."

"And dirty."

"Rachel, you are incurably unromantic. Why—I vow, there is a man out there in the shadows!"

I looked back quickly. I did not want her to see Livio. She would be most likely to remark on his presence to Lady Mira unless she realized, as she had this afternoon, that his presence would compromise me.

But it was I who was surprised. The figure that moved out of the shadows to the foot of the bridge, looked around and ducked back again—that figure in no way resembled Livio. It was the silent Turk. I had no doubt he was waiting to intercept Livio. The thought terrified me. I wanted to run out and stop Livio, to leave a message at the leather-worker's shop in the Merceria. But a moment's common sense told me that a man of Livio's skill in spying experience would certainly be on the watch for just such traps. What worried me most was the knowledge that if the Turk had been sent out to intercept Livio, it obviously meant that Mira had discovered Livio's presence, and his interest in Father's palazzo. I supposed now that it would be Mira's palazzo as well.

And what, actually, was Livio's interest—or that of the Serenissima—in the palazzo? Almost I did not want to know. It was certainly not the simple desire to protect me. Even in my sudden new love for Livio, I knew better than that. Before I had arrived Livio was already set to spy upon the people here. Was it possible he and his employers knew of the treason of my poor father and the others? In such case, how could I ever persuade him to save my father?

"Are you coming, dear?" asked Dacey, waving her exquisitely feathered fan in a big, generous sweep. I suspected it was a present from Mira Carewe but did not mention the fact.

In spite of my depressed spirits, I laughed and came with her.

Dacey not only looked her best but very shortly became a belle at the meeting of the wedding guests in the newly redecorated great vestibule. The altar and pseudoreligious decorations had been removed and in their place were elaborate gaming facilities, stiffly elegant chairs, divans, sideboards, tabarets, and individual tables for games of piquet. But the greatest crowds surrounded Lady Mira, their hostess who, on her wedding night, was presiding over the faro bank. And on this wedding night, she was also stunningly gowned in black with lace panniers and taffeta underdress, and an overdress of richest satin. And above it all, flashing and blinding us, was a parure of diamonds around her only slightly aging throat. In her carefully powdered red hair was set a great diamond crescent.

There was a good deal of buzzing about her. She was impossible not to notice. But curiously enough, while I was admitting regretfully to myself that she looked glorious, I heard many criticisms of her. Most stemmed from the obvious expenditure of her new husband's money. One thing I overheard I found more than a little trying to my pride, though I was in no wise surprised by it. It was a dialogue between two male guests who imagined their conversation was masked by the loud shout of triumph as Lady Carewe won a perfect torrent of ducats.

". . . all his fortune on her back. As for the daughter, the poor creature will be penniless."

"Not unattractive, though. The young creature will make a profitable marriage, mark me."

When they talked of me as penniless, they did not know of my mother's fortune which would be mine if I lived. If I did not live, of course, it would then belong to my father—and, by natural progression, to Mira Carewe, or to my husband.

A great many of the guests of both sexes were powdered and wigged, and put me in mind of scenes in Paris before the Revolution. The sight of them was saddening and faintly ridiculous to me. I realized how far I had come from those days. I did not belong in this masquerade world of the eighteenth century, after all. My ideas had been formed against my will, but they were now, unquestionably, of the glittering new century, with all its possibilities.

I had no money to play the various games of chance being so skillfully provided for the entertainment of her guests by my father's new wife, and in my present disturbed and suspicious state, I was not interested in games; so I went and sat by my father who looked older and more frail than ever in black satin breeches and a warm velvet coat, with an ele-

gantly embroidered brocade waistcoat and a great froth of
shirt ruffles and neckcloth. He was seated in a large milord
chair near a crackling fire in the enormous fireplace at the far
end of the hall. It was the first time I had seen a fire in this
great hearth and it did a great deal to add a pleasant feeling
of intimacy to that end of the room.

I said, "May I sit beside you, Father?"

Vaguely, he raised his snowy white head, gazed at me out
of pale, watery eyes. "Yes, of course, my child. Do sit down.
It is a trifle warmer here. Don't you find it so?"

"Very . . . comfortable." Sitting this close to the fire for
longer than a few seconds made me feel like a roast turning
upon the spit, but it seemed the only way to have a private
interview with my father, uninfluenced by his wife.

I pursued my advantage, speaking rapidly in a low voice
barely above a whisper. "Papa, are you happy? Is all of this
what you really want of life? Tell me the truth, I pray."

He rubbed his hands and held them toward the fire. They
were trembling and looked transparent. I waited and he
apparently grew conscious of my silence. He murmured, "I
thought I would be. I was sure I would be when—"

"When you were married?"

His hands jerked. He turned and stared at me. "When—?
But . . . yes. Naturally."

"Do you love her?" My voice was so low I was surprised
that he heard me. I scarcely heard it myself.

"Always. Until . . . always."

Hoping against my own convictions about him, I repeated
hoarsely, "Until?"

"I meant—my age, you understand. Nothing else." But he
looked over his shoulder in the most furtive way, and I had
no hesitation in suspecting he was terrified of being heard.
His manner convinced me that his conduct was based upon
his fear of those who now guided his life since his illness.

"Papa," I began, hoping to have him relate the whole of his
entrapment by this band of Austrian spies, "how would you
like to be free of this place? Free of the pressures over you.
In just a day or two you might be taken away from—"

Behind me, Captain Dandolo stood resplendent in uniform
with the candlelight gleaming on his sleek, black, carefully
clubbed head of hair. "Taken away? Are we to understand
your dear Papa wishes to leave his post here? Your Excellency, are we to understand this?"

I winced at the terrible, cringing servility of my once-bold father. He reached out a palsied hand, denying it violently. "I had no such notion. None whatever. I cannot imagine what possessed my—my little girl to suggest such a thing. She knows quite well how important it is for me, especially at the moment, to remain at my post."

"Father!" I cried, but it was useless to be cross with him. When the time came, I would simply have to persuade him to go with Livio and me, and the time must be secret, when there was no likelihood of his being terrified by these people who controlled his life.

The Captain, favoring his arm in its fresh silken sling, asked me if I would care to take supper with him. As I hadn't eaten in many hours and was mortally afraid to touch any food furnished for me by my Father's wife, I accepted his offer at once. However, when we went to supper in one of two salons opening off the great striped vestibule with its full complement of gamesters, I preferred to choose my own food. I felt that it was highly unlikely that Lady Mira would poison the entire list of guests just to kill me.

The Captain made no objection when I chose to fill my plate with tempting morsels, a delicious little creamed shellfish, some tender, succulent white flakes of a fish I was also unfamiliar with, and innumerable other delicacies, some with the thick, too-sweet coating that announced their Near-East derivation. And afterward, there were cooling ices, glaces, and candied fruits. Since I was not sure when I would feel free to eat again in this house, I must have startled the Captain with my appetite.

He pointed out his helplessness with one arm useless, and I heaped his plate as well. While we ate, he pointed out how tolerably we dealt together.

"And you will have the benefit of my strength with your unfortunate Father. You must see that your life is impossible until you are married, my lovely one. Afterward, you will know all the freedom of other Venetian ladies in your position."

I asked ironically, "Are there any other ladies in precisely my position?"

He ignored that, or did not understand the allusion.

"Has Lady Carewe told you how I feel about you, the happiness with which I view your affections, Bellissima?"

I could not resist waving my hand and remarking slyly, "And when I am married, think of Mama's fortune that my husband and I will share! What gaming and splendid masques and routs we may have!"

He grinned but remonstrated carefully, as if to a child, "But I am not so foolish as to permit you to waste your inheritance. It shall be carefully—husbanded, so to speak."

I laughed at this truth so untruthfully spoken. Since I was in possession of a fact he could not possibly know, that he would never be my husband in any circumstances, I could afford to joke with him about it. "And would I be permitted to have a wardrobe as resplendent as that of my stepmama?"

"By all means," he agreed promptly. "And may I say, you would do greater justice to it?"

I took leave to doubt that, but I pursued the joke because I wanted to keep his mind off the subject of Father's imminent and secret departure upon which I was now determined.

"And Papa shall have his favorite chair by the biggest hearth in Venice. And then," I added, more or less at hazard, "he will probably never need the rest of his boots and we may toss them away, too."

"What on earth can you mean, Madonna Rachel? Toss away his boots?"

I began to suspect I had touched upon something dangerous; so I tried to dismiss the matter as something unimportant. "Like that collection of Father's boots in a chamber on the second story that Mrs.—pardon me—Lady Mira removed to the refuse pile."

This time I could not mistake the rigid lineaments of his face or the hard glitter in his eyes. Beginning to be concerned for my own safety, I explained, "Old boots, I imagine. She merely—"

"Stupid!"

I jumped. His smile had a distinctly malign twist. "What an incredibly stupid thing!"

"To have destroyed the old boots?" I asked, all bewildered.

"To have saved them," he said between his teeth in a voice that gave me chills. A moment after, he began to eat his candied fruit and to complain about the awkwardness that attended such an operation, with only one arm available. Like an actress schooled in her part, I played to his mood, but I could not shake off the terror he inspired in me after that curious outburst.

CHAPTER FOURTEEN

TOWARD THE END of the evening, the Captain deserted me while Dacey and I were gossiping about the gowns present. I did not immediately understand and made amused remarks to Dacey, pointing out his "infidelity" and the fact that he had made his way, eventually, to the side of Lady Mira, who had left the faro table and was taking midnight supper in company with several male gallants of assorted ages. This did not annoy me. I was somewhat afraid of the Captain now, especially after his absurd outburst to me about the boots we had seen. But I was curious as to whether he had a part in the Austrian conspiracy that occupied Father, Fortman-Truscott, and undoubtedly Lady Carewe.

Observing my attention upon the Captain, Dacey rapped me under the chin with her fan. "You are seriously interested in that young officer? What a delightful creature, to be sure!"

"Don't be a goose, Dacey. He is all you say, and he knows it. And furthermore, I have a great attraction for him."

Dacey smiled complacently. "I do not make doubt you have an attraction for him. I have seen him hovering about you."

"But you have not asked what my special attraction may be."

"Now, Rachel, you must not seem to display immodesty. Well . . . well, what is this attraction?"

I said, with triumphant cynicism, "Mama's estate."

She was crestfallen and would have denied me vigorously, but at that instant we were besieged by two of Venice's many strikingly attractive males, of various ages, who wished to "stroll about the hall" with us. The more sophisticated and older of the two addressed me, while the younger, callow but friendly, sought out Dacey. And so we "strolled about the hall," an absurd pastime popular in my youth as a means of making the closer acquaintance of members of the opposite sex, but its purpose seemed so obvious to me now, I could not think how much simpler and straightforward customs had become in Paris.

We were in the midst of this stroll and I was trying hard to look interested in my companion's description of a naval engagement against Barbary corsairs when I was a good deal surprised to be approached by the Captain again.

He was almost rude in relieving me of the companionship of my nautical friend. "Your stepmama wishes you to join the tables. I suspect, lovely Rachel, that she is about to let you *punt on tick.*"

"Thank you," I said, "but I do not play games on borrowed money."

"Nonsense. She insists on your having the money. She is an excessively generous female."

. . . *With Papa's money,* I thought, ashamed of my constant negative reaction to her. It was even possible she meant to be generous. But I doubted it.

Aware that I was suddenly the center of considerable attention from those at Lady Mira's table, I could only refuse as politely as possible until, against all my inclinations, I allowed myself to be led to the table where I was given a quantity of golden ducats and, following Captain Dandolo's advice, rapidly lost them all. I could not keep my mind upon the rapid turns and winnings of the game. Behind Lady Mira's chair I kept seeing my father at the far end of the room, alone and forgotten. I tried to conceal my bitterness but I fear it was there for all to see.

"What a pity you persist in losing, my dear!" Father's wife remarked several times, with one of her sad, elegant little moues of sympathy.

The Captain's manner was curious. He complained that I had not been given enough to make it worth risking, which

was absurd, as I would have won no more than an even
greater outlay of money that was not mine. The curious
thing about it was the single quick flash of fear I thought I
caught in Lady Mira's eyes before she offered a *rouleau* of
money and I refused it. Why should she be frightened of
Captain Dandolo, and why should she take orders from him?

The long, ghastly evening ended at last and after kissing
Papa good night and allowing Lady Mira to press her cheek
to mine, I was permitted to retire to my bedchamber. Dacey,
bless her, was having much too good a time with her young
swain to join me, for which I was grateful. I rushed into my
room where the tired maidservant was turning down my bed
and had left a large silver ewer of hot water on the table
and a steaming glass on a tabaret near the bed. I spoke to
her but I was much more interested in whatever might be
happening along the canal outside.

I rushed to the portieres which she had closed, and opened
them abruptly. The canal looked desolate and beautiful, the
glistening waters reflecting in weird, exaggerated form the
buildings that bordered the canal. After several seconds of
tension I made out movement at the far end of the humped
bridge. Then I saw the Turk's tall, thick-shouldered form and
was enormously relieved. Obviously, he had not caught his
prey. I forgot myself enough to exclaim joyously, "He's
escaped the fellow!"

"I—I beg pardon?" A crash followed. I swung around
startled, to see the maid kneeling on the floor, crying
nervously as she picked up bits of glass.

Wondering how she had tipped over the glass of hot negus
or mulled wine—whatever it was—I said quickly, "Just clear
the glass away. Thank you."

But she went on sniffing loudly and sobbing, "I drank so
little . . . so little . . . I was tired and cold and I drank so
little, and then you spoke, Madonna, and I was frightened . . ."

"I understand. It doesn't matter. I won't need it tonight."

I set about helping her collect the last pieces of the glass.
A minute or two later, still inordinately nervous, the woman
stood up, then took my arm in a grasp that made me wince.

"It is most strange, Madonna Rachele. A light across the
canal in that loft."

I stood up quickly and followed her pointing figure. A
light, no larger than a candle, flickered, then was gone. I went
to the long balcony windows and stared across. For a fleeting

time the moonlight illuminated Livio's face at the window between the broken shutters. I saw his fingers against the window, and then one forefinger, and I was sure he smiled. Trying to be nonchalant for the benefit of the maid behind me, I put my hand against the glass and then my forefinger. I felt infinitely better. He was close, after all, and yet he had not fallen into the trap set by the Turk, probably under the instructions of my father's bride.

I was so happy at the knowledge of Livio's nearness that I felt I could cope with the problems here in the palazzo. Besides, Lady Mira had not attempted anything against me tonight. Now that she possessed the key to Father's fortune as well as to his household, she might not feel so virulent against me. If this should prove to be the case, I need not rush to escape in the next day or two. I would have more time either to persuade Father to go with Livio and me, or to satisfy myself that I had been wrong about his wife's intentions.

"Who can it be, Madonna?"

"Probably a seneschal. A steward who oversees the building." I began to worry over the woman's knowledge of Livio's presence. I added quickly, "Some old man working there."

"Yes. Only—it did not look to be an old man. Excuse me . . . I will remove the bits of glass. Again, I regret, Madonna. Good night."

I wished her good night, thanked her once more for arranging the room so cozily, and saw her leave. I decided not to draw the portieres, so that whenever I looked at them in the night I would know that help was near.

With a modesty I found absurd, even as I practiced it, I was very careful that when I bathed with the aid of towels and that silver basin of water, I did not make a parade of myself past the uncovered windows. But when I dressed for bed, I wore my best bedgown and over it my good robe of white wool nipped in at the waist, with a low, V-shaped decolletage. Ashamed of my own sudden attack of sensuous awareness, nonetheless I walked across the room at least three times, always hoping Livio was on the watch. When I finally made my prayers for Mama in heaven and for Papa to see the light, I suddenly remembered that Livio had undressed me to my petticoat. He would scarcely be impressed by the sight of me in my night-rail.

No matter. Perhaps he meant it when he called me his love. I hugged to myself the memory of this afternoon, that brief time with him, the way he looked at me, whimsical and sad and loving, all at once, and especially the feel of his mouth, the feel of his arms, with their unexpected and surprising strength.

And thus, with a mind that seemed to have banished troubles and suspicions for the night, I went off to sleep. So comforted was I that I did not even dream of Father's voice calling to me as on the first nights in the palazzo.

Curiously enough, it was the only night I had forgotten to bolt the door, and when I was awakened at a time that seemed much later, I sat straight up in bed, staring into the half-dark. Only the reflection from the late moonlight on the canal gave the slightest illumination but after a few seconds I made out a bundled figure, rustling in a strange rhythm as it moved across the room toward me. My first reaction was to rise up in bed and scream in the most cowardly way. Surely, this was Mira Carewe, stalking me even in my bed, perhaps with some thought of choking or smothering me!

And then a whisper through the darkness: "Rachel . . . Dear? Are you awake?"

Dacey! What a tiresome thing to do, sneaking in here, frightening me out of my wits, in the middle of the night! "No!" I muttered crossly. "I am asleep. What is the hour?"

"A trifle after two. The last of the guests who are not staying the night have gone. Oh, Rachel! What a city to live in, where ball guests go home in little cockleshell boats!"

I yawned elaborately. "Is that why you woke me up?"

"No, dear." She peered over her shoulder toward the door, which stood open. The hall beyond looked dimly menacing, illuminated by only one already guttering candle. "I didn't want to disturb anyone on the lower floors. It might be bad for your Papa's position here if those guests in the first-storey bedchambers heard about it."

"Heard about what?"

Dacey was her usual patient self. "About the woman lying there. Simply lying there."

"Lying where? What woman?"

"One of the maids, dear—lying on the landing above the first-storey gallery. It was too provoking! I nearly trod upon her hand."

This time I did sit up in bed. "Was she taken ill? Perhaps she tripped and fell."

Dacey was feeling for my bed candle. "I won't take the time to light this. We can light it by the hall candle."

"Yes. I'll be with you as soon as I can find that blasted robe." It was on the floor, under Dacey's feet. She fetched it up, and I swung it over my shoulders and followed after her. She was still wearing her elaborately panniered ballgown and it was the swish of taffetas that I had heard in the darkness when she crossed the room.

In the hall we lighted my candle. "Are you certain she did not fall, or simply faint?" I asked again. The truth is, after my quiet hours, I was still under the illusion that only a natural accident could explain such a simple matter. It was unfortunate, however, and I was sorry for the poor maid. She had been nervous enough when she dropped the glass in my room.

Dropped the glass.

I said quickly, anxiously, "Hurry . . . hurry! She drank from a glass in my room. Hurry!"

Dacey was tripping along as well as she could in her tight blue silk slippers and I passed her and rushed ahead toward the door leading to our now familiar steps.

But Dacey, confused by my sudden excitement, corrected me breathlessly. "No, no. The servants' stairs. I came up by the servants' stairs. They were closer to my room. Rachel, what is it? You are acting most peculiarly."

All the time that I was running, barefoot, through the hall, I was reminding myself that my loving stepmama may not have been satisfied with my Father's estate, after all. I found the woman crumpled across the stair landing and knelt beside her, trying to rouse her. At all events, she was not dead. I was grateful for that much. But, of course, she had not drunk the entire glass of mulled wine that had been left for me.

"She doesn't seem to be hurt," Dacey said as we examined the woman's limp, unconscious body by the light of my candle, which Dacey held high.

"No. It appears to be something like laudanum. She seems asleep, but her breathing is so heavy."

"Laudanum! How stupid of the woman! She should have taken it only after she was in her own bedchamber."

I laughed without humor. "I don't think she took it by choice."

"Whatever do you mean? Rachel! What are you saying? We must fetch up Lady Carewe. She will be very shocked."

I shook my head, thinking better of my first inclination to tell Dacey everything. It was a sickening, disillusioning truth, but I confessed it to myself at that moment: it was highly unlikely that my beglamored friend would believe anything that reflected upon the integrity of Mira Teotochi Carewe. Dacey was, like Father, a prisoner of her own belief in the woman.

"Well, Rachel? Shall I go and fetch up Lady Carewe?" She was on her feet, groaning a little at the pressure exerted by the too-tight slippers.

"By all means. If you think she would be interested. Otherwise, we had best try to rouse the woman. If we can make her walk, that should help."

Dacey started down the stairs, then stopped, appalled. "But I cannot call upon Lady Carewe. This is her wedding night."

I doubted very much if the wedding night of Mira and my Father would be in any way full of passion and maidenly seduction. But then, life had made me cynical, until I fell in love myself.

In the end, while I got the unfortunate maidservant onto her feet and tried to make her walk back and forth on the landing, Dacey went down to summon Lady Carewe. It was while she was rapping on Father's door, she later told me, that Lady Mira appeared in the gallery behind her. So the tender passion of the wedding night had not been quite as romantic as Dacey pictured it.

I had just gotten the maid to walking under her own power and she was descending the stairs shakily, when Dacey and Lady Mira came upon us, in the doorway to the first-storey gallery. Remembering the guests asleep on that floor, Dacey was careful to lower her voice, but to my surprise and puzzlement, Lady Mira sounded unnaturally loud.

"Really, Serafina! You must organize your work so that you will not fall asleep during its performance."

I said stiffly, forgetting all resolutions to be clever, "She drank a glass of mulled wine meant for me."

Already her voice had aroused several guests behind her. I saw doors opening along the gallery and people peering out in various absurd states of undress. Most of these heads, both male and female, were crowned with nightcaps and frilled bonnets. Of us all, Lady Mira, in her smoothly elegant green velvet overrobe, was by far the cynosure of eyes. Almost as though she had dressed for the role.

"Really, my dear child," —this to me, "you should not play

about with dangerous drugs, even to sleep well. Surely there are better ways."

I was so enraged I very nearly forgot myself and all my good resolutions to match her own shrewd game. "How dare you! You wretched woman—twisting everything—!" Words were rapidly failing me, due in part to my indignation and in part, also, to all those infernal eyes staring at me in that shocked way. I was still sputtering, crying out, "No! It is you!" when Dacey took my shoulder in a hard grasp quite unlike herself.

"Rachel! That will do. Everyone is looking at you."

I knew that. It was maddening and stupid. I should never have betrayed my real suspicions, but I had been pushed so far! I knew that if the maid Serafina was poisoned with laudanum drops, they had been meant for me.

Lady Mira had taken over the care of Serafina and with an arm around her, reassuringly, said, "Come, now, I will take you to your room. You will recover, Serafina. Be quite yourself . . . Adelaide, will you get Rachel to her chamber? She is overwrought."

"I am not overwrought. I am in perfect control. It is you who—"

People were buzzing around me, hustling me away toward the steps. Afraid I would strike the hateful woman, I make no doubt. I was still protesting when we reached my own bedchamber. I rushed inside, slammed the door on Dacey, whose persistent misunderstanding made me frantically angry. I threw the bolt and then rushed to the balcony windows just as I was, disheveled, in my night-rail.

Thank God I would not have to go clear to the Merceria leather-worker's shop to find Livio. I had been at the window a couple of minutes when he appeared at the window directly across the canal. I saw his hand raised, pressed against the window. I did the same. Then I rushed to my armoire, took out a dark blue travel gown and petticoat, put them on, stepped into my walking slippers, laced them over my ankles and then, with a deep breath, I opened the balcony doors.

There, far below me, was the Turkish mute, now walking up to the foot of the bridge and back, obviously chilled and probably bored by his inaction. I made motions, wild but silent, so that the moonlight gleaming on my hands and face caught the Turk's attention. I made frantic gestures, motioning to him, calling upon him in dumbshow.

He looked up at me, clearly confused. Then, just as I was

ready to give up in despair, he bundled his jacket closer around himself and hurried across the bridge in great strides toward the palazzo. Good!

Meanwhile, I must see that he did not catch me here. I unbolted the door as quietly as possible and looked out. The hall was silent, the candle flickering as if burned low. I hurried to the circular steps that were open at the top to the night sky. I had guessed correctly. The Turk would take the servants' stairs. In a minute or so I had reached the ground level where the servants had evidently completed their work of cleaning up after the gaming party, and various ghostly objects remained carefully shielded by holland covers. I had to study each of them for several seconds before deciding that they were all inanimate and could not betray my presence.

There was a light burning somewhere on this floor, providing me with a dim but adequate illumination. By this time the Turk must have left the ground floor. It would ruin everything if I met him now. I made my way through the doors that opened upon the water steps. Then—I gasped with terror when a hand reached out of the darkness to touch mine. It took an endless moment before I recognized it as Livio's.

"Thank God!" I whispered. "It is you." And then I was briefly enveloped in Livio's arms, half-smothered by his black travel cloak. "I must get away today." I whispered then. "She gave me laudanum in my wine tonight. The maid drank some. If I had drunk the entire glass, I should have died."

"That creature!" he muttered, his hands closing painfully around me. "I thought we had her when she took money from me . . . But your arrival precipitated matters, and now she has all she needs, she and that gang of cutthroats. Come along with me, darling. Now! We can't afford to leave you in that house for another day."

I wanted to go with him. I intended to go, at least in a very short while, when I was sure about Father's safety. But I must be assured of that first. "Don't you see? Father's life is the last obstacle. I couldn't stand to see anything happen to him now, after all we had both suffered, he and I, in being apart. I couldn't stand it! And to gain control of his estate and mine, she must first be rid of him. We must find a way to get him out. Mira's gang won't give him up just because we knock on the door and ask."

"They will surrender him up to a detachment from the French Army," he said grimly.

"But how can you be sure? They will arrest him—they will put Father in prison. Or worse."

He looked down at me with that compassionate, almost sad expression I had observed in his eyes on other occasions and which had always puzzled me.

"I promise you: if, after he has been questioned, you still wish to save him—"

"Of course I do."

"Then he shall have an amnesty."

I raised my head, not so much suspicious as confused. "How can you do that? An Italian. A Venetian like you."

He gazed at me. I remember how very slowly I began to release myself from the warmth and safety and tenderness of his embrace.

"Who are you?" I managed to ask, finally, my lips dry and my whole body stiffening for the blow, the answer.

It was as if he wanted to spare me. He did not look frightened, or angry, or alarmed, but tender, as if he wished he might spare me. Before he could prey upon my sympathy, I went on in a ragged, harsh voice, "You are as bad a traitor to your country as any of them. You—a Venetian born! Tell me whom you really serve!"

He put a hand out, slowly, as if he knew it would be rejected. Before he spoke, I understood why I had always felt that compassion and the deadly unknown in his eyes. For me, as for the others who thought they knew him, "Messire Livio" did not actually exist.

"I am not a Venetian born, Rachel, so I have not betrayed my own people. My name is Marcus Livio. I was born in Ajaccio, Corsica, twenty-eight years ago, the same year as my general. That makes us both Frenchmen, by one year. I have never served any country but my own, which is France. And our war is with the Austrians. Not the Venetians. You must remember, sweetheart, as a French citizen yourself, that the Austrians attacked us. We did not begin this war. And we do not need the conquest of Venice. We want the Serenissima neutral, as she is now. A buffer state, if you will. But ruled by her own people. Not by the Austrians. Have you ever heard of a double-spy?"

I hated the word. "You are a *double-spy?*"

"To serve my own country, I constructed a background, a past that made the Council of Ten hire me as their catchpole, their spy. And I discovered that the Ten would rather sell out the Serenissima to the Austrian Empire than permit free elections by the citizens of Venice. I have not betrayed Venice. It is the Ten who have—"

I thought of the others, the Englishmen, Fortman-Truscott and my Father; the woman, Mira Teotochi Carewe, who might be any nationality. I despised them for their treason and in this moment of anguish and shock I wanted to despise Livio. For whatever his reasons, however loyally he served his true country, he was, by his own admission, a double-spy. A man who would not hesitate to pretend to love me if that would achieve his end . . . No! I believed he must love me. Yet, as I now realized, he was a threat to my Father's life. From the first moment I saw him spying on this house from the bridge outside, he must have been the enemy of all within it. Since Father was the head of the house, Father must be his prime object. But Livio was too clever for me and his influence over my senses was too great. I had to dissemble.

I felt for my handkerchief, found one in his hand, and tried to patch up the damage of my tears the while I smiled faintly at Livio and lied. "I think I understand. But I will go only on one condition. You must promise me you will intercede with your General Bonaparte for Father's safety."

He looked so relieved, to touchingly glad at my apparent surrender, that I wanted to break down and confess the truth, that I too could play his game of dissimulation. I too could pretend. And without those silly, disfiguring spectacles he so often wore in his masquerade. Before I could draw away, he kissed me lightly yet tenderly, on my lips, which quivered nervously at his touch, for I wanted him as I have never wanted anything in my life before.

"Dearest," he said urgently, "you cannot go back into that place. You would never get out."

"I escaped from your lodgings," I reminded him, and saw his rueful smile. But then I added, "I can't leave Dacey!" I knew it was Father I must save, but clearly, Livio would not take him too; so I used poor Dacey as my excuse. Livio might be the man I loved, but that must end now—else he would destroy Father. I did not believe him for a minute when he spoke of an amnesty. He was a bloody Revolutionist.

"Can you count upon her keeping the secret of your escape?"

I knew I could not. She had been too badly taken in by Mira. But it did not matter. I must save Father, even at the cost of betraying Livio. I must convince Father that he must come with me and send for Mira afterward; that she was perfectly safe, being Italian. Unless he knew, as I suspected, that she was Austrian-born. . . .

"Dacey must come with me," I insisted.

"Very well."

"After Dacey and I escape without being seen, what then? The Turk will have roused everyone out to find you when they realize what has happened."

He shook my hand a little as he made rapid plans, and a part of me wanted to hold his touch forever, but the sterner part reminded me of my duty to Father.

"After their revels, they will sleep late, despite of the Turk's excitement. But you are right. After they have searched for you, the Turk will come out again, and this time they will undoubtedly remember that loft across the canal. Can you start walking toward the Merceria early this morning? I will be there, at the leather-worker's shop. After that, you must trust me." He put his hands on my shoulders, turned me to face him, and I found his warm, dark gaze hard to resist.

I managed to utter only a half lie. "If—if you will help me about Father . . . afterward."

"Your Father—" He broke off.

"But you will help him? You promised!" It was the kind of plea he would expect of me.

He was going to say something. I was sure of it. Some ghastly new confession. Probably that he could not save Father, after all. Instead, after an instant, he said, "Very well then. Now, *chérie,* will you meet me as soon as possible at the shop? Simply pretend you are going for a stroll. Take nothing. If you fail to get away, drop something onto your balcony. Some piece of furniture. Books. Something I can see from across the canal. If necessary, I will create a diversion and get you out."

I could afford to promise! But it was not a promise I intended to keep. . . . He kissed me again. This time, though I despised my own weakness, I responded with all the desperate longing that I felt for him, knowing it was very likely the last time we would ever meet.

"Be—careful," I warned him as he looked around and then, with a wave and that warm smile I loved so much, seemed to be absorbed into the darkness.

I went inside to betray him and his mission to my father. It was that, or the inevitable; to have Livio and his Army win, and destroy my father instead. I went quietly up to Father's suite of rooms, tried the door of his sitting room, and, as I only half believed my luck, found it open under my touch.

He was sitting up in his big armchair before the fire, trying vainly to work up a bigger flame with half-burned kindling and some old papers. He did not seem in the least surprised to see me. He looked around, complaining vaguely, "It is so cold! So very cold here. Could you start up the fire for me, my dear?"

"Of course, Father. Let me help you." I went over and knelt to blow on the little flame, and it caught at last. Father put his frail hands out, but instead of holding them to the flame, he caressed my hair. "You are being very good to me. Better than I deserve."

"Nonsense." There were tears in my eyes and I had to clear my throat to reply but I managed briskly, "You and I are going to run away and go where it will be warm, and you need not worry. Not ever again. I don't know how we will manage it. But we will. Through the Venetian government, I think."

He looked up at me, so trusting, so eager. "But how, my dear? Nothing would give me more pleasure. But how? We have nothing to make them help us. And they may find out things. Bad things."

"No, Papa. I have a secret we can use." I broke off, sickened by my own words, but the sight of my father, so frail and needing me, made me go on stiffly, unemotionally. "They have hired a French spy who is working in the Inquisitor's Office itself. For that secret, they will certainly give us our freedom."

He shook his head slowly. "How can we tell such a lie? We must have proof. They will demand proof."

"Let them find it at the leather-worker's shop in the Merceria. A French spy: Marcus Livio. Now, Papa, you must get warm and then you must dress and we will escape to the Doges' Palace and see the Grand Inquisitor."

Gradually color began to reappear in his face, behind that fragile, aged flesh. "A little more warmth first, my child. Just a little more. Ah! That is better." He brushed aside the brocaded bedrobe he wore. Under it was his wedding suit, the black satin breeches, the black silk stockings. But his feet in their stockings were surprisingly small.

I stared at them and him, remembering the old days, the days of my childhood. The long walks with my father, the way he had taken great strides in those large boots of his. Large because his feet were the large feet of a man used to the out-of-doors.

Large—like those boots that Mira had discarded in the room up on the second storey. Like those boots she had later found it necessary to discard before I became suspicious. Because, of course, this man who was so like my Father in every way could not wear my Father's boots.

I backed away from him. He looked up at me, puzzled, almost hurt, I thought. Poor man . . . The horror of my discovery, and with it the realization that I had betrayed Livio, numbed me. I could feel only pity for this man.

"I must go," I said, and repeated it with dry lips. "I must go."

"Please, don't leave me," he murmured, and extended one of those wasted hands. "I am so afraid!"

"Later," I found myself saying, without knowing what I meant or what were my plans. "I must go now." And I ran from the room.

Someone in the gallery opened a door, peered out at me. I ran past, not caring. I stumbled, heard another door open, and saw the Turk standing before the door to the steps leading down. I found the servants' stairs and ran up toward my own chamber and Dacey's. "I must think . . . I must plan," I kept telling myself. But I was numb. My brain felt numb.

CHAPTER FIFTEEN

DACEY'S DOOR WAS CLOSED, of course, but it might have yielded to my pressure. I did not use it. Livio was a double-spy. Obstinately, I believed he loved me—yet I had betrayed him. . . . My Father was not my Father . . . Oh God! What had really happened to my Father? And Dacey must have betrayed me, too, just by believing a little more than I had believed in Lady Mira and Sir Maitland Carewe!

I made my way to my bedchamber, closed the door behind me, and went to the long balcony windows. Livio was no longer in the building across the canal. He was gone, as he had said he would be. He was with the French, not the Venetians or the English.

What had he said to me? *You are a French citizen.* . . . But I was not. *Citoyenne* Rachel Carewe? No! Yet, what was I? No longer English. Not Venetian. What, then? My life in France had brought me far beyond the Reactionary world I had known in my childhood, the ignorant, horribly privileged and one-sided world I had glimpsed in Venice. Repeatedly during the last few days I discovered that I had gone too far with the new French Republic ever to return to the world I saw around me, the old world of the eighteenth century.

Livio . . . Livio . . . I had betrayed him to Father! No. Not to Father—to the poor creature so like and yet so unlike him. I did not know what to do. Surely that poor, weak, cowardly old man who was not my father would ignore what I had said about Livio, what he is and where to find him. . . .

I knew as I looked far out over the canal from my balcony that if I had it to do over again, I would not betray Livio. But maybe that man who looked like Father would forget what I had said; perhaps he had not really heard me at all. I prayed that he had not. I looked hard in every direction but saw nothing, not even a gondola to dapple the dark waters of the canal. And Livio was gone. Out of my life forever.

Ironically enough, as a French citizen, I myself might be safe if Livio was right about the French Army treaty with the Doge to set up a democratic government in Venice. But as for Livio, in the meanwhile there was what the Inquisitor's Office must call the crime of double-spying, the guilt of Marcus Livio. Corsican officer of the French Republic One and Indivisible. A terrifying title to anyone as reactionary and oligarchic as the Grand Inquisitors.

I could not go to the Inquisitors for help. Nor could I remain here in the palazzo where I might be poisoned at any moment. But there was one way in which I could right the wrong I had done to Livio. I could try to go and warn him before it was too late. I looked around at the brightening sky. Dawn had come. Never had sunrise been more welcome to me. I looked straight down at the water steps. No one from the palazzo was stationed there, or around the little bridge to the east.

I went quietly out into the hall and to the open stairs. No one was about. I moved down step by step, passed the door to the first-storey gallery, and went on. If the Turkish mute was still standing before that door, on the gallery side, I could not tell. I only prayed he would not hear the faint scrape of my walking slippers upon the stone. Once more I went through the long, high vestibule to the water doors. Curious, I thought, that not a soul was abroad, not even the servants who would normally be about at dawn, cleaning or preparing the trays of *cioccolata* for the guests. I told myself this slackness must be due to the festivities of the wedding.

There was a huge bolt for the doors but I found it shot back just as it had been in the night, when I went out to speak with Livio. I let myself out and stood on the water steps for a minute, assuring myself that no one from the palazzo was in sight. Across on the narrow quai a man in a dark smock over striped, loose pantaloons, was sweeping the cobblestones. He paid no attention to me. I went to the bridge, crossed over and began to run, passing him rapidly, holding onto my high-crowned bonnet whose ribbons caught in the bright morning air. The cleaner gave me a startled glance but I ignored him.

Breathless, I came to the Merceria. Already there were numbers of workers passing, and an occasional beggar propped against the high, windowless walls, watching me with lackluster eyes. A glazier passed me going toward the shops of San Marco, carrying a great rectangle of glass in its frame, on his broad back. I began to run again, along that tangled, narrow *calle* which was the most important shopping street in Venice.

As I made a sudden, right-angle turn around the corner of a forbidding gray palazzo, I saw the leather-worker's shop on my left, looking harmless and silent, deserted. I was enormously relieved until I reached the shop itself. The shutters were all closed, as I might have expected, but the shutter nearest me was rattled suddenly, almost in my face. I leaped back, suddenly aware than an eye was regarding me with a startling intensity from between the wooden slats.

I turned, half inclined to run from the spot, when the door opened and a tall, handsomely uniformed man strode out to hail me. The rising sun glistened on the sleek head of Captain Pietro Dandolo. He flashed a brilliant smile of greeting. And triumph?

"Good morning, lovely Rachel. You have come to receive our thanks in your own delightful person; isn't it so?"

"Why—" I moistened my dry lips, my stiff, terrified lips, and went on hoarsely, "—why are you here? What are you doing in a shop like this? Oh, of course! You are here to buy some leather-work?"

"Please, Rachel, dearest Bellissima, no jests at this hour." He was striding toward me, holding out both hands. "You are angry because we have not yet thanked you for your service to the Serenissima."

"I don't understand a word you are saying. What am I to be thanked for?"

He spread wide his long arms. "But for informing us as to the identity of the French spy, Marcus Livio. And even for informing us as to the place of his assignations—this leather-working shop." He smiled, the false tenderness that sickened me. "Indeed! But for these important developments, I should be at my rest in your new Mama's house, sleeping off the effects of that delightful wedding."

I backed away but he came on, relentlessly, his smile never varying. "How did you ever manage to learn his secret? We thought him quite innocent; he has been successful this age and more. We thought him an absurd little catchpole for the Inquisitor. Who would have believed that ghastly fellow with the spectacles could be so important to the French Army? He very nearly ruined all our plans."

"Your plans to turn Venice over to sack and pillage by the Austrian Army?"

The smile became more fixed, less spontaneous.

"Ah! You have been told that absurd story. What an unwise chattering little female you are! And so lovely, too." He sighed, a great, false sigh. When he would have touched me, I pulled away, revolted by his nearness, his smile.

"You are talking perfect nonsense, you know," I said, when I could speak, for the horror enveloped and smothered me. "I came on a walk to the Rialto Bridge, and you stop me, make accusations, and talk rubbish—"

"And you did not betray your lover to the old gentleman, your Father, last night? Or should I say—early this morning?"

"I have no lover. And that old man is not—" I recollected myself, "—he is not 'the old gentleman.' That is very rude." I was doing my best to backtrack from my original anger and terror. But to pretend now that it was all pique, all a silly morning walk . . . I was not so good an actress, and apparently he knew it.

"Rachel, you are foolish. Your tender heart does you credit, but does not say much for your intellect. If you had not confessed the French spy's identity to your Father, how do you think we were able to seize him and to take him prisoner, him and his precious leather-worker?"

"It is a lie! You made my—my Father tell you a lie! How would I know that Messire Livio is a French spy? If, indeed, he is, which I strongly misdoubt."

I saw a pair of powerful men, the Inquisitors' secret police of Venice, come out of the shop looking inhuman and chill as they regarded me. "What have you done with him?" I screamed. "What have you done?"

And I saw them look at me and each other with contempt. I controlled myself with an effort as the *sbirri* went their way and Captain Dandolo took my hand in easy command. I did not resist. The repeated shocks of the night were as nothing compared to this—the horror of Livio's danger, as a result of my betrayal. Was there any way I could erase this ghastly Judas trick of mine? I could deny it. I must keep on denying, keep saying that "my Father" had made up the whole tale. Of course, Livio had already been found at the leather-worker's shop, so there could be no question but that the information about him was correct.

"I will escort you home," the Captain explained politely when I tried to pull away from his grasp.

"I don't wish to go home. Not that the palazzo is my home! I wish to lay my evidence before the Grand Inquisitors."

"Your evidence?"

"That it is all a lie. I never said Messire Livio was a spy. Besides, if the French Army will be signing a treaty with Venice in a few days, I should think you would not dare to convict someone you accuse of being a French spy."

The Captain's unpleasant smile broadened. "My dear little *Française,* have you never heard of provocation? The garroting of a Frenchman close in the councils of General Bonaparte is a provocation sure to provoke reprisals."

"The reprisals being that the Venetians, under your persuasion, will open their doors—and canals—to the Austrians!"

"You are not as innocent in these matters as I thought. The best hope we have against the influence of a spineless Doge is to provoke the French against the Serenissima. And with your betrayal of Messire Livio you have provided us with that provocation. For which, many thanks."

I tried to recover the lost ground, to retreat, as it were, into an ignorant stranger who had blundered in upon this palace of intrigue and betrayal, but I knew it was too late. I was sick with worry about Father—my real Father—but I found myself thinking constantly of Livio. Father had been the past. I had tried again to love, certainly to compassionate, that old, frail man in the palazzo—but Livio was the present. Livio, as I knew now, was the dearest person in my life. And I had betrayed him.

I had a dozen thoughts of breaking from the Captain, running away, trying to reach the Doges' Palace or the prison behind the palace, but it would be stupid. The two *sbirri* were marching ahead of us now, and the Captain's grasp was relentless. Much better to play a part, try to fool them all as they had so bitterly fooled me. I was aching to ask what they had done to my father. But that would be to sign my death warrant, I was sure, and it would gain me nothing, since they were hardly likely to tell me the truth.

He is dead. I knew it must be true. . . .

The anguish of his loss was compounded by my pity for the unfortunate old gentleman I had accepted as my Father. The resemblance had been startling. But then, it may have been strongly aided by my absence from him for eight years, and my knowledge of his critical illnesses. . . . And one of those illnesses, I knew now, must have been fatal. Since the conspirators never knew of my escape from the guillotine, in all likelihood Father had died believing Mother and I were gone as well.

What was it the boy from the embassy had said during the wedding ceremony? *I would never have known him.* . . . And even to me, his frailty had been shocking. My own Father, the man I had known and loved as a child, would never have allowed a woman like Mira Teotochi to reorganize his life and to order him about like a slave. I should have seen at once. But the years had been so long, in some ways an entire lifetime, that we had been apart.

And what was to become of that poor old man who had tried so valiantly to play the part of my Father?

The immediate and most frightful danger, however, was to Livio. There must be some way, some effort I could make, to save him. As I walked with Captain Dandolo, I made an enormous attempt to remove all my passionate concern from my voice as I asked, "Would it not be more politic if you used Messire Livio as a hostage for your own safety from the French? It is stupid to murder hostages."

"Execute is the word you are seeking, Bellissima."

"Well, then, isn't it more clever to hold hostages than to—to—"

"Strangle them. That is the customary method of disposing of spies." He stopped and turned.

I was startled by his action and nearly fell into him before stopping on the edge of the canal that ran past the palazzo. "Do not use that word—strangle! Let us think of something pleasant. I can help you all." The idea came to me suddenly and I poured it out in desperate anxiety to gain his good will. "My Mother's estate, for example."

I could not mistake the gleam in those opaque olive eyes as they narrowed in suspicion, and in thought. "I do not understand. What is this about your estate?"

"Mother's estate," I corrected him, with a sweetness that made me feel ill. "Think how simple it would be, to assume all rights to my mother's estate without being forced—you will pardon me—to deal through my beautiful new Mama."

This gave him something to think about. I hoped devoutly that it might drive a wedge between him and his fellow conspirators, Mira, Fortman-Truscott, and possibly the old gentleman I had grown to care for as my Father. We were approaching the palazzo, and I did not want him to catch a glimpse of Mira before he had thought over my appeal to his greed. I was still more terrified of Mira Teotochi "Carewe" than of any of the other conspirators.

I was also thinking frantically of the fact that my father's estate and fortune, as well as Mama's, was being enjoyed by villains, traitors and murderers. Yet I was willing to give it all to these creatures if I could ransom Livio. My Father must, almost certainly, be dead—but perhaps I could make a legal arrangement, and buy Livio's freedom and that of the frightened old man who had, to the best of his feeble ability, enacted my Father's role. Yes, I thought, he was so frightened, so pitiful, I would make the poor old man's safety a part of my dealings with them.

I said, with a ghastly cheerfulness, "Even a Republican government set up by the French would be forced to recognize a paper signed by me, properly witnessed, giving to you my Father's estate and my Mother's."

"Why your Father's? he asked sharply.

I shrugged. "The old man is feeble. His brain may fail him. And you. Would it not be better to be assured of the estate legally? Think—if you could better prove your right to the estate than Mira could prove hers?"

Recalled to himself and to my meaning, he said, as we walked over the little bridge to the palazzo, "What you imply is singularly unpleasant. Your father is in fair health, in consideration of his age. And as for your Mother's estate, it will go to your husband to cosset and care for in your name. Your husband, Bellissima . . . Now there is a matter where there is room for discussion. Think about it. We are at the palazzo."

I was so enraged, so haunted by the events of the night and the morning that I did not even reply. I rushed inside and slammed the doors in his face. I had scarcely turned around when I found myself the cynosure of innumerable

eyes. There must have been a dozen of the wedding guests
staring at me in various stages of dress and from various
corners of the vestibule.

"What is it? What has happened?" Even as I asked the
question, vaguely addressing them en masse and blinking at
all the shadowy faces after the bright sunlight on the canal,
I did not really expect an answer. They went on gaping,
mouths open, but incapable of uttering a sound. I recognized
one or two. Surely, that was Messire Fortman-Truscott over
by the cross-foyer and the door to the circle steps. He was
staring at me like the others but he looked less stupid, more
sinister, even though he, like some of the others, was still in
bedrobe and absurd nightcap. Obviously, the palazzo had been
visited by calamity. I had no idea what that calamity might be
but it could not equal my anguished thoughts.

What was happening to Livio at this moment in the prison
called the Wells, those cold, wet dungeon cells open to the
waters of the canal at the city's frequent high tides? How long
did they hold spies in prison before they . . . strangled them?
Did the Inquisitors' Office torture its victims first? Oh, Livio
. . . Livio . . .

I made my way between staring, idiot faces to the door
opening upon the stairway. The Turkish mute was on the
steps, with his gypsy mother, the cook, beside him, her earrings glistening in the light as I opened the door. I screamed.
The Turk grimaced. I think it was meant for a smile. He
walked beside me up the steps clear to my chamber, leaving
his mother behind, chuckling in a senseless way. He opened
the door for me. I was terrified that he would follow me
inside but he left me there. It was not until I turned to face
the room's interior that I saw Mira Teotochi standing there
in severe and funereal black. Dacey was with her, her eyes
swollen with tears, her face unnaturally pale. Dacey was not
so providentially dressed in black. She wore one of her
pink gowns, heavily decked with bows. But her manner to me
was excessively strange.

She hurried toward me, enclosed me in her arms and
sobbed, "Darling child! Why?" And then she added an odd,
disquieting whisper, "Forgive me! It is for your sake."

Over her head I looked at Mira whose basilisk eyes
watched us while she seemed absolutely motionless.

"Why——what? What is this about? Dacey, stop crying and
tell me."

Dacey tried to pull herself together, and between sniffs

and sobs she told me. "Your Father has been—is dead."

"Oh, no! That poor, tortured old man!" Actually, his death was not surprising to me. Regrettable, but not surprising. He had been so frail, so helpless, and I was sure he suffered bitterly from his part in the deadly masquerade.

"Poor old man!" Dacey shivered, aghast. "You can talk that way about your own dear Papa? What has come over you?"

I looked at Mira Teotochi. I surprised the faintest flicker of expression—apprehension, or surprise—cross her flawless face. I said, "We will talk about my feelings later, Dacey. How did he happen to die? Was it his heart?"

Though I spoke to Dacey, I stared hard at Mira. There was another meaning in my voice as I repeated, *"How did my Father die, Miss Teotochi?"*

"I don't understand you at all, Rachel," Dacey fumbled on. "How can you talk like this? And so rude to dear Lady Carewe. It's all the fault of that dreadful Revolutionary upbringing you received in that heathen France."

"But Lady Carewe understands, doesn't she?" I asked, speaking directly to Mira who recovered with admirable promptness from her first surprise at my attack.

"I fear we all understood, my child. My unfortunate husband died of laudanum poisoning."

I was shaken by that and though I hated her knowing it, she was much too clever to miss it.

"Laudanum!" I repeated, startled. "Like the maid."

Mira and Dacey exchanged glances. Dacey patted me anxiously. "Yes, dear. Like the maid in your room. Was that—were you only testing it?"

"Testing it! Are you mad? Don't you realize that laudanum was meant for me?"

Dacey let out a shriek. "Not—dearest, were things so bad you were driven to suicide? Believe me, things might have been straightened out. It was not hopeless. Mira and I—there are ways. You will not pay the supreme penalty! Mira says your mental state is the explanaion."

"The explanation of what? I tell you I did not intend to kill myself." Bewildered, feeling the trickery at work, I tried to fight it in the worst possible way, with passionate denials. "That glass of mulled wine was intended for me, but I did not order it. It was meant to poison me. Or if not, to connect me with the death of the man you call my Father. Was it not, Miss Teotochi?"

"*What* is that?" Dacey sniffed mightily. "I can't understand anything you say. Your Father is dead and you were the last to see him—my dear Rachel, dozens of people saw you run from your papa's room, so angry! Crying out things against him. And then . . . he was dead. And you know you did put the landanum in your mulled wine last night. To make you sleep, I daresay. . . ."

She clapped her stout little hands excitedly and turned to Mira Teotochi. "But that explains it! She never meant to kill her poor Papa. Somehow, he drank a glass she had intended for herself. To help her sleep."

I said, "This is the purest rubbish! Would I prepare for myself a draught of a drink strong enough to kill me? I was *not* the last to see my Father—I mean—that old man!" Yet I saw it all now, from my arrival in Venice until this moment, as one long, single-minded plot to destroy me; I also saw that it just might work!

Dacey cried, "Rachel! Not '*the old man*'—your very own loving Papa!"

Ignoring her, I spoke to Mira. "How you must be enjoying this! Did you kill him because he no longer served your purpose?"

"Come, Adelaide," Mira said calmly. "The Turk will guard the unfortunate child. Everyone knows she was the last to visit her father in his sitting room. Everyone saw her leave in that dreadful state of violence against him. The Serenissima takes a severe view of that worst of crimes—parricide."

Dacey tried to reach me again—doubtless to whisper some other absurdity—but failing, she let herself be taken from me, weeping, protesting, sniffling. I knew there would be no earthly purpose served in my screaming about my innocence. I would tell my story to the Red Inquisitor, that fearsome, gray-faced creature in his blood-red robes. Surely there was some way by which I could convince the Venetians of my innocence and point out to them—yes, offer them a deal—for Livio's life. I would point out how grateful Livio's General Bonaparte would be. And conversely, I could show them how stupid it would be to destroy Livio and me, two French citizens, when the French would be joining Venice's pitiful defense Army in a few days to offer a bulwark against the Austrians. And I could inform them of the Austrian conspiracy here at the palazzo. That ought to count for something.

But all the same, while I waited to be arrested, not quite

believing it would happen, I walked up and down my room, went to the balcony, saw that two of the *sbirri* guarded the water steps beneath my balcony. No hope there. I went to the door, looked out into the hall. The Turk stood with his back to me. I wondered if I could crash a silver basin or a small statue over his strange, hairless skull. I was perfectly inclined to do so. Unfortunately, across the hall there were three of the wedding guests, fully dressed this time, buzzing among themselves about me, as I discovered when I listened to them speaking in Italian. They were watching for me as people watch the poor mad creatures of Bedlam in my native England.

"What a monster!" one of the women exclaimed. "To kill her own father! I saw her in the night. Quite mad! Screaming through the halls about her hatred for the poor man—ah! There she is. Monster!"

I slammed the door shut, sickened by their suspicions, their eyes, their greedy pleasure at being witness to such a ghastly crime. While I stood in that bedchamber—I think it was a little over an hour—I kept asking myself what had happened to my Father, though I knew he must be dead. And when that thought proved too painful, I had my betrayal of Livio to haunt me.

Presently, when the morning sun was pouring in through the high balcony windows, the door opened. I stiffened, assumed a cold, masklike expression. Heads were peering in. Then they were thrust aside. Two of the *sbirri* stepped inside the door, one on either side, and between them Captain Dandolo strode in and saluted me smartly.

I said, "How curious! The Captain of the Port comes to escort a prisoner."

"It is a convenient title, Captain of the Port. I have others," he admitted, and offered his gloved hand to me. I rightly assumed that this gesture was less gallant than official and I permitted him to take my arm.

No one told me precisely where I was to go, whether I was to be interrogated or simply imprisoned; or, indeed, if I were to be given a trial at all. As the Captain escorted me out into the hall past endless staring faces, Dacey came fluttering toward us.

She threw her arms around me, sobbing, "Rachel, my poor child! I know you are innocent. I'll never stop until I prove it. I'll not rest until you are free, if I have to go to the French to do it." And then she murmured. "The Doge is seeing the envoy one day this week. Messire Livio told me last night. I will try to see them both."

"No!" I whispered, pretending to console her. "The Ten might find out and throw you into prison as well. They rule Venice, not Doge Manin."

With her arms around me, she whispered, "Doge Manin can still sign the treaty with the French. He has that power. I will tell the envoy about you and Messire Livio." And then, loudly moaning, "Oh, my poor child! We must do what we can."

"Thank you, Dacey dear." I hugged her, trying with an enormous effort not to break in front of those curious, greedy eyes.

But the truth was, even if the French envoy visited the Doge, he would have no way of knowing Livio and I were imprisoned. And Dacey was scarcely the kind of belligerent female to push her way past the guards to reach Doge Manin. Even if the Ten were loyal Venetians, they would never surrender to the rule of the people. They had held their secret power too long.

The two officers came to separate us. Dacey was led away, helpless and protesting. The last words I heard from her did not reassure me: "We mean to have you freed. I swear we shall. Lady Carewe agrees with me that there must be a way. She will find it. Never fear . . ."

We passed others on our way to the gondola below the water steps but I did not see or identify the faces. I remember only that the wind had swept the sky, which was a vivid blue, but the sun felt less than warm on my hands as I was helped into the gondola. The opposite side of the canal was swarming with curious spectators. I sat very still, trying not to move a muscle in my face. I hoped they did not guess my hands were twisting in my lap.

CHAPTER SIXTEEN

BY THE SECOND DAY I came to know when it was noon. Even in the stony depths of the cells behind the Doges' Palace, I knew that much. There were the great, clanging gongs in the Piazza San Marco nearby. Those were the hours, between ten in the morning and midday, that I looked forward to. It was then that daylight poured into the cell across the narrow, scummed canal flowing past my windows. I had been placed here before ten o'clock in the morning. Under the benign influence of the sun I could feel encouragement about my situation, about our imminent rescue by someone— the French?—and the outcome of our civil trials. Livio's and mine.

For there *would* be trials, surely! They could not condemn Livio without calling me to repeat the betrayal I had made to my "father." Or were spies simply executed and buried?

Those scarlet-clad officers of the Serene Republic of Venice who executed murderers by garroting them . . . the Stranglers. I tried to close my mind to the picture of such an ignoble and hideous death for Livio and me, and without ever being allowed to see each other again.

I prayed a good deal during those first prison hours, often by rote and repetition, over and over, but not to the God of my childhood. The Revolution had removed that God. I could never recover Him again. I prayed instead to my more immediate Father, who was dead, surely. I prayed to him, Sir Maitland Carewe, who had been British Ambassador Plenipotentiary to the Court of the Serenissima. Absurdly, to the man I was accused of murdering.

"Papa, please help me, you who died alone and secretly, far from those who loved you. You, of all people, must know I am not guilty. . . ."

The prison authorities were kind enough to send me the petit point work for a firescreen that they must have found among my belongings. Of course, the design was meant for Papa's study, so there was no point in doing it now. Nevertheless, I worked on it briefly, until the light faded each day. It pleased the turnkey who brought it and who kept passing the grated window, smiling at me as I worked, and nodding, "Good, good, Madonna." But he would say nothing about any other prisoners here in the dungeons below the level of Venice.

When the light faded and I had to put away my petit point, that meant it was afternoon, with night to follow. The first night had been frightful. Even the daily candle they left me would not drive the rats away—huge, wild, long-tailed creatures as big as a cat and far more fierce. I shivered and concentrated on thinking about the two hours of sunlight which would return tomorrow morning, if the day was fair. I had learned that anticipation exceeded realization.

And sometimes it kept me from wondering if Livio was somewhere nearby in these dungeons, if he had been tortured, or if he had already been executed.

The turnkey brought my dinner tray at precisely the moment darkness settled over the narrow canal beyond my window, as if he wished to take my mind off the night to come. My meals were paid by the widow of Sir Maitland, he told me, reminding me without saying so that I ought to be grateful to her.

I averted my mind's eye from the memory of my arrest, and the fact that I had not been formally charged, but my imagination peopled all the shadowed corners of my cell with the movement of the Procurator's blood-red robes, his long, bony fingers like blanched spiders playing over the hem of his sleeve as he ordered me to the cell and would not listen to my pleas for a trial, a hearing.

Each time the turnkey assured me of my Father's widow's "interest" in me, it was on the tip of my tongue to issue a fiery denial, and an accusation; but this would mean nothing to a poor turnkey, who meant well, so I only repeated my request to see and confront my accusers, and the turnkey nodded, looked surprisingly sympathetic, and then went away. I heard his wooden sabots for a long time until he had left the stone corridor and was gone. Then I went back to my thoughts as I ate.

Some time later, having prolonged the eating of some ambrosially light little cakes sent over from the Caffé Florian, I heard the nerve-wracking rattle of the ancient cell door and did not look up, knowing this would be the turnkey, come to fetch the supper tray. It was therefore a frightening instant when I reached down to pick up my fallen napkin and saw the narrow-toed crimson slippers and the full-skirted crimson robe of an Inquisitor. I tried as rapidly as possible to recover some kind of dignity and courage.

"Good evening, Messire Adorno. Am I to be hounded even at night?" I wanted to say sharply that I thought I was living in the enlightened eighteenth century, not in the Dark Ages! But the pale, inhuman look of the Inquisitor, accentuated by his crimson judicial hat, made him look uncomfortably like some blood-stained apparition from those same Dark Ages.

"Madonna Rachel Carewe, citizeness of the French Republic, you will come with me."

I stood up so rapidly I overturned my chair, the only good article of furniture in the cell. I was shivering, but I hoped Messire Adorno, the Inquisitor, could not guess the extent of my terror. "Am I being taken to my . . . execution, Messire? Can you tell me—may I speak for Messire Marcus Livio? I lied about him. I lied!"

"Come," he repeated in that same glacially impersonal voice, indicating with the faintest gesture of a bejeweled forefinger.

"It can't be," I told myself desperately. "It can't be that they will strangle me for a hideous crime I could never have committed, and no one will stop them!"

I expected to find two of the Inquisitor's half-naked torturers out in the damp stone passage, but found myself walking up a flight of time-worn, uneven steps alone with Messire Adorno. Gradually, I lost my freezing terror. Whatever the Serene Republic's ultimate plans for me, they certainly would not execute me tonight with so little ceremony.

A minute or two after I had decided this, I found myself stepping out into the blessed night air, crossing a narrow canal over a humped bridge in company with the Inquisitor.

"Where are we going?" I asked finally, having recovered enough courage to try to conceal my previous terror.

For the first time Messire Adorno's stern facade split into a thin smile, like a vein running across marble.

"A conversation, Madonna. A little conversation in my study."

The Inquisitor waved me into a narrow passage in the fine palace opposite my prison, and I soon found myself ushered into a small room lined to the high, vaulted ceiling with books, and sparsely furnished with a huge fifteenth-century table and several equally impressive high-backed chairs. A gaunt, priestly looking young man, also in crimson, sat at the table with a book as big as a ledger before him and his lean hands busy carving a fresh point on his pen. He looked up at me, appearing to my frightened glance like a death's head.

"And now, please to be seated, Madonna Carewe," said the Inquisitor, just a shade less icily than was his habit. "I think we may spare you more indignity in certain circumstances."

"Circumstances?" I echoed, obeying him by dropping into the chair farthest from the skull-faced secretary. It was just as well the order had been given, because my legs were shaking, and weak as water. "If I can—in any way—"

"You may recount to us once more every action of yours since your arrival in Venice to join your Father, the late British Ambassador."

"Yes, sir. But I am afraid it is not quite the story you expect. And afterward, will I still be released? I mean—am I to be released?"

"In custody."

I stiffened and sat up straight. "Into whose custody?"

"After certain considerations, we will provide you with a—guardian. You must understand that in view of the heinous crime of which you are accused, you will be, in a sense, her prisoner."

I moistened my lips. "*Her* prisoner?"

"In a manner of speaking. A gracious gesture on the lady's part. She will keep you safe until your recovery. . . . Madonna! This is not amusing."

I suppose my peals of laughter must have startled Messire

Adorno and the secretary more than any amount of tortured cries from their victims. They both stared at me, appalled.

I think I must have been hysterical. But it was so excessively funny! "I beg to contradict you, Messire. It is more amusing than you know. It was this gracious gesturing lady who committed the murder of that old man. It is this gracious, gesturing lady who had my real Father secretly buried and substituted this old man in his place, in order to manipulate him and the English government to please their Austrian allies. Mira Teotochi and the others in that household are Austrian spies!"

I saw the quick look exchanged between the Inquisitor and his secretary. I had the sudden, burning hope that they believed me, or at the least, wondered at my tale. And I went on pouring out the truth which sounded so improbable, even to me. "I wish to God I knew where they put my Father, what happened to him. He was very ill some time ago. That I know. But I believe he never recovered. Or else they murdered him as they murdered this poor fellow who took his place."

Messire Adorno caught his breath, moved his fingers nervously in their long crimson sleeves. Whatever he said, I could see he had been shaken by the vehemence of my accusations.

"Do we understand, Madonna—" He snapped his fingers at the open-mouthed, astonished secretary. "—kindly inscribe this—do we understand that you accuse another person of the murder of your esteemed Father?"

"That was not my Father," I said firmly.

Messire Adorno started to rise again, and sat abruptly. "Let us be certain we hear exactly what you wish to say. You deny that Sir Maitland Carewe was your Father?"

"Not at all. I say that poor old man at the palazzo who died of laudanum poisoning was not Sir Maitland."

"I see." Clearly, he did not see at all. In other circumstances I might have thought this entire misunderstanding was ludicrous. "Then who is he? Or who are you? You have admitted you are Rachel Carewe, have you not?"

"I am sure Your Excellency has my passport papers. They give my full description. I arrived here after having been separated from my Father for eight years." I went on to explain my Father's odd behavior, the efforts they had made to plant doubts of my own identity. "So that if I discovered the truth of the masquerade, I might be denied, even accused of masquerading as myself. They have also kept this old

man away from the secretariat at the British Embassy headquarters, so that no members of the clerical staff might recognize the substitution. I make no doubt that is why poor
Peregrine Watlink was killed. He knew my Father too well."

"You can swear to me that the dead man was not your
Father?"

"I swear it."

"And the members of the embassy could likewise recognize
the so-called substitution?"

"No longer—they are gone, I believe, like Mr. Watlink.
Except, of course, for Fortman-Truscott, the present First
Secretary, who is part of the conspiracy."

Messire smiled, an unpleasant, chilling smile. "I was expecting that. I am afraid you are outnumbered in your claim.
Would you care to change your story now?" He added on a
sudden persuasive note, "Why not explain the truth of the
affair? You were overpersuaded by that French scoundrel to
poison the British Ambassador. The Serenissima can understand that. A simple, lonely young Frenchwoman pursued
by one of her own countrymen, doubtless persuaded that her
lover would marry her if she obliged him by destroying the
British Ambassador, a great obstacle to French success."

I wanted very much to scream a denial but forced myself
to say calmly, "You are mistaken, Messire." And then, covering my throat with my hand to prevent the telltale pulse
from revealing my panic, I added, "If I may be permitted
to speak with Messire Livio, you will see that we are innocent
of anything to do with the death of that old man."

Much to my astonishment and overwhelming relief, the
Inquisitor agreed thoughtfully. "Something might be learned
from your meeting. God knows little has come from the spy,
though you yourself have proved more helpful, Madonna.
Yes. I would say a meeting may be in order."

So Livio was alive, at least! I was so grateful I thanked
aloud that God I forsworn long ago in the cell of the
Conciergerie. My limbs were so weak with the anticipation of
this moment, both the terror and the joy, that I grasped the
edges of the long table very hard with both hands while,
over my head, all arrangements were made to bring in
Political Prisoner Number 173.

The Inquisitor rang a small bell with one of those graceful
motions of the hand that I might have admired in other
circumstances. The order was given to two toughened, evil-
looking rogues, nude above the waist, whom I suspected to

be torturers, and they disappeared, their heavy sandals
noisily slapping the stone floor of the passage until they were
out of our hearing.

While we waited, the Inquisitor and the secretary ignored
me, speaking over my head. "Is it true, do you think, Messire
Adorno? His Serenity, the Doge, has made a commitment
that Venice will become a Republic with the protection of
the French?"

"We are a Republic now," the Inquisitor corrected him
coldly.

"Ay, but—a Republic with votes for the merchant class
and others, and the right of the mob to sit on the Council of
Ten? A true democracy?"

"A rule of the *canaille,* you mean? What is this world
coming to? Next, beggars and females will have the vote. That
is what comes of Revolutions and the like. A dangerous business, to put one's future in the hands of the populace."

The secretary persisted timidly, "But if the rumors are
true, would it not be wise to save the life of this French spy?"

Messire Adorno's bare palm hit the table so hard my own
hands jumped nervously. "No! *Per dìo!* No one has seen fit
to inform me of the plans and treaties made by His Serenity.
I am answerable only to the Council of Ten! Therefore I
shall set about my business as always. And that double-
dealing Bonapartist spy goes to the Stranglers, at dawn!"

"But if the French arrive, Messire, we will be answerable
for the life of their man."

"By then he will be dead. Nothing could matter less. The
French are a practical people."

"Oh, no!" I cried in panic. "Give him another day. He, at
least, was serving his own country, unlike those other spies,
Mira Teotochi and the Captain, who are Venetian citizens.
Her crime and the Captain's crime, those are greater—for
they have broken their oath of allegiance to the Serenissima."

The Inquisitor's thin upper lip curled. "Assuming that were
true, at the least they are on the side of lineage and aristocracy. Not the common clay. I might admire this French
spy's courage, but he is, after all, a Revolutionary!"

I looked at him in amazement. How curious, I thought,
that as I spent each day away from Paris, I grew more certain that my sympathies and my common sense called me
back to that very government I had sought to escape. I had
lived there too long. My future, if there had been one per-

mitted to me, would have been in Revolutionary France. I
no longer thought like the Inquisitor.

And then we heard footsteps in the passage and as my
heart raced, in my anxiety, Livio stepped into the room between the two guards. The passage had been ill-lighted and
he blinked momentarily, then looked around the room, saw
me, and smiled the special, warm, faintly sad smile I had
learned to love. Except that he was disheveled and his white
shirt dirty and bloodstained, he looked almost himself. His
black hair was tangled, matted, I thought, with blood, and I
shuddered. There was a curious red welt across his forehead
which showed plainly against his olive skin, and I guessed
that they had used a cord around his head, tightening it as a
method of torture.

I loved him all the more for the jaunty way he ignored
this painful wound and the pain his right hand and arm
must be giving him, because his hands were bound behind
him at the wrists and there were brown stains over the cuffs
and torn lace of his shirt. I tried to run to him but was
prevented by the Inquisitor's long arm.

Livio said, "I hope, Messieurs, you do not think this lady is
a bloodthirsty French assassin. She had not the least idea of
my true profession."

"Look here, rogue," said Messire Adorno sharply, "You
will have much ado defending yourself. I suggest you do not
waste the few precious minutes remaining to you in defending
a parricide."

"Nonsense," Livio persisted in his light, easy way, "we all
know the girl is being made a scapegoat so that household
can acquire her father's fortune."

"She was the last to see him alive, I remind you."

"Not at all." Livio took a step forward and his two guards
reached for him clumsily, but Messire Adorno, obviously
puzzled, waved them away. "What do you mean by that?"

"But I ask you to consider, Messire. Madonna Rachel went
to visit her Father—or him she thought to be her Father."

"Yes, yes. Get on."

"Just before his death, she visited her Father, and betrayed
my identity to him—"

"You admit it!"

Livio said impatiently, "Do you wish to carry on the inter-
rogation, Messire?"

"If you please . . . get on."

"Very well. Madona Rachel betrayed my true identity, and left the sitting room."

We were all watching him, puzzled. Messire Adorno urged. "And then?"

Livio ended, in pleasant triumph, "But you say that was the end. Madonna Rachel left the old gentleman, having betrayed me; and thereafter, no one visited him again until he was dead. This fact is the strongest evidence you have against her."

Messire Adorno saw the point before I did.

"Y—yes," he agreed slowly. "That is the evidence we have received."

It was clear to me that the Inquisitor had already leaped to some conclusion I did not follow. While I was sorting out Livio's words, the Inquisitor glanced from Livio to me.

"Obviously, Madonna, someone must have visited your Father after you left him. Else we should not have known of Messire Livio's identity."

He snapped his fingers at the skull-faced secretary. "How were we informed of Messire Livio's identity?"

"By Captain Dandolo, I believe, Your Excellency."

"I need not linger over the obvious," Livio said in that easy pleasant voice that suggested so much more, to me in any case.

Messire Adorno looked at the secretary. "How did Captain Dandolo come to know?"

The secretary riffled through the big ledger. "Captain Pietro Dandolo was informed by—Sir Maitland Carewe. Lady Mira Carewe also testifying to the facts that led to the capture of the spy, a Corsican named Marcus Livio."

"Exactly," said Livio.

"But, Messire Adorno," said the secretary in some puzzlement, "how could the Capitano and the Lady Carewe know the identity of this spy, if no one saw the dead man after Madonna Rachele left him?"

The Inquisitor sat down abruptly. "This does not mitigate your guilt, Messire Livio . . . but one wonders about the guilt of Madonna Rachele."

"No!" I cried quickly. "I lied about Messire Livio. He is not a French spy. I only said that because—because—"

Livio smiled tenderly. "My darling, it is quite useless. My comrade, the leather-worker, has already been induced to confess."

"But if the Doge has made a treaty with——" I caught Livio's eye and flushed at the warning he gave me.

The Inquisitor persisted, "Yes, Madonna Rachele?"

I said quickly, "Mira Teotochi told me Doge Manin might make an arrangement to free the political prisoners." I added in a lame way. "But that was several days ago."

Livio looked at the Inquisitor. "What does His Serenity say to these rumors?"

Instead of ignoring the impudence of this question from a prisoner, Messire Adorno surprised me by his cynical reply: "Who knows? I am only the judicial authority. Ludovico Manin has very likely tucked his skirts into his boots and taken flight to the French camps."

The secretary appeared astonished at his imprudence, but Livio took quick advantage of it.

"Surely, Messire Adorno, it would be wise to examine more closely the evidence against the young lady. You are, perhaps unaware that a large fortune was involved in the accusation against Madonna Rachele?" The Inquisitor's eyebrows raised in obvious interest. "The very persons who testified to you are the last to have seen the dead man, and by odd coincidence are also the heirs to the dead man and his dead wife. *If,* Messire, they are able to convict Rachel Carewe."

"He was not the first man they killed," I cried suddenly, half-rising in my chair. They looked at me. Maybe now they would believe my charge. "That man they killed—he was not my Father. They had killed my Father earlier—killed him or let him die, the same thing—so they could use the British Embassy to conspire with the Austrians."

The poor secretary had begun to scratch his pen over the page, but soon lost himself in my babbling. Finally he threw down the pen, raising both hands wildly. "Messire Adorno! I pray you . . . slowly. Slowly."

The Inquisitor reached past me, his crimson sleeve falling across my hand. He ordered the secretary, "Later. We deal with one case at a time here. I regret, Messire Marcus Livio, Representative *en Mission* for the French Republic, you are a gallant fellow, but you must know the penalty for your sort of activity. At dawn, the Stranglers. If this meets with your convenience."

I gasped, too horrified to get out my frantic protest, as Livio replied to the Inquisitor with equal politeness, "I would prefer the dawn following. But I daresay . . . No. I can see that it would seriously inconvenience your office."

The Inquisitor shrugged and flashed his thin smile. "Alas, Messire! One is besieged by these cases. They must be taken in order and . . . dispatched." He made one of his spidery gestures and the two guards took Livio's bound arms.

All my frenzied insistence that I had lied about him went for nothing. These two impossible men, Livio and the Inquisitor, continued to exchange compliments even in the doorway where Livio regretted cutting short their "interesting conversation," and the Inquisitor bowing him out. "Again, my regrets, Messire Livio. In a sense we are in the same business. It is always sad to see one's competitors cut down. My compliments on your behavior under stress."

But Livio's last warm glance was for me. I could scarcely see him for my tears. I could not bear it when he smiled at me, then was gone. I hated men's proud acceptance of the inevitable. I wanted to scream out my helpless fury at God, the Venetians, and even at Livio's French employers.

In the end I retold my story of my arrival in Venice and the substitution of the old gentleman for my Father. I pointed out that my Father was a sturdy walker, a man with large, competent feet.

"It was the only way the conspirators failed. I had not seen him in so long I might believe all other changes in him. But I noticed the man's feet for the first time only hours before his fellow-conspirators killed him."

"Absurd, Madonna. We could never prove it."

"Has he been buried yet?"

"Tomorrow, I believe." Messire Adorno motioned to the secretary.

"Tomorrow, Messire. The Ile San Michele."

"Then," I said quickly, "ask at the Grand Canal embassy. The name of his bootmaker. See what size his boots used to be. And then try such a boot on that corpse!"

The Inquisitor appeared to care little for what I said, but I could tell by his thoughtful air that he had not so lightly dismissed my suggestion.

I dreaded the return to that damp, dark, rat-infested cell to count the hours remaining of Livio's life, but I was as ready as I was like to be. On the way back across the bridge I pleaded again for Livio: "Give him but one extra day, Messire—it may be greatly to your advantage and the advantage of Venice . . . I pray you, Messire . . . but one day . . ."

By that time, I was hoping against hope, the treaty between the Doge and the French Republic would have been signed, and General Bonaparte's Army would arrive to secure the democratization of Venice. Surely, one of their first missions would be to save their own secret agent!

I fumbled my way into my cell, then realizing that the lean, crimson-robed figure was about to depart, I clung to the rusted bars and called to him until a distant clanging told me that the passage door had been locked. I pressed my face against the bars.

"Livio . . ."

Any answer was muffled by the whine of the night's wind blowing through the corridors. Several of the other cells were occupied. I heard an occasional groan and senseless murmurs from the cell next to mine. But no one answered me. Did they take the condemned to other corridors?

As the minutes passed, I found my frantic energy subsiding into a kind of frozen calm. I had repeated delusions that I was living a nightmare and would awaken to the sunlight sparkling on the canal past Father's palazzo. And Father was still Father, and Livio was that delightful young scoundrel whose motives I suspected. But in the midst of these dreams I fancied I heard screams, hideous and close by. I awoke to my surroundings with a start.

The moon had already gone down when the rusty passage door protested as it was unlocked and opened, and I looked out anxiously. It could not be time! But two guards appeared first, followed by the tall, cavernous Inquisitor in his crimson robes.

I screamed at him, "It is not yet time. You cannot take him. It is not time."

He spoke as he approached my cell. "Do not agitate yourself, Madonna. There are still some minutes. The condemned is making his Last Confession to Fra Antonio. I have here a bill of charges which may ultimately free you. It requires your signature."

"I don't understand. Will it free him, too?"

"Regrettably, no. Open up, there." One of the guards applied the key, pulled the door open and Messire Adorno stepped inside, frowning at the bad light cast by the one frail candle. "I trust you can read this."

I bent over the stiff parchment. It was extraordinarily difficult to read the Italian words while they blurred with my tears. It was something about the death of Sir Maitland Carewe and other names I did not immediately recognize, an Alistair Dreen, and Peregrine Watlink.

"What is it?" I asked dully, thinking only of Livio, who had only minutes to live. I looked at the Inquisitor. "May I see him once more?"

He understood at once. "In passing, Madonna. He will be brought up from the Prison of the Wells for the execution of sentence. You may glimpse him from your canal windows as they cross the bridge. Now, Madonna! We have the confession of one of the murderers, Gerald Fortman-Truscott, who has implicated Pietro Dandolo and Mira Teotochi. The *sbirri* are ordered to bring them in."

"Confession! How—oh, my God, no!" I had heard the screams in the night. Hence, the confession. I had never thought I should pity the supercilious Fortman-Truscott . . . "But who is this Alistair Dreen? A victim, also?"

"It seems you were quite right about your father's boot size, Madonna. And this wretched Dreen was the creature you took for your father. The bootmaker, Vacelli, swears his boots made for Maitland Carewe would never fit the body of the man at the palazzo. This corroborates your statement and the confession of Fortman-Truscott, who seems to be in the pay of the Austrian Empire."

"What—" I tried again. "What did they do to my father?"

A trifle impatiently, Messire Adorno pointed to the document. "The whole of it is related here. He was smothered during a typhus attack."

"No!"

"I fear so. And buried secretly on the Ile San Michel under cover of the funeral of an uncle of Capitano Dandolo. According to Fortman-Truscott's confession, the actual murderess was your father's housekeeper, this Teotochi. She has fled with Capitano Dandolo, probably toward the Austrian borders. But they will undoubtedly be halted within Venetian boundaries."

Distant sounds, shouts and laughter intruded vaguely upon us in my cell. I clutched the Inquisitor's crimson sleeve. "What is that?"

"Carnival, Madonna. A series of gondolas, no doubt, full of revelers. One more matter. The so-called attack upon Capitano Dandolo: this Fortman-Truscott has been persuaded to tell us that the knife, thrown by Dandolo's gondolier, was meant for you, Madonna. Rather an irony that the Captain took the blow in your stead. I would like to have been present when he chastised his careless gondolier!"

Another sound, much closer, made me stiffen with terror.

The clang of iron-bound doors. I rushed across the cell to the canal window, and standing on my toes could just see the stone bridge in the first pale light of dawn. I saw the two brutal guards, then, between them and slightly taller, Livio's head, dark against the dawning sky. I called to him but another burst of noise and laughter along the canal blurred the sound of my voice. He stopped, looked in my direction as if listening. His face appeared pale but composed in the early light. I thought his dark eyes sought my cell, but he could not be sure where I was. I called again, thrust my hand out, just as his guards pushed him on across the bridge.

Suddenly, ahead of them, the door leading into the palace burst open. Stupefied, I thought for a moment that I was seeing a street mob out of Paris pouring onto the bridge. But the three men leading that mob were in the uniform of the French Artillery, ragtag and bobtail, like most of the uniforms of our Army, but unquestionably our saviors tonight.

"Behold that rogue, Livio," shouted the Captain in their lead. In French he went on, "You make it easy for us to find you, Livio. You send old women and old Doges to direct us to you. Is that Madame Dace your new mistress, *mon garçon?*"

The officer threw his arms around Livio, saluting him on both cheeks. Livio raised his bound hands behind him, said something, and they all looked in my direction. One of the French soldiers quickly slashed the cords that bound Livio's wrists, and Livio turned, thrusting aside the confused Venetian guards, and ran back across the bridge toward the corridor leading to my cell.

Inside, I started to run to the door and collided against the tall, crimson barrier of the Inquisitor.

"All in good order, Madonna Carewe. Doge Manin seems to have gotten his way, and the French are here, their efficient selves, as usual. The Council of Ten badly underestimated Ludovico Manin. I wonder how the French knew of your plight, and Messire Livio's."

But, from the French Captain's words, I thought I guessed. Dacey must have gotten through to the Doge, who had informed the French envoys, after all.

"Will Livio be free?" I demanded. "They can't carry out the sentence later, can they?"

Messire Adorno walked me calmly to the cell door, which was still ajar. He said with a certain irony, "On the contrary, Madonna. There is every reason to suppose I will take his

place in the cells. I did not have the foresight of our coura-
geous Ludovico Manin."

"The foresight?"

"His Serenity has brought democracy to Venice, but to do
so, he has sacrificed the ancient Republic."

I was surprised at my own pity for him, and perversely
enough, I admired him more than the Doge who had the
foresight to save his skin by calling in one Army to save the
city from pillage by the other.

But now, my heart was filled with the sight of Livio. He
was running through the passage and I pushed the door
open. It went clanging against the ancient, seamed, and water-
scummed wall. And then I was in Livio's arms and his blood-
stained hands closed around me.

"I was so afraid for you!" I kept babbling, while he kissed
my hair and my forehead and cheek and finally my lips,
thus effectively silencing me.

CHAPTER SEVENTEEN

In the Dandolo tomb on the cemetery island of San Michele they located my Father's body, and it was removed to a Venetian felucca to be transported to the British Fleet off Naples. Father would be buried, as was fitting, in his family's tomb in Devonshire.

"I know now," I said, "that when I heard his voice in my dream, Father was trying to warn me."

Livio was kind enough not to dissuade me from my belief. "But he will be far from you, my darling," he reminded me as we returned by gondola from San Michele in the lagoon.

"If only I could have seen him before—" I whispered. "If he could have known I was alive!"

I sighed and Livio took my fingers warmly in his hand. The fresh red scars along the fingers made me cringe. "Does it hurt terribly?" I murmured. My heart felt squeezed in a vise as I thought of his pain during those days and nights in the Prison of the Wells.

But he said lightly, shaking both our hands, "Not from the moment I saw those blessed uniforms on the bridge that dawn." He looked at me in the special, tender, thoughtful way that had first made me love him. "But Paris will be a long way from Devonshire . . . A long, bitter war away from

your Father, from his grave, and his country. Can you bear
to live in Paris again?"

I glanced out over the sunlit waters and then, keenly aware
of his intent gaze and a kind of anxiety in him, I smiled.
"Venice is beautiful. And romantic—I met Messire Livio
here; did I not? But I am not Venetian."

"Or British?"

Very seriously, I looked at him. He was studying my face
as though he would read every lineament. "Dearest, when I
was a child, I felt that Richmond Hill was my home. But the
eight years after were the years that formed the woman I
am today. My mother is buried in Paris. I don't belong to
the world of my Father, or of this eternally masquerading
Venice. I want to be part of the future. And France is the
future."

The enormity of his relief touched me with a joy that was
almost painful.

"Thank you, my darling." He kissed my hair and we drew
closer together. "France has had frightful birth pangs, but I
think she will grow into a healthy republic. At the least, as
you say, she is the future. And like you, I want to be part of
it."

Our gondola came between the Piazzetta's mooring poles
and Livio helped me out. Already, it was being snapped up
by three eager, excited young French soldiers seeing Venice
for the first time. They gave Livio careless glances and
grinned at me. One of them murmured to the others in
French, "The damned Italian civilians have all the pretty
ones."

I looked at Livio and we laughed. I said, "How quickly
your heroism fades!"

Adelaide Dace, looking twenty years younger in pale blue
with furbelows, waved to us from outside the Doges' Palace.
As we approached her, we were nearly swept apart by a
half-dozen more French soldiers headed for the gondolas.

Livio laughed, rescued me from a jolly, drunken sergeant,
and we finally reached Dacey in the forecourt.

"My dears," said Dacey, "it is too dreadful! Just because
I winked and minced my way to the Doge to tell him and
the French envoy about your danger, I am now called in
to sign charges against that awful Miss Tocki female."

"But how were you able to reach the Doge without being
stopped by the spies of the Ten?" Livio asked.

Dacey simpered. "I simply assured the guards that I was

not His Serenity's mistress and that I had merely been asked to read to him. I was so firm about it—and dressed in such frills as to leave no doubt in their minds—that they leaped to the notion I really was his mistress and let me pass. One of them even remarked that the Ten would be amused; for they had expected him to be plotting, not making love!"

"Dacey!" I cried, shocked.

But Livio gave her a great hug. "And His Serenity could not have found a lovelier—visitor."

Dacey blushed and disclaimed, returning to business. "In any case, the Doge and the new Council called me in today, and I reported what I knew."

"What did you tell them, dear Dacey?" Livio asked as he took her hand and thrilled her by kissing it.

"Everything about that Miss Tocki and the others. Everything."

Livio was amused but he said politely, "That is certainly comprehensive enough. And now they ask Rachel to sign?"

"I don't know," I said, drawing back, feeling once more the horror of my imprisonment. "To put someone else in those cells . . ."

Dacey was severe. "You must! The Inquisitor was very definite."

But I felt a kind of spontaneous revulsion of which I had not been aware.

Livio reminded me quietly, "It is not enough to run away from cruelty. There are others who may be victims."

I shuddered but felt his protection and love beside me as he drew me closer and we went together through the elegant halls, following a Venetian usher in silk hose and soundless brocade slippers. We came presently into that high-ceilinged, book-lined room where I had been questioned on the dreadful night before Livio was to die.

As before, Messire Adorno and the skull-faced secretary were there to greet us. So, in despite of the democratization of Venice, the Inquisitor had retained his post.

"I had rather sign a paper and have done with it," I protested.

The Inquisitor shook his head. He assured me in his urbane, yet authoritative voice, "These creatures have committed countless crimes, Madonna. You must not feel any qualms at their well-merited punishment."

It was thereafter necessary for me to watch the malefactors enter the room in company with their guards, and to see what had become of the supercilious, elegant Fortman-Truscott after torture and confession. He appeared an enfeebled old man, limping, unable to stand straight. I glanced at Livio, who had withstood torture, and saw that even he winced at this sight. I knew now what to expect of Mira Teotochi; but no matter what she had done to Father and to me, I prayed she would not be brought in under the same conditions.

I need not have worried. As we heard the click-click of a woman's sharp Venetian heels upon the passage floor, Messire Adorno said, with obvious disapproval, "Due to the supervision of General Bonaparte's personal representatives, we were not able to apply the usual persuasive methods to this murderess."

"Torture is not permitted under the laws of the French Convention," Livio said to him.

Unimpressed, the Inquisitor went on sharply, "You will bring the prisoner Teotochi to the desk, and await her on either side."

I steeled myself to see the worst, the degradation of the elegant Mira Teotochi. I myself, though well enough treated, had looked wretched, disheveled and drab when I was brought in to be questioned, but the Teotochi, in shapely emerald green, with her red hair neatly and beautifully coifed, entered the room as though it were the wedding feast in the palazzo.

She smiled at me disdainfully. Ignoring the others, she addressed me. "I see that you have made them believe your lying tale. Your unfortunate Father is dead at your hands, even a servant poisoned, but with the French to back you—" She shrugged. "What a pity the Austrians could not have won at Arcola and Rivoli!"

The Inquisitor looked at her coldly. "Your Austrian friends outnumbered the enemy two to one, Signora Teotochi. Perhaps more spirit was needed. Do you admit to the death of one Maitland Carewe by smothering him with the pillows from his bed?"

"Certainly not. This girl—his daughter—fed him laudanum. She was angry over his marriage to me."

I looked at her open-mouthed, almost unable to believe what I heard. She was so convincing, I could scarcely believe my own senses, my own memories. But Fortman-Truscott, half-hidden in the dark corner of the room, his arms bound behind his twisted back, muttered an obscenity in English and we all looked around at him.

"Fool!" he shouted then, and I saw Mira flinch in surprise. "Dandolo has fled to the Austrians. He will not help you. I have confessed . . . under persuasion. Confess and you will be saved the rack and the burning tongs."

Mira reminded him haughtily, "It will not be allowed. The French rule Venice now. Torture is not permitted in French territories."

Messire Adorno turned to me as if none of this had taken place. "Now, will you sign the charges you make, Madonna Rachel?"

Mira Teotochi stared at me as if she would mesmerize me with those deadly green eyes.

Thus challenged, I drew myself up. I said, "Yes. Please give me the pen." And I signed.

Mira spat at me like an angry cat. Livio raised his hand in a sudden access of rage unusual in him, but I caught his hand and smiled . . . Was that her best revenge?

I rubbed my cheek where she had spat at me, and motioned to Livio. "Come. We are finished here."

No one stopped us. We walked through the empty corridors and down the great staircase.

At the foot we met Dacey. "Dear child, is it done?" she asked me anxiously. "Will that creature be put where she can do no one else any harm?"

I nodded. Livio started to say more. I said wearily, "Don't. I don't want to know what will happen to them."

And we three started out across the lively square of San Marco. That great red and gold banner, the Lion of St. Mark, beat at its tall staff. Beside it was the bright *Tricoleur* of France, to guarantee, as I hoped, the liberties of Venice. After a few minutes, Livio and I looked at each other and smiled, and we were thinking not of the painful past, but of the future, of those glorious years to come in the new century.